"MIKE? HI. IT'S KELLY."

"Kelly!"

"Can we meet?"

"Tell me what you've decided."

"Look, Mike, I don't want to talk about this over the phone—"

"You're not coming with me."

"Oh, Mike, you know I'm not. I've told you I'm not. I don't want us to split up over this, Mike."

"You're just doing this to prove some bloody point, aren't you?"

If I had any lingering doubts about going with Jade and not Mike, they dissolved there and then. I slammed the phone down on him and phoned Jade and told her to count me in for definite.

Then I left the phone off the hook.

Also by Kate Cann

Love Trilogy

1: Ready?

2: Sex

3: Go!

Grecian Holiday

Or,
How I Turned Down
the Best Possible Thing Only to
Have the Time of My Life

KATE CANN

AVON BOOKS
An Imprint of HarperCollinsPublishers

Grecian Holiday
Copyright © 1999 by Kate Cann

All rights reserved. No part of this book may be used or reproduced in any manner whatsoever without written permission except in the case of brief quotations embodied in critical articles and reviews. Printed in the United States of America. For information address HarperCollins Children's Books, a division of HarperCollins Publishers, 1350 Avenue of the Americas, New York, NY 10019.

First published in the UK by Scholastic Ltd., 1999.

Library of Congress Cataloging-in-Publication Data
Cann, Kate.
    Grecian holiday or, how I turned down the best possible thing only to have the time of my life / Kate Cann.
       p.   cm.
    Reprint. Originally published: London : Scholastic Children's Books, 1999.
    Summary: Kelly's summer vacation at a Greek farmhouse is disrupted by the arrival of her boyfriend, with whom she has recently had a terrible fight.
    ISBN 0-06-447302-3 (pbk.)
    [1. Greece—Fiction.   2. Vacations—Fiction.   3. Sexual ethics—Fiction. 4. Interpersonal relations—Fiction.]   I. Title.
PZ7.C169 Fo   2002   2001045103
[Fic]—dc21   CIP
                                                                                  AC

First Avon edition, 2002

AVON TRADEMARK REG. U.S. PAT. OFF. AND IN OTHER COUNTRIES,
MARCA REGISTRADA, HECHO EN U.S.A.
❖
Visit us on the World Wide Web!
www.harperteen.com

To Hester,
with love

THREE WEEKS INTO JUNE, and life was great and I had everything going for me. Four weeks into it and I chucked it all in.

OK, that's a bit dramatic, but that's what it felt like. I look back and still can't believe what I did. So unhesitatingly. On instinct, I suppose. Survival instinct.

A-levels were over, and I thought I'd done OK in them. Good enough to get the college place I was after, anyway. But first—*euphoria*. Freedom. A whole gap year before I got down to real life.

It was high summer, and I was with Mike. We'd been together four months and that time had been intense. I'd felt like I was walking a tightrope all the time. On one side, Mike, and on the other, working for the exams, and me in between, swaying dangerously. Just about keeping my balance, keeping my head together.

But as soon as I walked out of the last exam I just *plunged*. I spent every possible minute with Mike. I couldn't keep my eyes off him, I couldn't keep my hands off him. Time spent without him was wasted, pointless. My friends accused me of dropping them, of being obsessed. But I didn't care. I'd worked my hide off and now I was going to free fall unthinkingly whichever way it took me.

Which was to him.

So there we were, blissed out, staying in, going out, making love, partying. Talking about every subject under the sun. Except love, we didn't talk about that. We just circled it, the whole idea of it. But we were falling all right. Well, I was. I felt like he was taking me over.

There were bad times, too, of course there were. He'd throw a fit over some comment, some attitude of mine, say stuff like, "I can't *believe* you think that way!" And I'd back down, because I couldn't bear to disappoint him. Or we'd row, and his temper would be spiraling out of control when he'd manage to stop, and say sorry. And then I'd say sorry, too.

Sometimes I felt we'd moved too fast, too soon. Everything was *so* intense. Little things, little differences—they took on an importance out of all real proportion. It was made worse by the fact that he was going away at the end of June, off across Europe in a souped up sleeper-van with four of his mates. Something that had been planned long before I came into his life. We felt like time was running out on us. He kept saying he didn't want to go, couldn't bear to leave me behind for the summer. And I was pleased and restrained, waiting to see what would happen.

Then one morning he rushed round, early, pushed past my indignant mum, and burst into my bedroom. I saw him first in the mirror, because I was standing there brushing my hair, and my stomach flipped, like it always does when I see him. He is so *fit*. Real strong features, wonderful eyes, sexy teeth. I spun around and he came bounding over and wrapped his arms around me, half lifting me off my feet. Then he stepped back, and smiled, hugely. "You're in, Kelly! The guys—they've said you can come on the trip!"

This scenario had not even entered my consciousness. I'd imagined him dropping out, or coming home early, to be with me—but not *this*.

I was so shocked I couldn't speak, but Mike filled in the silence for me. "This is the *best*, Kelly— it's perfect. We'll be together for like, *three months*! I've got a tent I can take. And if the weather's rough you can have my bunk in the van and I'll sleep on the floor."

"But Mike, this is—Jesus, this hadn't even crossed my mind . . ."

"I know. I didn't want to say anything to you until it was fixed. I didn't want to get your hopes up. But it's definite, Kelly. Everyone's agreed."

"They agreed? But I mean—they hardly know me—"

"What does that matter? They know you enough to say yes. What's the matter? Aren't you *pleased*?"

"Yeah—*yeah*—of course I'm pleased, it's just so *unexpected*, it's—"

"Bloody brilliant. It solves everything, Kelly, it's great."

And he took a step toward me again, grinning, but I stopped him saying, "You sure you didn't twist their arms?"

"Look—don't worry about *them*. You'll be with me, not them."

"Yeah, but I'll be *there*. Won't I throw the balance out?"

"What are you talking about? What balance?"

"You five guys."

"Look—they've said you can *come*!"

"Yes, but it's a big blokey thing, isn't it? They

wanted *you* along . . . if you're with me you'll have less time with them and—"

"Jesus, Kelly—stop making problems! I thought you'd be . . . I thought you'd be *really pleased*! Don't you want to be with me this summer?"

"Well, yeah you know I—"

"So stop worrying! It'll be *great*! I can do stuff with them. And we can all do stuff together. And you and me—we can do stuff too, yeah? *Really* do it."

And then he reached out, wrapped his arm around my neck, pulled me toward him and started pushing his face into my hair, and we stopped talking and went on to the stuff, despite the fact that Mum was singing very loudly in the bathroom on the other side of the wall.

SO THAT'S HOW IT WAS SET as the best possible thing that could happen for us, and that night Mike, Ben, Harry, Jim, Andy, and me all went to the pub. I sat close to Mike, holding his hand and listening to the plans the five of them had made months ago. They were a laugh, his friends, and they were nice to me, welcoming, funny. Only I couldn't join in the conversation much, obviously, because they knew all about what they were doing and I didn't. And there were a few too many cringe-making jokes about the "love tent" and Mike being too knackered to go hill walking with them for me to really relax.

However nice they were, I felt excruciatingly in the way. I wanted to keep apologizing for agreeing to come along. Plus they were all worryingly hunky. Like training was a way of life, and taking risks was the spice in it. This was one of the things that had drawn me to Mike, but somehow, multiplied by five, it was . . . daunting. They had this idea that they'd park miles away from anywhere they wanted to visit and then hike into it, to get the real feel of the place; and they kept talking about living wild and getting away from civilization.

The thing is, I quite like civilization. And I've got quite a bit of stamina but I had grave doubts about keeping up with these five. When I mentioned this to Mike in an undertone he just told me I'd be fine, then he added, stroking my hair, "But bring some books or something—in case you stay behind some days."

At the end of the evening the five of them got together and told me what I needed to get for the trip, what gear and what clothes, how much space or rather how little space I'd be allowed, and they all had a good laugh at the idea of me bringing a hairdryer.

Then the next day I was in Millets camping shop trying to make myself buy some walking boots when I suddenly came over all queer and had to go home. And when I got home I took a very deep breath and dialed Mike's number and when he answered I said, "Mike. Look. I've been having second thoughts. I just—I'm not sure I want to go on this trip. Really. I'm getting cold feet.

I mean—it's really not my scene, roughing it with five blokes."

There was a hideous, hideous silence. Then he said, "You saying you don't want to go?"

"Um . . . sort of. Well, yes, I am. I'm sorry."

"You saying you don't want to be with me?"

"No. *No*. That isn't what I'm saying. I'd *love* to be with you, I'd love it, you know that. It's just—not like this. It wouldn't work. I'd love to go traveling with you, Mike, I really would. But on your own. Just you."

There was another horrible silence. Then he yelled, "Shit, I don't believe this, Kelly. What're you saying? I'd got it all sorted. What the hell made you change your mind?"

"Mike, I never really *made up* my mind, did I? I got kind of—carried along by your enthusiasm."

"Don't give me that. You had a choice."

"I didn't feel like I had a choice. I didn't feel I had time to *think*. Look—it means *so much* to me, you know, that you want me to come, and you got them to agree to it and everything . . . but now I've let it sink in I just—I don't think it would work. I just feel—really embarrassed about it. I mean—they're being really sweet about it, but I'm always going to be an extra, aren't I? I shouldn't be there."

"Kelly—I want you there. What does the rest

matter? Can't you just ignore it, as long as we're together?"

"Yeah but—you and me—we don't know each other well enough. We're not *comfortable* enough."

"Who wants to be *comfortable*?"

"OK, OK, not comfortable. But it's too early to—I dunno. Take that kind of risk with each other."

He started swearing then, really tearing into me. I held the phone away from my ear and gritted out, "*Don't* yell at me, Mike."

"I can't *help* it! You make me so *mad*! This trip—it's going to be *amazing*. And I've worked my arse off getting it together—we all have. D'you know how much it cost us, getting that van sorted? And we say you can come and you just—turn it down! You *think* about it, Kelly! You won't get an offer like this again."

"I don't care," I croaked. "I still don't want to go."

"Great. Just—*great*! You're just bitching up everyone's plans at the last minute."

"That's not true. I've only been *included* at the last minute. If I don't go, it won't make any difference."

"It will to me."

"Of *course* to you. But not to the others. Come

on, Mike—you know I'm an afterthought."

"*Jesus*, you—*God*! If you knew the *time* I've spent, convincing the guys you'd be OK on this trip—"

"There you are," I said, triumphantly but quite upset, "I knew they never really wanted me."

"But *I* do," he said. "That's the whole point, Kelly, *I* want you there. Isn't that enough? I want to be with you, this summer."

"So come away with me on my own," I said.

Deadlock. Mike accused me of being spoiled, petulant, girly, scared. He went on and on and I couldn't get a word in and everything he said was steeped in how disappointed he was in me. Finally he said, cold as hell, "Look. Let's calm down, think about it. Talk about it later."

And I took a deep breath and said, "No, Mike, I don't need to think about it. I'm not going. *You* think about it. *You* think about doing something with just me."

"I can't let my mates down, Kelly. I'm not like that. I planned this trip with them first."

"*Exactly*," I said.

And he slammed the phone down.

I went and made a strong cup of coffee and walked up and down the hall a few times. Then I phoned him back and said, "Look. The last thing I want to do is stop you doing this trip with your mates. *I'm* not like *that.* You've planned this trip for ages, way before you even met me, and it's important, and you should go."

"I'm going."

"Right."

"Right. And I want you to come with me."

"Mike—it's *your* trip, OK? I can't just be slotted into it. I can't just do that and let go of . . . of everything I want to do."

"I thought you wanted to be with me."

"Oh, *Jesus.* If I come I'll be—excess baggage. In the way. Or like a camp follower or something."

"What's a camp follower?" he said, coldly.

"Oh, God. It's a—you know, a prostitute who tags along after soldiers on the move. Look, I didn't mean I'm—"

"You're *sick*, Kelly!" he erupted. "Sick to even let that thought enter your head. If that's what you think of me maybe it's good you're not coming. Maybe we're better off apart." Then he slammed the phone down again and this time I didn't call him back.

I went upstairs and flumped down on my bed and collapsed, crying and desperate. I thought: *If we're through, if he dumps you, you did it, it's your fault. That trip was everything to him, it was special, and he wanted you to share it, and you let him down, you dis-appointed him.* . . .

I cried for ages and then when I was too tired to cry any more I felt calm, washed-up, and these pictures sort of floated up in front of my eyes. One was me lying in a tiny tent at night, waiting, listening to the five of them talking outside as they drank beer by the fire. One was the five of them laughing and joking, setting off to do something macho while I stayed behind with blisters in the van. One was me and Mike arguing, because I wanted to stop walking and sit in a café for a while, and he wanted to keep pace with the others.

I looked at these pictures and thought maybe I'd made the right choice.

I knew what I was doing. I was drawing back from the edge, although I wasn't clear quite what the edge was right then.

WHEN MIKE TURNED UP on my doorstep that evening, glowering like a pit bull, I knew I wasn't going to get dumped. If he'd decided to dump me he wouldn't look that angry.

"We need to talk," he said, and I said yes, we do, and feeling weirdly excited, because things were opening up, and weirdly powerful, because I was the one who'd made it happen, I walked beside him in silence to one of our favorite pubs on the edge of town.

"You really . . . pissed me off, what you said," he announced, as soon as we'd got our drinks and sat down. "I thought you wanted to spend the summer with me."

"I did," I said. "I *do*. But not this way."

"I see. So if you can't have me all to yourself, you don't want to be there?"

"No. No, that is not it. It's just—"

"I can't let them down now. We planned this in January. I didn't even know who you *were* in January."

"I don't want you to let them down. I've told you—you should go."

"So what you're saying is—you want me just to go off. You don't want to be with me."

"That's not it. You know that's not it. It's just—we're—we're new together, and, I dunno, I don't feel ready to deal with lots of other people as well as you yet. Not in a camper-van for three months, anyway. It'd be OK if I was going to be just one of the guys, but I'm not, am I, if I'm with you?"

"You complicate everything," he said.

"Aren't *you* worried at all? Don't *you* think you'll be pulled two ways?"

"No. I think it'll be fine. I think it'll be *real*. What d'you want—some cutesy two weeks spent in a hotel—rubbing oil over each other on the beach?"

I thought that sounded kind of nice, but I said, "No. Oh, *Mike*! I love it that you want me to go. I really do. It's just—you're trying to have it both ways and you *can't*! It's just too *risky*. I mean—Christ. You wouldn't do it with my friends. You won't even *see* them."

"That's 'cos they're all kids."

"They're the same age as me."

"Yeah, but Kelly—you're different. You've grown up. Where it counts, you've grown up."

I gazed down at the table. Mike had this habit of running down my friends, my family, the way I spent my time—and then twisting it around into a massive compliment. It made me uneasy, but it was very seductive, too.

"Give it a try, Kelly," he went on. "I can't believe we can't make it work. What are you worried about—that you're just there as my girlfriend?"

"A bit," I sniffed.

"You should see beyond all that surface crap. Really, you should. I have to go on this trip, you know that. And I want to be with you. What's wrong with wanting both?"

"Nothing. But—"

"If you come, I *can* have both. What I want most." And he reached out and threaded his fingers through my hair down to the back of my neck. Then he started massaging it, working with strong fingers on the muscles.

"You're tense," he said. "All knotted up."

"I know," I said, as I rotated my head back against his hand, loving him touching me. "It's all . . . *this*."

"We'll sort it out."

"If only there was another girl going along . . ."

He dropped his hand from my neck. "Just what are you afraid of, Kelly? That you'll be bored? Left out? What?"

"Outnumbered," I muttered. "Shouted down."

"Jesus, Kelly, you are such a *kid*! Why can't you just see it as a new experience? Why can't you take the *risk*?"

"Oh, Christ, Mike, will you *listen* to me! I feel really uncomfortable about it, and if I come along feeling like that, well, it won't do *us* any good, will it?"

"*Us*? What's *us*? We're two people, who like each other, a lot, and this is something we can go through."

I sat silently, glaring at the table.

"I hate it when you *sulk*," Mike said, and went to get some more drinks.

CHAPTER 4

HE CAME BACK, A DRINK IN either hand, and we battled on and on, round and round. I began to feel like I was battling against a huge brick wall. I began to feel I might give in, after all, and go with him, just so we could stop arguing. Just so he'd put his arm around me.

We parted on bad terms. He told me to phone him when I'd thought it through and what he meant was—*phone me when you think I'm right, when you're ready to come on the trip.* He wouldn't kiss me goodbye properly. I reached for him, wanting him badly, wanting that contact, but he froze me off.

I drove all my friends demented talking it over with them. Everyone had different opinions but everyone felt the same reluctance to go over it all more than about four times. Mostly, people said I should trust my instincts and not go. And now

17

there was a new problem. Over the last week or so everyone's holiday plans had suddenly got firmed up, and I'd been left out of all of them. So if I didn't go with Mike, I didn't have a lot of other options.

Rebecca, one of my closest mates, said she could try and book me into their package trip to Crete if I was sure I wanted to come. "But you're not sure, are you?" she said. "You're not sure about anything."

Mike didn't phone me. I knew he wouldn't. That would have been weak, and weakness wasn't his thing. I tried to be strong, too, but I missed him like crazy. I missed holding him close, up against every inch of him, I missed his scent, his mouth. I'd got to the point when I thought I'd either throw a coin to decide, or maybe just myself out of the window, when out of the blue Jade turned up on my doorstep.

She grinned at me with a slightly insane look in her eyes and said, "Synchronicity, yeah? You know what it means? You up for it?"

I had no idea what she was on about, but I asked her to come in, and she did. Then I asked her if she wanted tea, and she said yes.

Jade wasn't exactly what I'd call a close friend. We'd been thrown together in art classes and got on really well, and we'd hung out together at lunchtimes sometimes, and had a real laugh. But somehow life was too full and complex for us to organize anything else, to take the friendship any further. Since we'd left college I'd only seen her a couple of times, at parties, when I'd been with Mike and not open to anyone else.

I'd always admired her, though. She had this strong energy about her, and she was incredibly attractive, but in such a different mold to me it was hard to feel envious. She was lean; I was curvy. She had short, spiky, blond hair; mine was long and brown. She was sharp-featured, with weird, blue, almond-shaped eyes; I was altogether softer. The one thing I seriously envied about her was her ability to chuck on anything and look stylish. She had that kind of shape.

"So," I said, filling the kettle. "Synchron . . . whatsit. What's it mean?"

"Two events," she said, "that happen separately, that seem to have no relation to each other—but they have. Or will have."

"What?"

"Like two canceled holidays. No connection. But they could have."

"Jade, stop spouting like some kind of psychic . . . *weirdo*. Tell me what you're on about."

"OK. Word is you've just split up from *Mikey*."

"Split up—?"

"OK, had a bust up with. Over this holiday you're meant to be going on. If you want my opinion, you made absolutely the right choice. It sounds completely *ghastly*, not a holiday at all, more like combat training. Or a boy scout thing. Who can walk the furthest on two sausages a day. Who can go longest without *washing*."

Despite myself, I laughed. "It is a bit like that. But—you know—they're into all that stuff. Stretching yourself, pushing yourself to the limits—"

"And are you? Into all that?"

"Well . . . no."

"But he still asked you."

"He wanted us to be together."

"Sure he did. So he could take his Boy Scout Shagging Badge."

"*Jade!*"

"Sorry. Anyway. That's one 'holiday,' not that I'd call it a holiday, more like straight masochism, that's been canceled, at least as far as you're concerned . . ."

"Well, I'm still not sure—"

"Yes, you are. And the other is—"

"Wait a minute. Who told you all this? About the trip and everything?"

Jade looked exaggeratedly, comically bored. "Kelly—ever heard of the grapevine? It's big news, you finally standing up to old *Mikey*."

I could feel myself gawping. "What d'you mean—finally standing up to him?"

"You know—not just doing everything he wants to do."

"Doing everything he wants to do?"

"Look, Kelly, if you're going to repeat everything I say I'm *leaving*! Here I am, all geared up to tell you my synchronicity theory, and all you can do is act like a parrot."

"OK, OK."

"There you go again. Everything *twice*."

Despite myself, I laughed. "*Look*, Jade, what you've just said *bothers* me. Does everyone think he pushes me around or something?"

She shrugged, smiled, kept silent.

"Because he doesn't, OK? He's a bit—"

"—overbearing."

"—*definite* about stuff, but I hold my own, right?"

"Right. Make the tea, kettle's boiled. Where was I?"

"Two canceled connected holidays," I said, picking up the teapot.

"Yeah. One is Mikey's *farce*. The other is my

brilliant, beautiful, absolutely no-rent house in Greece. With a spare bedroom."

Greece. Tiny stirrings of excitement invaded my stomach, and it felt good. Especially after all the angst and pain I'd been feeling. "Why a spare bedroom?" I asked. "And why no rent?"

"My cousin's dropped out. Well—had a better offer. She's like that, the cow. But it doesn't matter. It was through her I got the house in the first place. My aunt has all these stinking rich friends, and one of them has a beautiful, beautiful farmhouse in this empty bit of Greece. Just for holidays and stuff. I've been there before and it's *heaven*. Anyway, this year, Jill—my cousin—got the idea she wanted it as a base for the summer, and she got it all agreed, and she asked me, and her best mate. Only then she got invited on a grand tour of the States. She has that sort of life, the cow. So she's doing that instead."

"And now it's just you and the best mate?"

"No. When the best mate found out Jill had canceled she threw a wobbly and made other plans, too. So everyone assumed the whole thing had fallen through. But they reckoned without me, right?" Jade grinned, picked up her mug of tea, and took a sip, watching me smugly over the rim. "I got my ma to phone up, say how disappointed I was. How much I'd been looking forward to it. So my aunt groveled, said *please* would I still use the house, still no charge, take anyone I want, she couldn't bear to think Jill had spoiled my summer. So that's what's happening. I'm in one bedroom. My mate Sarah's in the other. You can be in the third. If you want to be."

I felt my jaw drop open. She made it sound so simple. She made it sound so tempting.

"I don't know Sarah at all," I croaked, stalling for time. I'd seen her, often enough. To me she didn't look life Jade's type—she was kind of non-descript, with pale red, rather frizzy hair, and noth-ingy features. She was always glued to Jade's side like a shadow. Not saying much; not smiling much, either.

"Oh, Sarah's great. No problem. You'll get on fine with her. And let's face it, Kelly, you don't know all Mikey's friends, either, do you?"

"No, but—"

"That's different, yeah. At least, Mikey's told you it is."

I turned to her, challenging. "Hey, Jade, what's with this 'Mikey' all the time? Why don't you like him?"

Jade shrugged. "Just an impression."

"Of what?"

23

"Of having a ramrod up his arse, that's what. Hey—I can say this now, can't I? I mean—you haven't snogged and made up yet?" I shook my head, silently. I wanted to hear what she had to say. "It's just—he always looks so *serious*. Like he disapproves of people having fun."

"He *is* serious," I said. "I mean—he's intelligent. He thinks about stuff. And—you know—reads. The papers and stuff."

"Whoa," said Jade. "Party guy."

"Oh, shut up! I like that he's not just brain dead, like most blokes are. We really *talk* together. And he *feels* things."

"I bet he does!"

"*Jesus*, Jade! I mean—he's not just superficial. He's got—he's got *depth*."

"Yeah, yeah. Maybe I'm prejudiced. I had a spat with him the other week."

"*Yeah?* He didn't say."

"No—he wouldn't. It was at that party—Dave W.'s? You were there . . . with Mike . . . and loads of his mates were there, too. Some of them are OK, I admit. Some of them are quite tasty. But one of them—talk about an unreconstructed male. Jim, I think his name was. Candidate for the original missing link. He came on to me, about as subtle as a building site. Kept trying to grab me and put his hand down my front. So I smacked him one, and then I shoved him backward and he lost his balance, 'cos he was so pissed. He fell back against a table and everything went flying."

"Jesus, Jade, I don't remember that."

"I think you were queuing for the bog. *Mikey* was right there, though. He helped Jim up, sat him down on a sofa. Then he started picking up the stuff from the table. And he turned to me and asked me if I wanted to help him."

"So did you?" I said, laughing.

"No I bloody didn't! I told him his stupid oversexed friend could do it! And he said—why did I wear skirts up around my crotch if I didn't want to turn guys on." She stopped, eyes sparking with the memory. "So I told him he was a total arse and he said something like—At least I'm not showing mine—*prat!*—and I told him he sounded like a rape trial judge. That shut him up."

I was silent. I remembered a conversation we'd had a couple of weeks ago, about a new dress I'd bought. Mike had said it was too short, too revealing. "What d'you want other blokes looking at you for?" he'd said.

"Sorry, Kelly," Jade said breezily. "Don't mean to slag off the love of your life or anything. Mr. Tall Dark and Ugly. No. *Sorry.* He's not that ugly. You've always gone for those super-masculine types, haven't you? Broken noses, the lot."

"Mike's nose isn't broken. It's just—"

"A bit bent. Fine."

"*All right*, Jade, what about the guys you go for? That one you ended up with last week, everyone thought he was a girl, I mean, *what* a sweety, with that poncey little floppy fringe and—"

"Don't you dare knock him! He was a babe!"

"Too right he was a babe! He was prettier than you!"

"Only after I'd lent him my lippie. God, Kelly, did you see him *dance*? Like an *angel*. Better than your Mikey. *Mikey* moves like Frankenstein's monster before it's had its shots of lightning."

"*Sod off!*"

"And I bet he lends you *books*," she added, witheringly.

"No. Well—yeah. A couple."

"And then he asks you about them? Come on, Kelly—admit it! Yeah . . . yeah . . . I can see from your face. *God*, what a pompous fart."

"Shut up, Jade—I like books."

"And how many have you lent him? Right! None!" Jade grinned at me, then emptied her tea mug. "So. Will you think about it? Coming to Greece?"

I smiled back. *Greece*, I thought. *Mike was traveling through Greece.* "Yes. Yes, I will. It sounds fantastic."

"It'd be great, Kelly. I mean, it would work out, the three of us. Sarah really likes you."

"She hardly knows me!"

"Well—she likes what she does know. Look— want me to show you some stuff on it?" And she sat down at the kitchen table, and started pulling maps and booklets out of her bag.

It's funny how the act of looking at pictures and brochures, and talking about what it's going to be like, can suddenly make the whole thing more real. Sitting down like that, discussing it—it makes an idea become a plan. I brewed more tea, and Jade started jotting down lists of figures, how much the trip would cost me.

"With the exchange rate the way it is, it's cheaper to live in Greece than here," she announced. "So I'm reckoning on spending most of the summer there. We can work if we need to— they love English girls in cafés and bars and stuff. The airfare's the big bummer. D'you think your folks would help?"

That night, I talked it over with Mum and Dad. They were both incredibly keen on the idea of me going to Greece with Jade, and I knew this had a lot to do with their reluctance to see me going off camping with Mike and getting even more heavily involved with him than I seemed to be already.

I didn't mention that he planned to drive through Greece and I was fermenting a plot to get us both together. I just exploited their fears mercilessly, wondering aloud if I could bear to be apart from him. Then I made out that the big decider between Mike's trip and Jade's trip was the airfare, and by the end of the evening they'd promised to pay it—plus coming up with quite a wad for expenses.

"MIKE? HI. IT'S KELLY."

"Kelly!"

"Can we meet?"

"Tell me what you've decided."

"Look, Mike, I don't want to talk about this over the phone—"

"You're not coming with me."

"Oh, Mike, you know I'm not. I've told you I'm not. I don't want us to split up over this, Mike."

"Look—neither do I, Kelly. Christ."

I felt this great surge of relief when he said that, but I fought to keep my voice calm, measured. "Look—something else has come up and maybe . . . well, it could be a solution. Maybe we can get to see each other this summer after all."

"What d'you mean?"

"I've been asked to share a house in Greece.

29

And you're going there, aren't you, it's on your list. So I thought, if *I* went there, too, we could arrange a place to meet and—"

"Whose house?"

"Jade's."

A great snort came down the receiver. *"That* slag!"

"Don't call her a slag. I like her."

"It's just descriptive. It's what she is."

"Yeah—and what about your mate Jim? He knocks off everything that doesn't get away fast enough."

"OK, so he's a slag, too."

"Look—can we meet? And talk? I'm going to be in Greece for eight weeks, nine maybe, we could easily have some time together."

"What's this house like?"

"It's a farmhouse, and it sounds idyllic, and it's practically for nothing and—"

"You're just doing this to prove some bloody point, aren't you? That slag's got at you."

If I had any lingering doubts about going with Jade and not Mike, they dissolved there and then. I slammed the phone down on him and phoned Jade and told her to count me in for definite.

Then I left the phone off the hook.

* * *

The next few days were mental. I banned myself from inward raging about Mike and I was so busy the ban almost worked. I went through all my clothes, pulling out stuff for a hot climate. I got the money back on a sensible sweatshirt and three big T-shirts that I'd bought for the camping trip, and bought one bikini with the proceeds. Then I drew out all my savings and bought two very thin, fabulous dresses, some shorts and some tops, and changed the rest of my cash into traveler's checks and drachmas.

Jade had booked our flights; we left in three days.

Mike left in four. I knew it, but I wouldn't let myself phone, I couldn't. It was a point of honor. He had to recognize *my* rights, *my* needs, *my* wishes, *me*. I was just working myself up into another rage one night, mulling it over yet again, when the phone went.

I picked it up and heard his name, his voice. It felt like my whole body sighed.

"Kelly—I'm sorry."

"OK. Me, too."

"Let's agree to be mature, yeah? Let's have a conversation where nobody bangs the phone down."

"OK."

"You want to meet me for a farewell drink?"

"Sure."

"No—a meal. Have you eaten yet? I'll buy you a meal."

And suddenly I felt so choked up I couldn't speak. I whispered yes, yes, when he suggested where we meet and what time, then I went and showered and made myself up as perfectly as I could. It was hot, so I put on one of the new dresses I'd bought, and slicked on a bit of bronze body gloss where I thought my skin needed it.

And when we met he said, "That new? God, you look fantastic." He wrapped his arms around me and buried his face in my hair and then he muttered: "You'll have everyone in Greece going after you. I'm so sodding *jealous*, Kelly, I can't bear it. I *wish* you were coming with me."

It was like the words were torn out of him. I forgave him everything on the spot.

We had a wonderful, tragic time, sitting in a dark, candlelit corner of a corny old Italian, feeding each other titbits, drinking too much wine, saying "I'm going to miss you *so much*" every other minute or so. We went over everything all over again, and he wound up coming over all magnanimous and admitting he could see why I'd made my decision. I felt so relieved, so happy. We talked

about how time spent alone can make a relationship better, stronger—only we managed to skirt
around the word "relationship"—and he made me
promise not to let Jade influence me too much and
not to get off with anyone else while I was away. I
gave him the address of the farmhouse and we
made plans for him to write when they crossed the
Greek border, and then we'd make our way
together somehow and book into a little *pension*
somewhere and have some time alone. We told
each other that being apart would be awful but
that would make getting together again all the
more wonderful.

It was a graceful, forgiving, adult arrangement.

I should have known it wouldn't work out.

CHAPTER 6

IT WAS LATE AFTERNOON when Jade, Sarah, and I got to Greece, and the sun was low in the sky and still scorching. The ground had soaked up all the heat of the day and now seemed intent on giving it back. I squinted ahead out of the car window, but it was hard to see through the dust-haze.

"*Where* say farmhouse was?" grumbled the cabdriver. "This road—is not a road. Is bad dirt track. Ladies—I can't go on now. Spoil car."

In the backseat, squashed between me and Sarah, Jade was gnawing her thumb, eyes swiveling anxiously from side to side. "It's down here," she said. "A bit further. I'm sure it is."

"Well, it better be, because—"

"*There!*" Jade squealed in triumph. She leaned forward, put one hand on the cabdriver's shoulder, and pointed past his ear with the other. "That's *it*."

"You sure?"

"'Course I'm *sure*. Stop here."

The car drew to a halt by a huge clump of parched-looking cacti. Jade bundled me out of the car and clambered out afterward. Sarah followed more slowly behind.

I turned to look where Jade was pointing. Ahead, half visible through a great fig tree, was a high stone wall, white paint flaking off in the heat. "It's behind that," Jade said, grinning with excitement.

I stood and stared, soaking in the impact of the place. The vivid light and the imposing heat. The smell of scorched thyme, growing by the roadside. The emptiness, stretching to the far horizon.

"Oh, God, Jade," I murmured. "I can't believe it. I'm *here*. It's *wonderful*."

Jade smiled at me triumphantly, then paid the taxi driver while Sarah and I heaved the cases from the boot. Then we picked up our luggage and started to walk down the sandy, overgrown path toward the white wall of the farmhouse.

"What's that noise?" whispered Sarah. A constant, lazy whirring was filling the air.

"Cicadas," said Jade.

"Bugs?"

"Yes. But nice bugs. Now come *on*!"

Jade dumped her cases in front of an arched

wooden door in the wall and rummaged in her bag. Then she produced a big iron key, and jammed it into the keyhole. She jiggled it, swearing, for thirty seconds or so, while Sarah and I waited anxiously. Then with a dry grating sound, the key turned and the door swung open.

And we picked up our cases again and stepped through it, into a perfect courtyard. A gorgeous tangle of flowering vines and jasmine covered three of the walls; the fourth wall was the front of the farmhouse itself. I sighed, ecstatic, and let my eyes travel upward. From the flat roof scrolled a crumbling stone staircase. It paused on the upper story, at a long balcony with two doors leading off it, then continued down alongside the courtyard wall and ended with a flourish, a great cracked urn at its end.

I stood there, looking at it all, absorbing it, smelling the scent of the flowers, until Jade began to cross the courtyard, and I followed. Its flagstones were worn and beautiful, and looked wonderfully cool in the shade from the fig tree.

"It's just like I remember it," breathed Jade. "It hasn't changed a bit." She turned to me, beaming, like a conjurer who'd just pulled off the best trick in the world. "OK, Kelly. Is this better than bumping around in some tatty van, or *what*?"

"It's better," I laughed. "It's *sooo* much better."

"It's wonderful, Jade," said Sarah.

"Come on. Guided tour." Jade started up the staircase and stepped on to the long balcony. "The bedrooms are up here." She flung open the door on the left, stepped inside, dumped her case and said, "This is mine, OK?"

I followed her into a dim, square room, stone-floored, white walled. I watched as she wrestled with some shutters on the opposite wall, then blinked as the shutters rattled back and the low sun streamed in. Everything was designed for the heat. The only furniture in the room was a big pine-wood bed, a wardrobe, and a dresser with a three-legged stool in front of it. On one wall there was a crucifix, and on the other a great, gilt-framed mirror. I could feel this great happy sigh starting up in me. It was perfect, everything was perfect.

I wandered over to the window, leaned my elbows on the sill, and stared dreamily out at the parched fields. "Look at that view. Look at those *trees*. We can have fresh figs for breakfast."

"It's lovely," said Sarah. "What's that weird smell?"

"Insecticide," said Jade. "Don't look so sick. You have to spray the beds, to keep the fleas away. What we need to do is drag all the mattresses out into the sun and let them air. Come on. I'll show you your rooms." She walked out onto the balcony, and pushed open the other door. "Now, you have to go through one room to get to the other, but I thought you might feel kind of safer sharing that way . . ."

"Safer?" repeated Sarah.

"Oh, God, I didn't mean—look, there's no reason why you *shouldn't* feel safe. It's just—it's really quiet here at night. I thought you might want the company. It doesn't bother me, being alone."

"No," I smirked, "and you might *not* be alone all the time if the holiday goes the way you want it to—right?"

"Shut up," she grinned. Then she wrestled the shutter open, and the sun glared in.

"There's no glass," said Sarah.

"No need," shrugged Jade. "These rooms were only used to sleep in. In the winter, they just bolted the shutters to keep the cold out. We can leave them open all the time. There's a breeze that gets up, in the evening—it smells of jasmine. It's heaven."

This room was just like Jade's, just as wonderful, but narrower, with a narrower bed, and an extra door in the corner. "That's through to the other room," continued Jade. "Come on."

This room was small and square, with a window at the back like in the other bedrooms and a second tiny, arched window at the side. The bedstead had ivy leaves carved on it. On the floor was a bright blue and rusty-red rug, and on the wall a silvery mirror with two candle holders on either side.

You could tell just by looking at her that Sarah wanted the room to be hers. She let out a sigh, wavery with wanting, and Jade laughed. "I thought you'd like this one, Sarah," she said. "All snug and tucked away."

"OK," I said, pretty nobly I thought, "I'll have the other one. Just knock before you come through, right?"

"Oh, no," said Sarah. "Oh, look—that's not fair on you. Why don't we swap rooms each week—or after two weeks—or—"

"Sarah, it's OK," I said, smiling. "I like the other one, it's got more floor space. And I need a lot of floor space 'cos I don't always hang my clothes up."

"But you won't be private if I have to keep walking through—"

"I don't need to be private. Remember? I'm on my own. I will be doing absolutely nothing that you couldn't walk in on."

"God, dull," said Jade. "Just 'cos *Mikey*'s not around, it doesn't mean you have to spend this holiday like a *nun*—"

"Yes, it does. I'm still *with* him, Jade."

"Oh, God," said Jade, witheringly, rolling her eyes skyward. "I s'pose for your sake I'd better hope he turns up then."

Sarah blinked. "What?"

"Oh, shut up, Jade," I said. "He won't. That's not the arrangement. I told you."

"But if he and his mates get this far, and they want somewhere to stay other than that stinking van—you going to be sour enough to say no? Deny them a few days of luxury? Don't be selfish."

"It's not selfish! If they wanted luxury they shouldn't've—"

"No, no—selfish to *me* I mean. I told you I think a couple of his mates are quite tasty."

"You are im*possible*, Jade!" I gave her a playful shove hard enough to send her staggering backward onto the bed. "That should sort out your nits," I crowed, as the smell of insecticide wafted up.

"Oh, *God*," spat Jade, rolling off at speed. "This one's absolutely *drenched* in the stuff. Come on, you *cow*, grab the other end. Let's get this outside to air and I'll show you the rest of the place."

Together we bumped the mattress down the

stone steps. I went fast, dragging Jade along beside me, because I was angry with her. Angry about her mentioning Mike. I didn't want to think of him here, in this new place that had nothing to do with him. I didn't want to miss him too much.

We cleared the last two steps and dragged the mattress across the courtyard, then we propped it against the sunniest bit of the wall. "OK," said Jade. "Now the ground floor. This bit's been modernized—sort of." She pushed open the main door and went into a big, cool space. The only light was from floor-length windows on the far side. A worn suite of cane furniture was looking lost in the center; a sun-bleached wooden table and six chairs were ranged against one wall.

"Minimalist, eh?" said Jade. "We'll shift the table outside and eat in the courtyard. We needn't use this room much—unless *Mikey* and his pals turn up, of course. Then it'll be their bedroom. Well, not Mikey's bedroom of course. He'll be—"

"Jade, will you shut up?" I said.

"Yeah, why d'you keep saying that stuff?" put in Sarah. "Kelly's said he's not coming here."

Jade pulled a face at her, then turned back to me and laughed out loud, and I couldn't help it, I had to laugh back. "Let me show you the bathroom," she said. She took four steps across the room, and flung open a door revealing bath, shower, toilet, basin. "Like the avocado green tiles? It does its job, anyway—except when the water pressure drops right down."

"Does that happen a lot?" I asked.

"No. Only when someone's watering his tomatoes or something further down the track. Usually when you've just shampooed up. Here's the kitchen." She walked over to another door, us following. "Basic again—but it's got all its bits." Then she yanked open the fridge door and muttered, "Oh, shit."

"Oh, shit?" I echoed.

"They said they might get us some stuff in, but they obviously . . . haven't." She turned brightly to me and Sarah. "But that's no problem, OK? We'll get the bus into town and have a drink and maybe eat there and stock up."

"Get the *bus*—?" wailed Sarah, as though Jade was suggesting a moon launch. "Oh, God, Jade, I don't want to *go* anywhere. I'm *knackered*." She looked it, too. Strung out with nerves from the journey and the excitement. She'd spent the whole of the flight in a state of barely-contained panic, as far as I could tell, although whenever I'd asked her if she was OK she'd said she was fine. But I knew all she wanted to do now was go up to her room and sort her stuff out and curl up on the bed and settle in. Like a displaced cat.

"Oh, come on, Sarah. It's either that or starve," Jade said. "Or you could stay here alone, I s'pose."

Sarah looked nervously over at the kitchen window, like she expected an ax-murderer to appear. "No, it's OK. I'll come, of course I'll come."

"Good," said Jade brightly. "Kelly, just give me a hand getting the other two mattresses down, yeah?"

"I'll help," I heard Sarah say weakly, but we'd already headed out to the courtyard.

As soon as we'd propped up the mattresses Jade said, "Let's go. The buses are about every half hour, from the bottom of the track. Keep your fingers crossed we haven't just missed one."

THE TRACK SEEMED FAR longer and dustier now we were walking than when we'd arrived in the cab. The great red sun was nearly on the horizon; the evening was about to start. Goats, grazing on scrubland, looked up blankly as we passed; big-leaved plants and dead, dried flower heads waved above us.

"Alien landscape," I murmured.

"What?" said Jade.

"Beautiful, alien landscape."

"Oh, blimey. Kelly's getting poetical."

We walked slowly in the humming silence, and I drank it all in.

"You sure you know where the bus stop is?" Sarah asked.

"Yeah, down here where the road forks. Look—there." Jade headed over to a weather-beaten pole with a sign on the top and sat down beside it. "Now we just pray they haven't changed the timetable," she said. "And catch the last of the rays." And with that she tilted her face up toward the sun and shut her eyes.

I stayed standing, next to Sarah. "I'm getting hungry," I announced happily. "I can't believe it. After that foul meal on the plane I thought I'd never eat again."

"Yeah," said Sarah. "Know what you mean."

"Jade'll find us somewhere good to eat. Hey— Jade—know somewhere good to eat?"

"The best," said Jade, eyes still closed. "The best wine, the best grub. Definitely the best waiters."

I laughed, and Sarah said, "Won't we have to get the food first, before the shops shut?"

"Nah. There's some little tourist supermarkets on the main street, they stay open till midnight and beyond. More expensive and filled with drunks— but OK."

"Oh." Sarah gulped, as Jade went on, "Anyway, with any luck we'll be drunk, too, by the time we get the shopping done."

"What time does the last bus go?" asked Sarah. "Back, I mean?"

"Sarah, *stop fussing*. We'll get a cab. I'm not lugging a load of groceries along that track in the pitch dark."

"The *pitch dark*—?" repeated Sarah, shrilly.

"Look," I cried diplomatically, pointing. "Is that the bus?"

Jade jumped to her feet, shading her eyes with her hand. A small coach was rattling toward us, half hidden by its own dust cloud. "Looks like it," she said, and started energetically flagging it down.

The bus was very crowded. Half of it was taken up with sun-sore holidaymakers heading back from the beach, half with stocky matrons with bulky shopping bags. We all three had to strap hang for the first ten minutes, then the bus stopped and several people struggled off, leaving empty seats. Jade, giggling, pushed Sarah down next to a well-developed blond bloke in tiny white shorts. Then she turned and dealt with the conductor, asking for tickets to the town center, handing over the right amount of strange, Greek coins. She was so *confident*—it amazed me. I felt unsure, inadequate—like my first days at sixth-form college, when I'd so wanted to fit in and be part of it, but I didn't know how to act.

I watched Sarah as she gazed unhappily down at the red-brown muscley thighs taking up most of the seat beside her and thought that she was almost certainly feeling more inadequate than I was, and that kind of cheered me up. Then I wondered for the millionth time what it was that kept Jade and Sarah's friendship going. Longevity, I supposed; they'd known each other a long time before I'd come on the scene. That, and loyalty. It certainly wasn't what they had in common. Jade was all energy, excitement, taking risks, taking charge. Sarah—Sarah wasn't.

The bus shuddered to a halt. "We're here," Jade announced. "That's the market square." She jostled her way to the bus exit, and Sarah and I followed, and we hopped down onto the pavement.

"Last bus ten-thirty!" the bus driver shouted after us, sternly.

"Thanks, *Dad*," Jade called back.

I looked around me, savoring the foreignness of everything, the sheer sensuality. The sun had gone and the light was dwindling rapidly, but the evening was still hot with a sweet fragrance you could almost taste. The square was ancient and pretty; low trees surrounded it, loud with their cargoes of cicadas. Everywhere, little restaurants and bistros were getting busy, with pavement tables set up under strings of white fairy lights.

"Wow!" I breathed. "This is . . . spacey! I don't feel as though I'm really here! It's like . . . watching it on a film or something!"

"It's 'cos it's so different to home," said Jade.

"Yeah . . . it's like . . . it's like everyone else can't see you!"

"Well, they can. Try flicking some Vs and see the reaction."

"And I expect you're tired," said Sarah. "From the traveling."

I didn't feel tired, or inadequate, anymore—I felt charged. I stepped further into the square, revolved, ogling everything, loving it all.

"Want to wander around a bit first?" asked Jade. "We can get a drink—and I'll see if I can remember where that bistro is."

Sarah and I nodded, totally in her charge, totally dependent on her. We toured around the little side streets, looking at the shops with their leather bags and silver jewelry for sale, smiling nervously at the black-clad grannies sitting in doorways with their crocheting. Then we agreed we wanted a drink and drew up outside a smart-looking bar, all huge square cream-colored umbrellas and palms in pots.

I could tell it intimidated even Jade, a bit. She stood at the door assessing it, noting it was waiter service, spotting the menus on the tables. Then she sailed inside and sat down confidently at an empty table, with us shuffling admiringly behind her.

A waiter appeared almost immediately. "One minute," she said, raising an elegant hand, and he smiled and loped away again.

I examined the glossy menu. "Let's have one of these cocktails," I said. "The ones with the swizzle sticks and the little umbrellas."

"They're expensive, aren't they?" said Sarah. "How many drachmas are there to the—"

"My treat," I interrupted. "Come on—it's our first drink here."

"You're on," Jade replied and I was just summoning the courage to call the waiter back when she hailed him, and ordered. Within minutes he returned with three tall, festive-looking glasses full of ice and peachy liquid. We each took a sip, and then Jade sat back and grinned in a kind of triumph. "Well?" she said, eyes sparkling as she looked at us. "How d'you like it here?"

"It's utterly utterly fabulous," I said. "It's *whoa*!" I leaned over the table toward her, suddenly flooded with excitement. "When you think that this has been all kind of last minute, I mean, you know, *unplanned*, accidental . . . I can't believe it. I can't believe it's all worked out so well. Your farmhouse is gorgeous."

"Yeah," said Jade. "It is. What I really like about it is, the farmhouse itself is all simple and peaceful and away from the oiks—I mean, there's a beach nearby that's so *quiet,* even in August. But there's loads of action and nightlife nearby for when you want it."

"It's going to be a *great* holiday." I sighed.

"Yeah. But it isn't just a holiday, remember. Nine weeks counts as *living* here."

"D'you think we'll end up having to work?"

"Dunno. Depends how much partying we do. How soon the cash runs out. Don't worry about that now."

I turned to Sarah, trying to infect her with my enthusiasm. "Aren't you glad Jade's cousin skanked her?"

"Skanked?" repeated Sarah.

"You know—let her down."

"Oh, right. Yes."

"Look," said Jade, "I want you both to know this is not second best for me. It's first best. Jill's OK, but her best friend . . . no way. You two are a massive improvement. I was delighted when they dropped out. The whole thing is just— *serendipitous.*"

"Oh, my God, not another long word. D'you have vocabulary bog roll or something?"

"What's it mean?" said Sarah.

"Serendipitous? It means a happy accident.

Cheers." And Jade chinked both of our glasses loudly, spilling some of my drink.

"Is it a happy accident for you, Kelly?" Sarah asked suddenly.

"Yes," I said immediately—and I realized I meant it. "I was feeling like I was in a meat grinder, you know? Everything with Mike had got very . . . pressured. Like I didn't know what I really thought anymore, or felt, or . . . or anything. This is perfect. Being part of . . . of all *this* . . . it's perfect. It's like things are opening out."

"I'M STARVING," Sarah suddenly announced, from behind her little paper umbrella.

"Right," said Jade. "Let's eat."

I paid the drinks bill and we wandered out into the street again. It had got really dark, and the atmosphere had changed. Families with kids had been replaced by loud groups of people our age and couples holding hands. Beachwear had been swapped for something altogether more glamorous. The nightlife had started.

We started to stroll down the street, enjoying the buzz, the undercurrent of expectation everywhere. We were still feeling kind of post-cocktail heady and reckless and celebratory. It didn't matter that we were in our crumpled up flight-clothes with pale smudged faces; we weren't part of all this yet, we were watching, waiting to begin.

"You can't do this in England," said Jade. "Not

even in the hottest weather. Just . . . *promenade.*"

"Yeah, you can," said Sarah. "If there's sea nearby. When I visit my grandma—"

"Where's she live?"

"Skegness."

Jade and I burst out laughing, and Sarah, to her credit, joined in. "You *can*," she insisted. "When it's hot, you *can*."

"Look at all these people," Jade gloated. "I bet they spent months planning their holidays. They should learn to be spontaneous."

"Like us." Sarah giggled.

"Yes. Now come on, I'm sure that bistro is down that lane there."

It was, and it looked brilliant. Crowded, noisy, smelling wonderfully of grilled lamb and herbs. A waiter welcomed us enthusiastically, saying, "You just arrived? You are beautiful, but white, so I guess." We smiled at him, told him he was right, and he directed us toward a tiny table for two right at the front, on the pavement. Then he turned to the taverna interior and imperiously summoned another chair. A second waiter obligingly produced one, hefting it with a flourish across the diners' heads.

There was just enough room for us to squeeze around the table. "You want the lamb," the waiter told us. "Is excellent."

"It smells excellent," said Jade. "Yes, please." She looked over at me and Sarah. "Three?"

"Definitely," I said, but Sarah picked up the menu and started scanning it.

"Have pizza if you want," Jade said. "No one'll think you're sad."

"Shut up," said Sarah. "I'll have the lamb."

I got the feeling they often did this—these little power battles. It was part of what linked them together. I wondered briefly, anxiously, how the three of us were going to work out. Up till now, there'd been no connection between Sarah and me, apart from Jade. And whenever Jade and I had spent time together I'd been aware of Sarah there, in the background, watching me, monitoring my growing friendship with her friend.

Well, it would just have to work out, wouldn't it? Because we were here now. And whatever happened, I was going to make the most of it.

Three fragrant plates of lamb arrived with a basket of bread; then a big bowl of salad, glasses, and a jug of wine. We set to as though we hadn't eaten for a week. We didn't say much but as we chewed we kept grinning at each other like conspirators, as though we couldn't get over being where we were.

"Well," said Jade, wiping her mouth and putting her knife and fork down, "I'd like to say let's search out a club and have fun—"

"Oh, *no*." Sarah groaned.

"—but I think we should call it a day. We need to buy teabags and milk or I shan't be able to get up tomorrow. Also—more important—I'm not dressed for a club. Let's get the stuff and get home."

"Home," I repeated happily.

"Yeah. We need to make our beds up and stuff. *God*—I hope they've left us some sheets!"

We left the bistro and wandered back to the old central square where we'd got off the bus. "There's the taxi rank," said Jade, pointing, "and there's a supermarket. See? Simple."

Once inside the shop, Sarah came over all active. She picked up a wire basket and collected croissants and crusty bread, thyme-scented honey, pasta, tomato paste, garlic and onions, butter, tea, coffee, milk, olive oil . . .

"What's all this for?" complained Jade.

"We ought to stock up while we can," said Sarah. "If we're getting a cab home. Look how cheap this oil is! Let's get some Greek yogurt for breakfast."

We stood and watched as she scooted around

the shelves, loading up her basket, adding to ours.

"Can you cook?" I asked Jade.

"No, but—"

"Sarah can. Thought so."

"She does great stuff. Tasty but healthy. Semi-vegi. Whenever she stays at my place Mum just lets her take over. I think her family are all pies and chips all the time."

"You think? Haven't you been there?"

Jade shrugged. "Only a couple of times. It's pretty dreary. I feel really sorry for her, stuck with that lot."

Sarah was heading toward us, triumphantly waving a box. "Candles!" she exclaimed. "We can put them in jars in the courtyard."

"Romantic," said Jade.

"And I can put them either side of that mirror in my room."

"Spooky," said Jade.

"Yeah," I agreed. "Like a spell, Sarah. You might see another reflection—behind your own!"

"Just so long as he's fit," added Jade, and Sarah tossed her head, smirking, and the three of us headed to the till.

The goods filled five carrier bags and came to an awful lot of drachmas, but we agreed with Sarah that it was necessary. It was the basis of our larder. We staggered off to the taxi rank and found an empty cab without difficulty, and this time the driver knew our farmhouse.

"Just to the end of the track, is all," he said, warningly. "I nearly got stuck in a ditch last time I tried that track. You be alright walking—there's lights."

The lights, we discovered (once we'd paid the cab off and he'd reversed back onto the main road), consisted of a dodgy-looking string of naked bulbs suspended haphazardly along the lane. Only about one in three were actually alight.

"The electricity out here," said Jade, "is not high-tech. It cuts out at the slightest excuse—like a storm. I think these lights have been run off some mains somewhere. All very illegal."

"Great," I grumbled.

We tottered forward slowly, weighed down by our bulging carriers. The thin electric light cast eccentric shadows on the ground, so that you were constantly stepping over holes that weren't there—or into ones you couldn't see.

"I wish I'd left a light on at the farmhouse," Jade muttered.

"But you will find it, won't you?" asked Sarah, in a voice much higher than her normal one.

"Yeah, course I will. Come on—not far now."

We all quickened our pace a little. Then suddenly, to my left, something very large huffed out a great breath, and my heart seemed to stop with fear at the exact same time my brain told me it's OK, it's OK, it's a horse.

"What's that . . . chewing noise?" Sarah quavered.

"Chewing," said Jade.

"It's goats," I reassured her. "Other side of the fence. I've just had a *horse* blow on me."

"Nearly there," said Jade.

At last we got to the courtyard door, and we all put down our bags while Jade felt her way across the wood panels to the keyhole, swearing extravagantly.

"Whatever you do, don't drop the key," I said. Sarah and I waited, trying not to look as though we were scanning the blackness all around us for signs of movement. Which we were. Desperately.

"It's weird not having a front door, isn't it?" breathed Sarah.

"This *is* the front door," said Jade.

"Yeah but—it's—you know—*open*. It's like the bedrooms—lead off the *garden*."

"So lock your bedroom door. And if you hear the sound of a grappling iron being thrown over the wall in the early hours—just give us a shout."

"Oh, ha *ha*," snapped Sarah.

Then we heard the welcome sound of the door grinding open, and Jade laughed. "Sarah, I'm *teasing*. There's zilch crime rate here. Nothing to steal."

"It's not stealing I'm worried about," muttered Sarah, pushing past me so I was the last to get into the courtyard.

We made our way like the blind, step by slow step, across the courtyard to the kitchen. Then Jade snapped on the light and we all laughed at each other in relief.

"OK, OK, I admit it," I said. "That walk scared me!"

"You know what we need, don't you?" said Jade.

"A torch," said Sarah.

"Actually I was thinking along bigger lines," said Jade. "Like—a car."

There was a brief, awed silence. "A car?" I echoed.

"Yeah. I got my test six months ago. You don't drive, do you, Kelly?"

I shook my head. "Not yet."

"I know a garage in the center that does OK old bangers—Jill said they hired motorbikes there last summer. She said he was cheap. By the time we've forked out for cabs to get food and to get back from clubs and stuff—we may as well be running a car. Then we can go to loads of different beaches as well."

"Wow," I breathed. Jade certainly thought big. I had this brief vision of the three of us in some flash open-top, like a road movie. Singing along to the radio and cat-calling good-looking blokes on the pavement.

"But you can't drink, if you're driving," said Sarah. "So it wouldn't be fair."

"Sarah, you know I don't drink much when I'm clubbing. I get high on—"

"—attention from men. Yeah, I know. But what about that rutty old track we just had to *crawl* down? Not even the cab driver would touch it, and he's experienced, he's—"

"Sarah, the reason he wouldn't touch it was he was worried about his stupid suspension. If we get an old wreck, it won't matter. I can go slow and avoid the ditch at the side. I can *drive*, you know, Sarah!"

"Yeah, I know."

"Have you started learning, Kelly?"

"Well—I've had about four lessons, but—"

"Look, it would be OK with just me. We're not talking about massive distances here. Just convenience and the ability to give attractive guys lifts and—you know—*freedom*."

Freedom: the word hung happily in the air as we hoisted all the bags on the table and started unpacking the provisions. "Let's make some tea," I said.

"If there's any water." Jade twisted the tap; it banged irritably for a few seconds, then spewed out some water in a thin stream. Jade let it run for a while, then she filled the kettle, and banged it down on the stove. "We're cooking," she said.

Sarah, meanwhile, had found some spray stuff under the sink and was wiping out the fridge before she stacked it with the perishable stuff. "We can sort the rest out tomorrow," she said. "We need fruit and *vegetables*."

"There's a sort of streetmarket nearby," said Jade. "Well—a few big stalls on the side of the road to the beach. All fresh stuff. Oranges, peppers, tomatoes as big as melons . . . melons as big as . . . um . . . *huge* melons—"

"What about courgettes?" interrupted Sarah. "And aubergines?"

"Sure to be. All that stuff is cheap here. It's boring English crap like cabbage that costs you."

"Ratatouille!" said Sarah, pleased.

"You saying you'll cook tomorrow night, Sarah?" Jade grinned as she pulled a huge red teapot off the shelf and swilled it under the tap. "Cool. We need to save money if we're getting a car."

We took our mugs of steaming tea out into the courtyard, and stood looking up at the pure black sky with its stabs of starlight. There was a really good feeling between the three of us. "I'm wiped." Jade sighed contentedly. "Let's shove the mattresses back on the beds and get the sheets and turn in. Tomorrow is going to be long and hot!"

The owners might not have got us any food in, but they hadn't let us down over the bed linens. Jade went to an old wooden chest in the corner of the living room and pulled out six crisp white cotton sheets that still smelled of the sun. Then we spent some time running up and down the old stone steps: up to our rooms with the mattresses, down to the bathroom with our toothbrushes, into the kitchen, making a lot of noise to scare away the last of the fear from that long walk along the dark lane. And also just because we could make a noise. There was no one to tell us not to.

Then we said our final goodnights, and went into our separate rooms.

I thought of the other two as I shook out the sheets over my bed. Jade, stripping off at speed; admiring the reflection of her body in the mirror.

Unpacking all her bottles, lining them up, then religiously cleansing, toning, moisturizing her face. Jade was casual about a lot of things, but her looks weren't one of them. She'd discussed with me at length the type of suncream I should buy. Beauty routine complete, she'd collapse on the bed and be asleep within minutes.

Sarah had carried the candles up to bed with her. I imagined her pushing them into the two brass holders either side of the mirror, lighting them, and then just sitting there, lost in thought, before curling up under the sheet like an embryo not too keen on getting born.

And me. I cleaned my face off tiredly, pulled on my thin nightie and flicked down the coarse cotton sheet, ready to get into bed. Then I stopped, crouched on the floor by my case and began to rummage. I pulled out a framed photo. It showed me, smiling straight at the camera, crooked-but-nice teeth, long brown hair pulled to one side. And behind me, arm around my shoulder, smiling but serious, always serious, Mike. Darker hair than me, cut really short, strong nose, sexy mouth. Gorgeous.

I sighed, and propped the photo on the little chest of drawers. I had a sudden sense of him, his arms around me, his mouth moving across my face, getting lost in him, drowning in him, and I felt clenched up, aching, with missing him.

I went over to the narrow bed, to get in. Then I went back to the chest of drawers, picked up the photo again, kissed it, and shoved it back at the bottom of the case.

CHAPTER 9

I WAS WOKEN BY HOT SUN shining through the open shutters and straight on my face. My watch told me it was nine o'clock but that didn't seem to make sense; it felt earlier. Maybe the time zone was different; I hadn't checked.

Normally, mornings aren't my best time, but this was different. I was fizzing with anticipation as I swung my legs out of bed. The door to Sarah's room was shut and I didn't want to wake her by looking in, so I just slid, barefoot, out onto the stone balcony.

The sun hit me, blissful and strong, pouring over my skin like honey. I leaned my elbows on the balustrade, Juliet-style, and gazed down at the court-yard. It was even more beautiful in the morning light. Swags of green leaves cooled the white walls; the flowers hung down, still wet with dew. I turned to go down the steps and a tiny

65

green lizard with gorgeous, cartoon sucker-feet slipped out of a crack in the wall and skedaddled along beside me.

The courtyard was checkered with patches of shade, vivid patches of sun. I walked over it slowly, savoring it, then I went into the kitchen. It, too, was filled with early sun. I put the kettle on to boil, rinsed out three mugs, pulled the cold milk from the fridge. Somehow even these little jobs were enjoyable here.

"You beat me to it!" Sarah was standing in the doorway in dark blue pyjamas, her unbrushed gingery hair bushing out around her head. "I was going to bring you tea in bed."

I smiled at her. "I couldn't stay in bed. I wanted to get out in the sun."

"Me, too. Let's have it in the courtyard."

"Mmm." The kettle still hadn't boiled. Casting for something to say, I asked, "Did you sleep OK?"

"Yes, brilliant, thanks. I didn't expect to, somehow, after the flight and all the excitement and everything, and being in a new place, but I did. My room—it's got this really calm, really kind atmosphere—" She broke off and glanced away, embarrassed.

"Are you into atmospheres then?" I asked. "Can you sense them?"

I expected her to laugh and deny it, but she didn't. She looked back at me and said, "Sort of. In houses. When I first go into them. It's partly the vibes of the people who live there, but it's the people who used to live there, too."

"Eew—ghosts?"

"No—just a—you know. A feeling."

"So what did you feel from this place?"

"Well—it's hard to say. There's a lot been going on here. It's got lots of energy. But it's not bad energy. And it's got this lovely calm, too. Especially out in the courtyard. And my room."

"What about *my* room?"

"Ah. Active again. And that staircase—it's buzzing."

"Blimey, Sarah—creepy! You can really sense that?"

"Yeah . . . well. You know. But it's not *bad*, Kelly. It's just a place where a lot happened. Which isn't surprising, when you think how old it is."

The kettle finally boiled and I made the tea and we carried it out into the courtyard and sat on the steps. "We'll have to move that table outside," Sarah said. "You know—the one in the living room. Like Jade said."

"Breakfast in style." I laughed, and I was about

to ask her more about what she could sense about the farmhouse, when a door slammed up on the balcony. We looked around to see Jade catwalking elegantly down the stone stairs. Her hair was slicked back smoothly and she was wearing a fantastic turquoise bikini. She had a jet anklet on, with matching studs in her ears, the sharpest sunglasses, and eye-aching fuchsia toenail varnish.

"Go away," said Sarah.

"What?"

"You look too good. It's not fair."

"No, it's not," I agreed. "You make me feel like a fat schoolgirl. Sitting here in my nightie."

"So go and get your swim gear on," said Jade. "This is in my view one big plus of a hot holiday. You get up and get straight into your beach gear. No washing, no fussing—not even eye-makeup, 'cos you've got shades. You do all that stuff at night, after a day swimming and sunning. But not too much sunning, because we all know what the sun can do to your skin."

"We ought to," groused Sarah. "You're always on about it."

"Midday, we'll get out of it. There are the best cafés here—right on the beach, plenty of shade, full of gorgeous guys drinking beer. Food's cheap, too. You just hang out in the heat of the day. Dead sexy. Then you drift back to the shoreline, until the sun goes down."

It all sounded so glamorous it gave me the shivers. "It's *the* lifestyle, darlings!" Jade said. "I thought, today, we could go to the local beach. It's a ten minute walk or so. Easy."

"Sounds great," I breathed. "I'm glad you've got it all so sorted."

"What's for breakfast?" Jade grinned.

Sarah got eagerly to her feet. "If you two can bring the table and chairs out here, I'll get the brekky," she said. "I'll heat up the croissants."

"OK," said Jade. "One croissant equals twenty minutes extra swimming. Let's go."

Together we carried the bleached-wood table out to the courtyard, plus all six chairs, because Jade said we'd be having lots of fantastic people dropping round in a few days or so and we had to have room for them. I started to laugh, but she looked like she'd meant it.

There was still no sign of Sarah and the promised brekky once we'd set out the table, so I ran upstairs to get into my black bikini. I was feeling quite self-conscious about it. Jade looked so lean and streamlined . . . she'd make anyone feel dumpy.

I put it on, then I tied my hair up in a big high

ponytail, and hooked the silver rings I'd bought for the beach in my ears. The mirror in my room was tiny, and you could only check yourself out in quarter-sections. As I pivoted, I thought each of my quarters looked gross. And white. Oh, shit. Still, the bikini was the best I had and it had looked OK in my full-length mirror at home.

I walked self-consciously down the steps to join Jade, reining in my stomach for all I was worth. She smiled up at me encouragingly. *"All right*, Kelly! You look great!"

I grinned, pleased, and sat down at the table with her. "What's it like having tits?" she asked.

"Oh, come on, you've got tits."

"Not like yours. You've got a *cleavage*. I've always wanted a cleavage."

"Well, can't you get one of those bras that—"

Jade shook her head. "No bra would do it. Surgery—possibly. Hey—you know everyone here sunbathes bareback, don't you?"

"Bareback?"

"Topless."

"No way!"

"Yeah, it's great. It's the only way to avoid a load of crisscrossing strap lines on your skin. Everyone does it, so you don't get any stares." She stopped and grinned at me. "OK, I bet *you'll* get stares."

"Topless—blimey."

"It's OK when you're used to it. Although personally I don't go for all this strutting-around-flashing-it-all stuff. Call me prudish but I just do it when I'm lying down."

We were both giggling over this when Sarah staggered from the kitchen with a large, laden tray and placed it impressively on the table in front of us. Guiltily, I stood up to help her unload it. Coffee, croissants, Greek yogurt, honey, fresh figs . . . "I picked these round the back," she said. "The trees out there are *loaded*. These looked the ripest."

It was delicious, that breakfast in the growing heat. We felt we could take as long as we liked over it. "The big mistake people make about holidays," Jade announced, chewing, "is hitting the junk food. Or totally changing from what they do at home. That's one of the problems with staying in a hotel—no food control. So they feel ill, and bloated, and they put on weight, and it spoils their fun. *We're* not going to do that."

"No," Sarah and I echoed, mouths full of fig.

"And we'll get some serious exercise in," she added. "In the sea. Not just farting around in the shallows like most people. That way, when we hit the nightlife, we'll feel we've earned it, right?"

"Right."

"Plus we'll look fabulous. OK. Let's go."

"Let's wash up," I said. "While Sarah gets her swimsuit on."

"Oh—OK," said Jade, a bit begrudgingly, and she followed me into the kitchen.

Jade was right, it was an easy walk to the beach. Up until the last few hundred meters, that is, which consisted of scrambling over rocks. "Don't complain!" Jade called back over her shoulder. "These rocks are why this beach isn't overrun with grannies and little kids! And it's worth it when you get there, I promise you."

We clambered on, wincing and grumbling, as our feet jarred against jagged stones and our ankles got scratched by thorny low-growing plants, and finally we made it to the shore.

Jade was right, again. It was worth it. We walked onto a long, smooth sandy cove, ringed by cliffs. Waves lapped the shore; out on the horizon, it was hard to see where the blue sea ended and the sky began.

"Oh, this is *beautiful*." I sighed. "This is—I can't *wait* to get in that water."

"There's no shade," said Sarah. "We're going to *fry*."

"You're not using your eyes, babe," smirked

Jade, and she started striding along the beach, us following, glad to let her take the lead once more. She was heading over to a group of haphazardly placed beach umbrellas, all with two sunbeds underneath. Sunbathers were stretched out on about half of the beds; a few people were splashing on the shoreline, paddling or playing pat-ball.

As we came to a halt beside a vacant set of sunbeds, I noticed a little shack café, set back against the rocks. The sun and salt air had bleached it to the color of the sand it stood on; it was beautiful, like driftwood. Tables and chairs were set out in front of it; shade was provided by a huge canopy made from palm leaves.

An almost-naked kid of about fourteen with a battered leather satchel came running out of it and down toward us. "You want hire umbrella? Two thousand the day. You need two?"

"No," Jade said. "One'll do." She handed over the money, and hung her bag underneath the umbrella. "We can share. No need to chuck money away. And I guess while we're about it, we ought to have some kind of a kitty, for things like this."

"Yeah," said Sarah. "It nearly did my brain in, splitting the grocery bill three ways last night."

Most of the sunbathers had turned to check us over. They all seemed very brown and young and good-looking. That first-day-at-college feeling came over me again; I felt quite self-conscious as I stripped my old T-shirt off and sat down on the edge of one of the sunbeds.

"I feel so white and *English*," I muttered to Jade. "Sainsbury's and traffic exhaust and rain and—"

"That," said Jade, "will go. Trust me. You will get into beach life." Jade looked completely at home already. She looked like she'd been born in a bikini. "I'm going to cook for a bit, then swim," she announced. She pulled the other sunbed out into the full glare of the sun, spread her towel on it, and stretched out. Lean, elegant, eyes closed.

"I think I'm going in the sea now," muttered Sarah, beside me. "I'm all sweaty."

"Me, too," I said.

We waded hurriedly into the water, trailing our hands to test the temperature, avoiding the rocks we could see lying in wait on the sea bed. The sea was cool and fabulous. Before long, it had lapped up to the top of our legs. Sarah turned to me, saying "Come *on*!" and together we launched ourselves, and started swimming.

We were both laughing with sheer pleasure as we moved forward in the water. I looked toward the shore, meaning to wave at Jade, but she was still staked out, flat and motionless.

"Shall we head over to those rocks?" Sarah said, pointing to the cliffs at the side, and I nodded. I was surprised by how good a swimmer she was, to be honest. Somehow I'd expected her to be the sort who'd not risk going out of her depth. I'm nothing brilliant, but I can keep going, and together we breaststroked side by side, keeping to the same pace. Soon we'd moved into the shadow cast by the overhanging rocks. The sudden shade made me blind for a second or so; I trod water slowly, waiting for my eyes to catch up.

"Watch the rocks underneath," warned Sarah. "Don't scrape your legs."

Carefully, pulling our way forward with our arms, we coasted over the top of the submerged rocks and came to one that was half in, half out of the sun's glare. Then we perched there like mermaids, dangling our legs, swaying in the lapping of the waves. There was an awkwardness there, a vacuum, because Jade wasn't with us. Then Sarah sighed and murmured, "This is *heaven*. I'm getting used to the fact that this heat is for real."

"You bet it's for real," I said. "Don't you love it?"

"Mmmm. But it's good in the shade. Not having the sun blasting down on the top of your head for a bit."

"I suppose it'll take us a while to adjust."

"Yeah. And not only to the heat. I don't think I've got over the culture shock yet."

"What d'you mean?" I asked.

"It's all so *different*. Doesn't it kind of . . . scare you?"

I shrugged, happily. "Yeah, I guess. I mean—I feel a real new person. But it's just so *exciting*. It's so . . . *exotic*. And Jade is brilliant, the way she sorts things. And really—we've got no worries, have we? All we need do is *indulge* ourselves."

Sarah hunched her shoulders, and looked as though she wished it was that easy. "I have a bad track record with holidays," she said. "When I was a kid, holidays were always awful."

"Oh, *family* holidays—yeah. This is different. Hey—Jade's coming out!"

On the beach, Jade had got to her feet, and was scanning the sea, one hand shading her eyes from the sun. I stood up on the rock, and waved energetically at her. She waved back, then started to move down toward the water. Two guys who'd been heading up to the beach café stopped in their tracks and stood and stared at her as she waded in.

"She's so *great*-looking, isn't she?" I sighed. "She just *gives off* being great-looking."

"She wasn't always like that," Sarah said, watching her stonily. "When I first met her—when she was thirteen—she was weird. Scraggy and weird."

"Well, blimey, she's grown up well, then."

"Yeah. It's confidence. She is *so* confident."

"Oh, come on Sarah—it's not *all* confidence! What about her long legs?"

Jade was doing a fast crawl toward us. I watched her shapely, bleached-blond head as it drew closer, and I wanted to ask Sarah about their friendship—about why they still hung out together. Only I couldn't think of a way of putting it that didn't sound like I was asking: How come someone as cool as Jade is friends with someone like you?

Minutes later and Jade was circling us, splashing. "Hey—come on—stop slacking! Let's go further out. Get some real swimming in before lunch."

One after the other, Sarah and I toppled off the rocks into the water again, and set off after Jade. We skirted the sides of the cliff, and watched big, solemn fish touring the rocks, under the surface of the clear water. Further out, in the open, a whole shoal of tiny blue fish flicked away from us, as if by radar.

"We have to get snorkels!" Jade shouted. "Just imagine what's going on down there—I want to see it!"

"I don't!" I yelled back. "Maybe it's giant squid!"

"Let's go back now," called Sarah. "I'm knackered."

In answer, Jade plunged off at top speed for maybe twenty meters more, then she turned around and the three of us headed back to shore.

There's something about exercise—it makes you feel good about yourself. Maybe it's the adrenaline rush or something. I swaggered onto the beach and flopped down on the sunbed, then I rung out my long rope of hair on the sand like I had every right to be there.

"Want to rinse off?" said Jade. "Look." She was pointing to the rocks beside the beach café, where a tall, fit-looking guy was standing sluicing himself down with a hose. "Fresh water. It's included in the price of the sunbeds. On most beaches they have a proper shower, but that looks like it does the job."

She started walking over. "Hang on, Jade," I hissed. "Give him time to finish!"

"What for?" she smirked, and we followed her. The guy was really tanned. He looked as though he'd had bleach-streaks put in his hair, but apart from that he was lush. As Jade stepped forward, he opened his eyes and grinned, said, "Nearly finished," gave himself one more spray across the head, and handed her the hose.

"Thank you," said Jade, huskily, then she started spraying herself.

"You know, your feet are going to burn on the way back across the sand."

"What?"

"Your feet," he went on, in a faintly Scottish accent. "They're OK now, 'cos you've been in the sea and they're cold, but you'll need sandals for the way back, or your feet'll burn."

"I'll get them," said Sarah. "I'll run back and get them." And off she went.

Jade handed the hose to me, and stood there, gorgeous and dripping, next to the fit bloke who was showing no signs of walking away.

"Thanks for the tip," she said. "We've only just got here, and you forget things like that."

"Yeah," he agreed. "I was burning my feet for a whole week before I got used to it. Where you staying?"

And they were off. Jade described our setup, he described his. This was the closest I'd ever been to Jade's pulling technique, and I stared and listened avidly from underneath the spray of hose water. She was relaxed, amiable, soft spoken. She laughed a lot. She listened to his opinion of the local night scene. And by the end of five minutes she'd agreed that we'd meet him and some mates of his at a nearby club that night.

I felt slightly dizzy with the speed of it all,

and all I'd done was watch.

Sarah came skittering up with the sandals. "You're right." She gasped. "That sand is *burning*."

The fit guy grinned. "Told you. OK. See you tonight, maybe. Hope so." And he was off.

"*Whaaaat?*" Sarah squealed. "What did he mean—'see you tonight'?"

"He's taking me out for dinner," Jade drawled.

"He's *whaaaat*?"

"She's winding you up," I said. "But it's still pretty shameless—and incredibly fast work. He told her about this new club, only been open a few weeks, and said he'd see us there tonight."

"Jade, he's like—the first male you've *talked* to!" Sarah wailed. "And already you're—"

"Oh, so *what*. Where's the sense in hanging about? He and his friends are well in here—and they're staying on for the summer, like us. And the faster we get into the scene out here, the faster things'll happen. Right?"

Then without waiting for an answer, she slipped on her sandals and sailed back to the sunbeds. Dumbly, Sarah took the hose from my outstretched hand, and then we both exchanged a look, eyebrows raised, and laughed.

Jade's got it all worked out, I thought. And if that means I don't get time to think, that suits me fine.

*　*　*

We oiled up and sunbathed for a while, then Jade suggested we follow the steady trail of people abandoning the scorching beach for the shade of the café. I'll say one thing for Jade. She was *equipped*. She unhooked her chain-handled beach bag from underneath the umbrella, pulled out a mirror and some lipstick and made up her lips. She slicked back her hair, and rubbed a little more cream on her nose. Then she pulled out a silky, patterned, red sarong, tied it at a sexy slant around her waist, turned to me and Sarah, still slumped on the sunbeds, and said, "Ready?"

I butted my way into my old loose T-shirt and vowed then and there I had to get this beach-culture sorted, just like Jade. I had to get a sarong, and a bag, and be cool, relaxed, and organized.

The beach café was buzzing. It looked like every table was taken, and the almost-naked fourteen-year-old kid had now donned a huge apron and been joined by his sister. Both of them were scooting in and out of the kitchen at the back, carrying plates of food and drinks. We stood awkwardly in the entrance, willing someone to leave so we could get their table. A group of four lads with shaved heads, who'd stopped talking the minute we'd arrived, stared at us fixedly.

"I think they're soldiers," muttered Sarah. "Let's come back later."

"No—look," said Jade. "That lot are going." She nodded toward a family in the far corner. They were stirring, making leaving signs. Jade walked over, and stood beside their table, smiling winningly.

"May we?" she said.

The family spoke French to each other, gesticulated, and finally vacated.

"Jade!" Sarah said with a hiss, as we sank gratefully into their seats. "You practically tipped that kid out of its chair!"

"Yeah, well, the brat was taking forever. Look—the menu's chalked up on that board over there. English on the right. All pretty basic but it's not the food we're here for, is it?" She was scanning the other tables as she spoke. I watched her, skimming over couples, lingering on groups of guys, assessing, getting herself noticed.

"Your Scottish hunk's disappeared," I said.

"Yeah. He said he had to go."

The four skinheads apart, there were some guys worth watching. Worth exchanging looks with, and a bit of long-distance energy. And they kept standing up, going to the bar, walking in, walking out, watching us. It was a real show. Jade was an expert at this kind of silent flirting. I got the feeling that any time she wanted, she could turn up the energy, and get into a conversation with whoever she chose. But she kept it long distance. We ordered salad, and stuffed vine-leaves, and ice-cold Cokes, and enjoyed the whole thing.

Well, Jade and I enjoyed it. Sarah didn't. She seemed tense, ill at ease. I directed a few comments at her, tried to get her to join in the conversation, but in the end I gave up. I couldn't work her out. Maybe Jade made her feel inadequate, maybe that was her problem. Jade made me feel inadequate, too, but it was less serious for me because I had Mike and all this guy-watching was just a bit of fun. *And anyway,* I thought, staring at Jade over the rim of my Coke bottle, *I was going to turn those feelings of inadequacy to my advantage, wasn't I?*

I was going to copy her style, her sarong, and especially, her attitude.

By three o'clock we were back on the beach. We had another long sunbathe, and another blissful swim, circled by three of the guys we'd been staring down over lunch. Then we dried off and Jade and I went back to the café for a cold beer while Sarah dozed beneath the umbrella.

"Don't look now," Jade said with a hiss, "but those guys are coming, too."

"They're *ancient*," I whispered back. "One of them is going bald."

"That means they have money. They can pay for our drinks."

"Jade—*really*!" I said, mock-indignant, but sure enough, they came up behind us as we reached the bar, and insisted our tab was added to theirs. We exchanged a few bright words, and they told us how gorgeous we were. It was like a sport to Jade, like fishing. She reeled in all she could, then she announced we had to go, to get ready for the night.

"Meeting someone are you?" the balding guy asked wistfully.

"Yeah," said Jade. "See you." We wandered back, and this time I swaggered over the sand. Then we woke Sarah, rolled up our towels and headed over to the rocky exit.

"I love the way the day divides up, in these hot climates," Jade said. "It's sort of like *two* days. You get up earlyish, when it's all fresh and not too hot, and you wind down as it gets hotter and hotter. Then you get a second lease of life, once the sun starts to set. What we'll have to do is start taking a siesta. On the beach, maybe. Then it's *really* like two days."

"I can't sleep in the middle of the day," Sarah

said. "I can't go off—and if I do, I'm all groggy till I sleep properly at night. I feel awful now, and I only dropped off for five minutes."

Jade and I exchanged a look. "Maybe you'll feel differently after you've watched the dawn break a few times," Jade murmured.

I could tell Sarah wanted to come back with something, but she just set her mouth a little and carried on struggling over the rocks. Jade and I reached the road a while before her and as I turned around, preparing to wait, Jade said, "Don't worry. She won't be a pain like this all holiday."

"I don't think she's a pain."

"Yes, you do. You must do."

"Just a bit—you know—quiet."

"Yeah. She gets these moods on. All uptight and boring. When she's feeling out of her depth. Which she is now. But she'll get over it."

Then Sarah drew up alongside us, and Jade started talking about how brown she thought she'd got that day.

CHAPTER 10

TO SARAH'S SATISFACTION, the roadside vegetable stalls had set up by the time we walked back to the farmhouse. She made us stop, and she picked out huge, cheap oranges, a bunch of grapes, red peppers, courgettes, tomatoes. "I'll do a pasta," she said. "I'll do a vegi pasta for before we go out."

"Great," said Jade. "We've got ages. We don't want to head out till after dark." Then she muttered to me, "Trust her to get turned on by bloody *vegetables*."

We had hours before dark. Absolutely no need to rush over anything. We meandered back to the farmhouse, feeling nicely tired and well spent. Jade let us into the courtyard and I wandered over and stretched out on the stone steps with the late sun on my legs.

Sarah headed for the kitchen. "Can I help?" I asked, just a bit too quietly for her to hear, splaying my legs more comfortably.

Soon she was out again, with three brimming glasses of ice and orange juice. "I just squeezed them," she said, with satisfaction. "Minutes ago, these oranges were *alive*."

"Oh, fabulous." I picked up one of the cool, water-beaded glasses and took a sip. "Mmmmm, beats longlife. *Thanks*, Sarah. Jade? Come and get your vit C."

In answer, from the living room, a slow, rhythmic beat started up. And then a sax came in, running up the scale, pausing, tumbling down again. And then the most wonderful mellow sexy music was filling the courtyard, and Jade came boogying out, swaying, dancing, looking pleased as hell with herself.

"I just found their CD player!" she crowed. "The choice of music is pretty grannified, but some's OK. Like this—*serious* seduction material."

And she started pulling this total tart's face, and bumping and grinding, stripper-like, until Sarah and I were hooting with laughter and clapping in time. The music went into a really funky bit, and in response Jade hip-wriggled wildly up three stairs, posed like Marilyn Monroe, and hip-wriggled down again. "All *right*!" she gloated. "And this is only *halfway* as loud as it can go!"

Sarah looked panicky. "Oh, God, Jade—won't people—?"

"Sarah—*what* people? This is an adult free zone! OK, OK, we might get complaints from the goats, but personally, I think they're cool about music."

"Music," I said, getting up to dance next to Jade, "is what they've been *missing* from their lives."

"Yeah—the babes! We'll ask them to our parties."

"Parties?" echoed Sarah.

"Yeah. We'll have great parties."

"Jade." I laughed. "Great, but we need *guests* for parties."

"Guests? We'll get guests. We're meeting some tonight, remember? Come on—think *big*. We're dug in here for the whole summer. We have this fantastic place. We can have a real *scene*."

The music changed to something my mum might slow-dance to at Christmas if she got plastered enough. "Some scene!" I giggled.

"OK, OK. It's got a tape deck, too. I brought tapes for my Walkman. We can listen to good stuff, too."

And she was off again, dancing around me, taking the piss out of the music so brilliantly she had us both in stitches. Sarah handed her her orange juice mid-gyration, and she took a sip and sprinted up the stone steps, then reappeared a couple of minutes later, waving a bottle of vodka.

"Never drink orange juice straight, darlings!" she caroled, unscrewing the cap and heading toward me. I held out my glass and got a generous splash, but Sarah pulled her glass back after only about a thimbleful had been added. Vodka splashed on the flagstones.

"Aaagh!" shrieked Jade. "What a waste, what a waste! Quick, Kelly—lick it up!"

"I'm going to start the dinner," said Sarah.

"Want some help?" I asked.

"No, it's easy."

"Well—I'll clear up then," I called out, as she stomped into the kitchen. "Oh, God," I muttered. "She makes me feel so *guilty*."

"Don't let her," said Jade. "Bags I first in the bathroom." She disappeared.

I sat back on the steps and basked in the low sun, making my drink last, and that feeling of being in a film, of nothing being quite real, came back to me. It was very relaxing, somehow. As if all that mattered was to be here, now, with my feet on the warm stone. I thought about Jade and Sarah, and how I didn't really know them, how I had no idea how the holiday was going to turn out. But somehow, right then, that didn't matter. It would be a discovery. Like a play, like a film.

Jade called that the shower was free, and I got my towel and washing stuff and locked myself in the bathroom. Mouthwatering garlicky smells were already coming from the kitchen next door.

I took time showering, admiring the tan line on the top of my legs, wondering if I'd dare go topless some time. Then I dried off and lathered about a pint of after-suncream all over. No way was I going to peel.

Sarah looked more cheerful as she headed into the bathroom after me. I sat down next to Jade at the table, both of us in towels like sauna clients, and said, "Sarah seems happier."

"I told you, she gets a real buzz out of cooking. Don't knock it. We'll get fed."

"It just feels a bit—I dunno. Exploitative."

"Not if she enjoys it. And you're clearing up, aren't you? I heard you offer."

"Jade—we're *both* clearing up."

"Yeah, yeah." Jade unzipped a very professional make-up bag, pulled out a big, square mirror, and started working on her face, like a painter works on a canvas. I watched, fascinated. She got this shimmery, clubby effect around her eyes, using a gel, three different powders, and a tiny pointed brush.

"Do me, too," I said.

"You serious? You trust me?"

"Sure."

"You're mad. OK. Let me finish this."

Sarah came out of the bathroom, disappeared into the kitchen, and came out saying, "Fifteen minutes till we eat."

"It smells fantastic." I groaned. "I'm starving."

"We need wine," said Jade.

"I bought some Pimms," I said doubtfully.

"OK. Do that. With cucumber."

We spent the next quarter of an hour in relaxed, pleasurable semi-silence, wrapped in our towels. Jade made me up, then Sarah; I fixed everyone Pimms, with courgette instead of cucumber, which didn't work, so we flicked it into the vines for the lizards. Then we cleared the table of makeup and had dinner.

Sarah could cook. Her sauce was succulent, and the spaghetti perfect. As we were mopping up our plates, Jade glanced at her watch and said "Jeez—look at the time. It's seven-thirty already. We have to get going. It's getting dark."

"We could just stay here," suggested Sarah. "We could put on your tapes, and party here."

Jade didn't even deign to answer. She headed for the steps, then came back when I yelled at her and helped shift the dirty plates into the kitchen. "Leave them in the sink," she said. "Just fill it with water and we'll do it in the morning. This stuff needs to soak."

I accepted her somewhat dodgy reasoning, and raced up the stairs with her. I'd already worked out what I was going to wear. My white, strappy sandals, the ones I could move in, not the really high ones, and the dress I'd worn on that last evening with Mike—

I stopped short, in front of the mirror, and gazed at myself, at the surprised expression on my face. Mike. I'd hardly thought of him once, all day. Everything had been so new, so exotic, so different—I'd just been moving from sensation to sensation, wondering at it all.

Mike. He'd be camped for the night, brewing up some sausage and bean mess around a fire. Or footsore, boots off, downing beers in a taverna.

Did I wish I was with him?

No. I didn't.

I got dressed quickly, excitedly, and sped downstairs. Sarah was already there, wearing a modest-looking short skirt and top. Nice, but nothing to make you catch your breath. And then Jade made her second grand entrance of the day. In this short, shiny sheath. Lizard-skin tight. Her fuchsia toenails matched a bangle just above her right elbow. Her earrings clashed, brilliantly.

"Let's go," she said.

CHAPTER 11

JADE RECKONED IT WAS STILL light enough to walk to the club, along the main road that continued on beyond the beach. "Then we'll get a cab back," she said. "Or a lift if we get lucky."

"Oh, Jade, don't be stupid," cried Sarah. "You can't just get in a car with someone you—"

"I was joking," snapped Jade. She hadn't been, though. I could tell from her face.

We walked for about twenty minutes, tottering a bit in our party shoes, and then, after a bit of jiggling down some side streets, and some directions from a black-clad granny who obviously disapproved of all clubs and all people who went to them, we arrived. The club was called *Ariadne* after that girl in the Minotaur myth, and it was so new it was still in the process of being built. It was a low, white, square building, sitting in a wasteland that would probably one day be a car park.

"At least we're not the first," said Jade, jerking her head toward the dozen or so cars parked haphazardly along the road. "I can't bear being the first."

We picked our way past heaps of sand and blocks of concrete and made it to the entrance, which was pretty neat. It had two black pillars and a great palm tree lit up by a white spotlight. The palm had a skew-whiff, surprised air, as though up until recently it had been growing somewhere else.

Loud music vibrated from the open door. The three of us paused outside it, nervously. Back home, you always feel scared, going into a new club. But you kind of know what to expect because all English clubs are—well, English. But here, we had no idea what it would be like.

"Come on," said Jade, determinedly.

Sarah and I followed her into the entrance. A guy behind a glass booth beamed at us. "On holiday?" he said.

"No," said Jade. "We live here."

"You do? You live here? Where? Where you live?" He was growing more excited with each question.

"Not really," said Sarah, and she nudged Jade sharply in the back. "Just for the summer." I knew she didn't want Jade giving our address away.

Then something good happened. When Jade tried to pay, the man insisted on letting us in for free. "On the house! On the house!" he kept parroting. "And you have good time and you come back!"

"Brilliant!" breathed Jade, as we walked along a wide corridor toward the music.

"Why did he do that?" said Sarah.

"'Cos we're gorgeous," answered Jade. "Or maybe he lets all girls in free. Some do."

"Yeah," I muttered. "It's probably a cover for the white slave trade."

We'd reached a little courtyard, open to the night sky, full of naff little sets of wrought iron seats and tables. No one was sitting at them. The courtyard was brand-new mock-ancient, with crumbling flagstones, shattered columns, broken terra cotta pots. "Look," I said, laughing, "it's trying to create the image of what the farmhouse actually *is*."

"Only it doesn't do it half as well," put in Sarah.

"Come on," said Jade again, and we crossed the courtyard to the dark, noisy mouth of the club, and went in.

You were aware of all the people before your eyes adjusted to the gloom and you could actually see them. A great mass, heaving in the center of the floor. And more, strewn around the walls.

The bar was at the far side, lit up by neon adverts for lager. Jade set out toward it and Sarah and I tagged along behind, trying to look relaxed, quaking inside. In a day or two, I told myself, I am going to take over from Jade sometimes, and buy drinks and order meals. Just not yet.

The bartender was Greek, and obviously employed for his looks and not his English. But luckily the language for booze is pretty international. Jade had no problem ordering three beers, or handing over the huge amount of money he seemed to be demanding for them. "So *that*'s why we got in free," she grumbled, checking the change. "They're building this place on the drinks' profit."

Then she turned, leaned back against the bar, took a swig from her bottle, and surveyed the scene. I followed suit, hoping some of her confidence would rub off on me. Some things were the same as an English club. There were the usual load of rhythmically challenged guys gyrating about, glittery girls in among them; and the usual cool set, leaning up against the wall. I preferred the gyrators. It really kills me when people stand about looking cool and bored in clubs. You've turned up,

97

you've paid for your ticket—so why pretend you don't really want to be there? Why not at least look *awake*?

"Any sign of Ross?" Jade asked.

"Ross?"

"You know—the Scottish guy from the beach."

"No," I said, scanning the floor. "But isn't that the four skinheads from the—"

"*Don't* make eye contact," snapped Jade.

"I hate this," muttered Sarah. "I hate just standing here like we're waiting to be picked up."

"Oh, for God's sake. We're not," said Jade. Then she craned her neck to one side, peering through the crowd, and said, "*There* he is. I'm sure that's him."

Ross had spotted her, too. He came motoring over, grinning, and behind him were two girls and two other guys.

"Jade—hi!" he said. "You made it then."

"Yeah," she said. "It's really near our place. Er—this is Kelly, and Sarah."

"Hi." He turned to his friends, and flicked his hand toward them, saying, "Jodie, Nick, Megan, Chris."

There was a chorus of "Hi." Ross was easily the star of the group as far as looks went. Everyone else was OK, but kind of average. Jodie and Megan were eyeing us a bit coldly, and I couldn't blame them. Girls now outnumbered blokes five to three, and it was no way clear from the body language if Megan and/or Jodie were teamed up with Chris and/or Nick. Ross was free, though—that much was clear. He was leaning toward Jade like a plant leans toward the light.

Immediately, Jade went on a charm offensive toward all five of them. Lots of general questions about the best beaches and clubs in the area; lots of comments like "We've hardly been here five minutes" and "Everything seems so new still." Megan and Jodie looked appeased, especially when Jade went on about how brown they were; Ross, sidling closer and closer to Jade as she spoke, looked completely smitten. Then some very hot music started playing, and Chris said, "Oh, come on!" and somehow, all seven of us were forming an untidy group on the floor, boogying to the beat. And it worked— it was amazing how it worked. Ross was one of these exhibitionist types, so he had a natural ally in Jade, and this somehow bonded the rest of us, and we all circled them, laughing, doing our own thing. I love that kind of dancing. I began to really enjoy myself.

After half an hour or so, Ross and Nick went off for more drinks, and Jade sidled over to me and hissed, "You worked out what's going on yet?"

"No," I whispered back, "except I think Ross may be in love with you."

"Oh, that," she said dismissively. "What about the others?"

"No idea."

"D'you think Chris likes Sarah?"

"*No* idea."

"What we need are little badges saying: *I'm taken* or *I'm free.*"

"Yeah, Jade. Except it would make us look like public toilets."

"Maybe. And anyway—which badge would *you* pin on?" She danced away, irritatingly, before I had a chance to answer.

I'm taken, of course, I thought crossly. I had a sudden vision of Mike here. He'd be standing by the bar, because he hated dancing. Actually, he hated clubs, period. So maybe he'd be standing outside.

Maybe he'd have refused to come in the first place.

Oh, sod it.

Nick appeared at my elbow. "Got you another drink," he said. "I know you said not to, but I thought I would."

"Oh—thanks. That's great. But I'm getting the

next round, OK?" I'd meant to sound all we're-just-friends, saying that, but it came out like some kind of pact or commitment. And then some slow music came on.

Oh, shit. I looked over anxiously at the others. Ross was curved over Jade, aching to touch her—any minute now he'd put his arms around her. Chris was slow-dancing with Jodie in the smooth, practiced way you do when you've been with someone a long time. Megan was nowhere to be seen. Sarah was drifting back to the wall, looking unhappy.

And then Nick took back my drink, put it on a nearby table, and said, "What about a dance?"

CHAPTER 12

IT WAS SUCH A SUDDEN, unwelcome invitation that I couldn't think of anything to do but squeak, "Sure!"

Nick put his arm around me and steered me toward a space on the floor, then he put his other arm around me and I kind of propped my forearms against his chest, hoping to show by their extreme stiffness that there was no question of me fancying him at all.

We revolved stodgily in place, and something very, very obvious hit me, something that should have hit me before I got on the plane to come here. One of the main objectives of this holiday for Jade was pulling men. Of course, I'd sort of known that all along, but the implications of it—the way it affected me—hadn't really dawned on me until now. I'd vaguely thought she'd be doing her stuff, and I'd be alongside, doing mine, and I hadn't realized until now that it just couldn't work that way. If Jade was on the prowl, we all looked like we were on the prowl.

It was OK when she was just chatting and flirting, that was fine. But when it got more serious . . . I heard her laugh and slid my eyes sideways. She appeared to have hold of Ross's ears and she was throwing her head back, laughing. He looked like he wanted to dive into her throat. Oh, *shit*.

I'll have to get my tactics worked out, I thought, so I can deal with situations like this. So I can send out the right signals. Nick pulled me in closer to him, and I stiffened up a bit more in response. It was a shame, him wasting his time on me. He was quite sweet: dark, and sharp-featured, but with lovely, soft, fazed-looking eyes. And I'd liked the way he'd let himself go—just enough, not too much—when we'd all been dancing in a group earlier.

Then the song ended. I shifted thankfully back out of Nick's arms and said, "Whew, I'm hot."

"We could go outside," he suggested. "Cool off."

An even slower record was starting up. I was trapped between going outside with all that that implied, or another clinch on the dance floor. "There's that little courtyard place," I said. "I'd love another look at it." Then I spun around, saw Megan and Sarah side by side, Sarah kind of grimacing at me, and called out, "Coming for some night air?"

I felt rather pleased with myself as the four of us wandered out into the courtyard and stood looking up at the ink-blue sky and the stars. As a detachment technique, it had style, I thought. The place had filled up in the last couple of hours, and nearly all the sets of wrought iron benches and tables were occupied. In the corner, a little fountain had been switched on.

"There's some seats," said Megan, heading over. Nick was looking a bit knowingly pissed off, but not too crushed, I thought. I let him sit next to me on the bench.

We chatted about this and that, and I found out that Jodie was Nick's sister, and Megan was Jodie's best friend, and Ross was Nick's best mate, and that's how come the five were sharing an apartment not too far from here.

"We weren't sure it would work," said Megan. "You know—Jodie and Chris being a couple, and everything. But it's been OK."

"Yeah," said Nick. "Ross and me, we let Meg come out with us, when the lovebirds want the place to themselves. Honorary bloke."

"Gee, thanks," she said, sarcastically.

"And we check out anyone she tries to pick up."

"Scare them off, more like."

"It's pretty cramped, though. There're only two bedrooms and me and Ross—being *major gentlemen*—are sleeping in the living room."

"Which means you don't want to eat in there, believe me," said Megan.

"There's a balcony. But it's more like a shelf."

"We can only sit on it lined up side by side with our knees up against the rail."

I found myself warming to them both. "God, you should see our place," I said. "It has a courtyard—whoa—just as big as this. And a huge balcony. *And* you can go up on the roof."

"Have you stopped boasting?" said Nick. "When can we move in?"

"It's full." I laughed. "But you'll have to come round and see it. It's really ace. Jade says it's perfect for parties."

Sarah had started to say something, but Megan broke in with, "God, a party'd be *brilliant*. You get kind of sick of these clubs."

"And you get broke," added Nick. "You could get a whole case of lager for what they charge for a bottle in here."

"Oh, well, that settles it then." I laughed.

"We'll have to have one. Not that we know anyone to invite. The guests might have to be just you. . . ."

"Exclusive. That's fine," said Megan, just as Jade appeared through the door, towing a blissed-out looking Ross. "We're just planning a party!" I called out, proudly.

"Oh, I've done that," said Jade. "Not this Friday but the next. That OK with you?"

We squeezed up on the benches and let Ross and Jade perch next to us, and had a great time discussing the party while we finished our drinks. Ross was really excited about it—I suppose he saw it as some kind of commitment from Jade, some sort of guarantee that she'd still be seeing him in ten days' time. He kept asking her about the "sound system" and she described how loud it could go. Then we went back into the main club, where happily the DJ was slapping fast music on again. Nick was really sweet. He'd taken the hint that I wasn't about to get off with him, and we had fun just moving around in a group.

Sarah didn't look too happy, but I'd given up worrying about her. I was a bit bothered by what was going on with Jade and Ross, though. He wasn't really her sort. He was good-looking but he was too eager, too puppyish—he didn't have the right style. And I knew just by watching her that she didn't fancy him much. When she fancies someone she's all focused, intent; all she was doing with Ross was working him, hard. All the details of where it was best to go, where it was happening, who he knew; she extracted them all. And then she'd wrap her arms around him, and laugh.

After a bit, I said we'd get the next round in, and I grabbed Jade, and we went up to the bar, Sarah following. "It's good, you know, this place," said Jade, as we waited. "It's dead near the farmhouse and the guy on the door took a shine to us. And it's only just opened. We can make it *ours*."

"What d'you mean, make it *ours*?" I said. It amazed me, the way she saw the world. Kind of just being there, for her use. Like the way she saw Ross.

"Oh, you know. Somewhere to arrange to meet up with people. Somewhere we're *known*. We're not on some package tour, with a rep organizing our fun for us—"

"Thank *God*."

"—so we have to put in a bit of work ourselves. We have to have places. Bases. Like here. And it's what I want for the farmhouse, too. It's just so *brilliant*, we have to use it."

"What d'you mean, you want it for the farm-house?"

"Oh—you know. So it's *known*. Like having the party. You two are OK about that, aren't you?"

"Bit late if we aren't," grumbled Sarah. "You've fixed it up."

"Yeah, well, it just kind of happened. Ross knows all these people—these guys he met, water-skiing, and this bunch of people in the flat next door to theirs he says he'll ask—"

"God, Jade," erupted Sarah, "what's the hurry?"

"What d'you mean?"

"Just—throwing a *party*. When we've just *got* here."

"Sarah, next Friday's ten days off. It's *ages* away. And—trust me—throwing a party is the quickest way to get stacks and stacks of invitations back. We can't keep clubbing every night. The money'll run out. We've got to get a scene going."

"Oh, God, you and your *scene*. It's just all so— *frenzied*."

"Yeah, well, I am frenzied, aren't I, according to you," said Jade sarcastically, turning back to the bar and waving a 5000 drachma note at the bar-man. "I like my life frenzied. It's better than being bored."

"God, Jade. I can't believe you're talking about being bored. Everything's so new out here, and different, and . . . and . . ."

"Yeah, well, Sarah. I adjust quick. You know that."

"And all these people you're asking—you don't even know them—you haven't even *met* them."

"We've met Ross and the others. We know they're nice."

"Not that nice. They've hardly said a *word* to me. Outside, I was standing next to Megan and she started talking to Nick and she just turned her *back* on me—"

"Oh, for Christ's sake, Sarah, if she turned her back on you, maybe it was 'cos she'd forgotten you were *there*. You probably hadn't *said* anything for the last fifteen minutes. You have to *make* people want to talk to you!"

Sarah was silent. I could tell she was hurt. Then the barman arrived and Jade gave our order, and as he was banging the lager bottles down on the bar I thought again how ill-fitting Jade and Sarah were as friends, and I wondered how the hell this holiday was going to work out.

At the end of the evening, Ross and the others said they'd walk us back to the farmhouse. They said they wanted to know where it was and they were going in that direction anyway, to get a cab.

By the time we got back, we were all too wiped to even think about anyone coming in for coffee. We stood shuffling about at the end of the path under the amazing Greek sky, saying our goodbyes, talking about when we'd next go to the club. I saw Ross tug Jade aside, into the shadow of the wall; then from the corner of my eye I saw him kiss her. She put her arms around his neck, and said something, and laughed; then he tried to kiss her again, but she pulled away.

"Come on, Rosso," called out Nick. "We have to go, or it'll be too late to get a cab and you'll have to carry me back."

"You girls going to the same beach tomorrow?" Ross asked.

There was an awkward pause, and not only because he'd called us girls. Jade was fishing in her bag for the door key. "Yeah," I said, after the silence had got too embarrassing. "Maybe."

Ross gave one more yearning look at Jade, then the five of them walked off, calling out their last goodnights.

"What're you playing at, Jade?" I muttered. "D'you like him or not?"

"Yeah, I like him," she answered. "He's OK. Why?"

"Just—oh, never mind. He's great-looking. Apart from those poncey streaks in his hair."

"What's wrong with those?"

"It's so *vain*."

"What's wrong with *vain*? Just 'cos your precious *Mikey* would sooner have his dick chopped off than submit to anything as feminine as hairstyling—"

"Oh, shut up."

"Or maybe he thinks it would just drop off," she went on, giggling, "if he had his hair cut properly."

"Shut *up*," I repeated, but I was laughing, too, now.

Jade jiggled the key into the lock. "I think that was a brilliant evening," she said, with enormous satisfaction. "Ross and that lot are great, and they seem to know some other good people, and *Ariadne*'s OK, and . . ." She swung open the door, and stopped dead.

"Oh, *shit*," she said. "Oh, holy *shit*."

JADE WENT THROUGH the door, swearing furiously. "What's wrong?" I squawked, hurrying through—then I braked, hard. Water was pouring out of the kitchen door, streaming across the courtyard, lapping at my feet.

"Oh, no," murmured Sarah. She looked absolutely panic-stricken. "Oh, *no*."

"Who left a tap on?" screeched Jade. "When we went out—who left one on?"

"Well—it was *you*, wasn't it?" I screeched back. "You left the plates to soak—you said—"

Jade had kicked off her shoes, and was racing for the kitchen. Seconds later, she stuck her head around the door, and shouted, "I can't've turned it all the way off. And then the water pressure rose when it got late, and the bloody thing started running again."

"Oh, *Jade*!" wailed Sarah.

"The kitchen's absolutely flooded out!" Jade squeaked.

Sarah and I splashed barefoot across the courtyard, into the kitchen. Water was lapping up the sides of the cupboards; the dustpan and brush were floating toward us. "I s'pose it's one way of getting the floor washed!" gurgled Jade.

"Oh, my God." Sarah sobbed. "Look at the damage!"

"Ah, there's no damage," retorted Jade. "It'll dry out, no time."

"It's gone in the cupboards. The wood'll swell."

"Not in this heat."

"It's in all the pans."

"Well, they'll wash. Look on the bright side— the food's safe."

"What about the fridge? What about the electrics?"

"Oh, Sarah, shut up! It's still working, isn't it? Its little light's still on?"

"*Yes*, but—"

"Look—I'm knackered. I'm going to bed."

Sarah and I stared at her in disbelief. "You're what?" I said. "Aren't you going to help clear up?"

"I'll help in the morning. When the sun's up and everything'll dry easily. Look—it's a stone floor. It'll be OK. Let's leave it to soak!" Then she laughed, turned and sailed out of the kitchen, calling back, "G'night!"

Neither of us answered her. After a few seconds, Sarah breathed out, "I don't know how she can *do* that. Just go to bed and leave us to do all the work."

"Well, she's not, is she," I snapped. "We're going to leave it, too."

"But we—"

"Look. She's got a point—it'll be better doing it in the morning."

"But these cupboards could get damaged—"

"Sarah, she's in charge. If they get damaged, she'll have to sort it out with whoever owns the place."

"But—"

"Look. Let's get the brush, and sweep all this water out into the courtyard. Then tomorrow, we can clean up properly. Yeah?"

Dumbly, Sarah fetched the sodden broom from where it stood in the corner of the kitchen, and I took it from her. Then I drove all the water across the kitchen floor and out into the courtyard, where it sloshed into the lake that was already there, slowly draining away under the wall. "Think how much good it'll do the vines and stuff," I said wearily, then I too went to bed.

* * *

The next morning, Sarah and I were forced to forgive Jade. She was up before either of us, mopping out the kitchen with detergent, emptying the cupboards and rinsing off the pans. "Have you had a brainstorm?" I asked.

"Yup," she said. "Don't knock it."

"Right," I said, pleased, "I'll give the courtyard a sweep. Most of the water seems to have drained away overnight."

"Told you," said Jade, smugly. I ignored her, and started sweeping the last of the floodwater under the trailing vines, pulling them up from the ground to make a neater job of it. I was lifting a great swag away from the corner near the steps when I spotted two sets of small wheels hidden in the foliage. I pulled the vines up further and saw that the wheels were attached to a skinny looking trolley thing, which I dragged triumphantly out into the open, calling, "Hey, you two! I've found a barbecue!"

Sarah and Jade came hurrying over to inspect it. It was made of iron, solid and serviceable, with just a bit of rust. "I reckon the vines just grew over it, in the spring," said Jade. "Hid it from sight."

"D'you think it works?" I asked.

"Bound to," said Jade. "I mean—there's the grill, there's the charcoal tray. Hey—let's try it out tonight. Let's go into town, get some charcoal. And steaks. Protein helps you pull. And while we're in town, we can see about a car."

"Jade—*Jesus*!" wailed Sarah. "Can't you slow down a bit? Can't we discuss it first?"

"We can discuss it when we've seen about it," Jade said. "Then we'll have some facts to discuss it with. Like—the cost."

Sarah was opening her mouth, about to object further, when I spotted something else behind the vines, and swooped. "Look, loads of clay pots," I said, drawing out a whole pile. "They must've got covered, too."

"Oh, shove 'em back, Kelly," Jade said, but Sarah had crouched down and was unstacking them one by one, cooing, "This is lovely. It must be really old. Oh, look—this one's got tiny lions' heads on it! And here's one with grapes . . . they're gorgeous."

Jade pulled a face at me over her head, and I grinned back and said, "Let's get some coffee." Then we crossed the courtyard to the kitchen. The flagstones gleamed wet and beautiful in the strengthening sun.

Over breakfast, we agreed we'd get into town before it got too hot, then we could go to the beach in the afternoon. "And tonight—we'll stay in?" said Sarah.

"I just—I really feel like staying here tonight."

Jade looked at her, exasperated, then she smiled and seemed to soften. "Let's see how it goes. You know—if we get a car, it'll be no big deal at all to get anywhere."

We got the bus into town and bought steaks to barbecue, and bread and salad, and several bottles of wine. Then we got a bag of charcoal and some lighter fuel, and staggered along toward the far side of town to where Jade thought the bargain garage was.

"Maybe we should've got all this stuff *after* we'd been to the garage," I grumbled. I was carrying the charcoal.

"Maybe," said Jade. We turned down a seedy looking side street where every other building looked derelict. Suddenly Jade gave an "Ah!" of satisfaction and pointed to a sign with a big arrow saying *Nikos's Motocars*. "That's it, I'm sure that's it," crowed Jade. "It began with an 'N'."

It looked more like a wrecker's yard than a garage, with half-demolished cars lying around everywhere. We walked slowly through the sagging gates and a dog chained in a kennel leaped and snapped at us.

"Fotis—*quiet!*" bellowed a voice, and a man came forward to meet us. He was about fifty;

stocky, deeply tanned and gray-haired. Jade slowly explained our mission, and his face lit up with understanding. His English was pretty good. Yes, he was Nikos, he said, and he knew of the farmhouse and its owners; Jade's aunt's friend often hired from him. Then Jade showed him her driver's license and papers, and he came over all avuncular and said he thought he had exactly what we needed.

"You no want *speed*," he kept repeating. "Speed dangerous. Just something to get your shopping, and take to beach—yes?"

"Yes," we agreed. He didn't need to know about the clubs and giving lifts to scrumptious blokes and so on.

"Follow me." In the corner of the yard was an ancient, open-top, four-wheel drive Suzuki jeep. "Now—this will get you anywhere. Over the roughest ground. Right down onto beach. It's a bit noisy, maybe. People turn to look, but you no mind that, eh? They look anyway, eh, with you girls in it?" And he laughed loudly, flirtatiously.

Jade smirked, then climbed up the side and slipped behind the wheel. "Can I try it?" she said.

"Sure. Wait, I get keys."

"How much is it?" asked Sarah suddenly, shrilly. "To hire? And is it safe? Can you prove it's safe?"

"Shut up, Sarah," said Jade, while Nikos turned and glared at her, as though she'd just committed the most appalling *faux pas*.

"I am not man to hire young girls cars that are not *safe*," he said, heatedly. "Of course it *safe*. I have—what is it? Like MOT." Then he stomped off to his broken down office, came back with the keys, and climbed in beside Jade. She started it up, let up the handbrake, and they bumped slowly out of the yard.

There was a long, long, pause. Then Sarah seemed to explode. "I don't know about you," she spat, eyes fixed ahead of her, "but I am just about *sick* of the way Jade takes over all the time. Like everything has to be done her way. We don't get a say in *anything*."

I was a bit taken aback by her outburst, although something in me had been expecting it. "We . . . ell," I said slowly. "It *is* her place. And—you know—she's been here before. She knows where things are and stuff."

"So you think that gives her the right to just *dictate* what we're going to do all the time?"

"No . . . oo. But—well, she's a natural leader, isn't she?"

"Leader? Dictator more like. *Tyrant*."

"Look, Sarah, to be quite honest I'm *glad* she's

taking over. I mean—I haven't got the hang of the money yet, or anything. It's only our second day here."

"*Exactly!* And she's charging about, hiring cars, picking up strangers, arranging parties—"

I was silent, battling with my mouth to stop it splitting in a grin. "And you don't like that?" I asked.

"No. Not all the time. I want to relax."

"Well—we're staying in tonight, aren't we?"

"*I* am. You two can do what you like, but I am." Then she stalked away from me, away across the yard, and I saw her crouch in front of the dog kennel, just beyond where the dog could get at her. I watched as she delved into one of her carriers for a loaf of bread, then tore off bits of it and chucked them to the dog, clucking over it as she did so.

And then the Suzuki rocked back into the yard and shuddered to a stop, and an ecstatic Jade jumped down. "It handles like a dream!" she shrieked. "And I drove like a dream—didn't I, Nikos?"

"Very good," he agreed, approvingly. "She very good."

"I made this little git back up, when we were jammed in this narrow street. And I parked it. And we gave it a trial run over some really bumpy wasteland and it coped *so well*. It's perfect, honestly. We have to have it."

"So how much?" I asked, excitedly.

"Look—he's giving us three days' free trial. And he's going to talk to his partner about costs. He reckons around fifty thousand drachmas a week. I've told him forty thousand—and we can afford it."

Sarah was making her way back toward us across the yard. "That poor dog," she said, as soon as she reached us. "Chained up all day."

Nikos drew himself up to his full height. "Excuse me! Fotis not poor! He fed best food! And every evening—he come out with me, long, long run." He thrust his face angrily toward Sarah. It was becoming abundantly clear she was not one of his favorite people. "And then he come to bar with me. Get peanuts. OK?"

Sarah turned away from him, frostily.

"Oh, Sarah, it's a working dog, for God's sake," said Jade. "It has a better life than a lot of dogs in Greece."

"Exactly!" Sarah bristled. "This country is—"

"So we can really take the car now?" Jade broke in.

"*What?*" said Sarah.

I decided it was time to help Jade out. I was

getting a bit sick of Sarah's doom-laden attitude. "It's a free trial, OK?" I said. "Three days and we bring it back, nothing to pay, if we don't want to keep it. And if you're not happy with even *that*, you can carry the bag of charcoal home, OK? 'Cos I'm not."

That seemed to settle things. Jade shot me a grateful look, then she went off to do a bit of paperwork in the office while Sarah and I loaded the shopping into the car in a kind of tense silence.

Sarah was the first to get in the car, and she got in the back. So I climbed in beside Jade and said, "OK. Ready to die," and we drove off.

It was hilarious. Nikos was right, the car was slow. And loud. But it traveled along, and people waved to us and were kind when we stopped to ask directions. We got back to the farmhouse in one piece, fizzing with success. Jade suggested grabbing our stuff and making it out to a beach she knew of ten miles along the coast. "We have to try this buggy out," she said. "We have to give it a proper test."

"What about Ross?" I asked. "Didn't you say you'd see him today, at the local beach?"

"No," said Jade. "You did."

"OK." I wasn't going to push it. After all, if she felt no guilt about drawing him in then cutting him off, why should I? Any more than I should feel guilty about Sarah and whatever was happening with her.

Float through it, Kelly, I thought. Not your business.

We packed the jeep, and set off along the coast road. Jade and I chatted to each other, checking the route, loving the speed, the freedom we had. Then Jade started doing maths calculations out loud, and wound up proving that the car would actually save us money, if you set it against cab fares and so on.

In the back seat, Sarah snorted. "Only if you intend taking about three cabs a day," she said. "Over huge distances."

"Yeah, but I want *huge* distances!" exclaimed Jade. "Don't you?"

There was a silence, and I said, diplomatically, "Look, let's go over it all tonight. With a pen and paper. I mean—somehow I'm just not secure about your maths, Jade."

"Yeah," said Sarah. "Let's decide then."

Jade shifted up a gear and started chanting loudly, "I-want-to-keep-the-buggy! I'm-gonna-keep-the-buggy!" like the worst-behaved brat in town, and made us both laugh. Then we got onto the coast road, and saw the sea ahead of us. Little salt-ruined signs pointed down to the shore. Cars were haphazardly parked along the edge of the road, in amongst the scrubby thorn trees and low-growing pines.

"Where are we going to park?" I asked.

"Anywhere!" Jade crowed. "Ain't no yellow lines on the beach." And she bumped off the road into a clearing.

We made our way down the cliff path and stood surveying the scene. Compared to yesterday's beach, it was an institution. Ranks and ranks of umbrellas lined up as far as you could see, changing from all green to all red to all blue as the management of that particular patch of sand changed. And behind them, along the cliff edge, enough professional looking cafés to fill a high street.

"I'm not so keen on this place," said Sarah, inevitably.

"Yeah, well," said Jade. "It's a contrast, right? Where d'you want to go?" Then without waiting for an answer, she set off to her left, promenading slow and sure of herself between all the sunbathers.

It was food for her, walking through people like that. All that energy and attention she attracted—you could see her bloom in it, like a plant blooms in the sun. I was beginning to get into it, too. Side by side with Jade, I walked like her, I felt like her.

"What about here?" said Sarah. "These red brollies? I mean—you going to walk along the whole beach, or what?"

"OK," said Jade. "Let's go here. Are there some free up near the shore?"

Jade's radar was out. She found a set of empty sunbeds well away from any families, and near, but not too near, three sets of unaccompanied blokes. A few scattered loving couples provided a chaperoned atmosphere and also sent the temperature up by example.

I sat down on one of the sunbeds and stared surreptitiously at a nearby couple, lying intertwined on the sand, and felt this sudden stab of loneliness, this longing for Mike. *When we get together*, I thought, *I want to spend loads of time at the beach with him, and we'll lie just where the sea meets the sand, and I'm going to wrap myself around him, just like she's wrapping herself around her guy. . . .*

I looked up—Jade was grinning down at me. "Oil my back?" she said.

WE DIDN'T LEAVE THE BEACH till early evening, and even Sarah had to admit it'd been great. The swimming was good, and we'd had lots of slightly scary fun touring up and down the outside of the cafés, deciding which one looked best. Lunch had been very late and very riotous. A gang of lads from Birmingham had turned up, taken the table right near us, and nuked us with their persistence and charm. They told lots of very blue, very funny jokes, and then they persuaded us to come and do "watersports" with them. Jade hadn't been keen at first—they were fun, but not quite up to her glamorous-guy standard—but they'd flattered and cajoled her into it, and Sarah and I—as usual—had followed her lead.

Watersports consisted of a terrifying ride on a huge, inflated, bucking banana, towed behind a speedboat. I fell off as soon as I could, because the ocean looked a safe bet compared to the ride, but then one of the lads insisted on rescuing me and I had to practically clock him to avoid getting groped. They wanted us to try some kind of speeding rubber ring torture after that, but Jade told them we wanted to sunbathe and I said I got seasick easily and Sarah just backed away, groaning. So then they made a great effort to get us to meet them in the evening, but Jade said firmly that we had other plans. They seemed to accept that—win some, lose some—but as they were shuffling off, saying goodbye, Jade asked, "You got a phone number?"

That made them stop. "Yeah. Our hotel," said one.

"Why? You going to take us out?" asked another.

"We're staying in this old farmhouse," Jade said, laughing, enjoying the impact she was making, "and we're having a party soon."

"*Yeah?* Classy!"

"And if you wanted . . ."

There was an immediate outcry. "We do!" "We'll come!" "Here—I'll write the number down." "You call us, OK?"

Then we left, and went back to our place on the beach. "I thought you weren't keen on them," I said.

"I'm not. They're reserves on the guest list."

"Jade—so far the guest list is ninety percent *male*."

"You complaining?" she said, and stretched out smiling on the sunbed.

I felt relaxed to the point of exhaustion when we got back to the farmhouse, and I thought I might add my vote to Sarah's when it came to deciding whether to go out or not. Just the thought of lifting a mascara brush made my arm ache in protest.

Sarah, animated as usual by the thought of cooking, suggested we get the barbecue lit up right away, because barbecues took forever to heat up. So we cleaned it off with some scouring powder we found in the kitchen and left it to dry. Then we opened the wine, and Sarah marinated the steaks in oil with bits of garlic scattered over. Then all three of us concentrated on getting the barbecue alight.

"The secret is not to get intimidated," said Jade, pouring a huge amount of lighter fuel onto the charcoal. "Barbecuing is seen to be a male thing like—you know, changing an electric plug. But when you try to do it yourself you realize how *laughably* easy it is."

"Is it?" I asked dubiously. The fuel flashed and

flared, but the coals still looked very black and unlit. Jade sighed and flicked another two burning matches into the center, Sarah poked in the bloodied paper from the steaks. Then, slowly, the charcoal began to shift, and glow. "It's taken!" I said. "We've done it!" And we chinked glasses triumphantly across the grill.

"Right," said Jade, "let's take it in turns showering and . . . and *nurturing* this thing. Bags me first. I need to cream up. I can feel my skin peeling as we speak."

She headed off, and Sarah turned the meat in its marinade, and I finished my wine. The barbecue steadily heated up, and before long, the steaks were grilling and the salad was made and we'd all showered. We sat there in the twilight, tearing lumps off the loaf of bread and devouring them while we waited.

"OK," said Jade. "Car decision time. Let's do the maths again."

Jade covered a sheet of paper with incomprehensible lines of numbers, then shoved it under mine and Sarah's noses; then she took the paper back and added more and more numbers, until Sarah and I gave in out of sheer exhaustion and agreed that we should probably hire the Suzuki. Then Jade made an impassioned plea that it wasn't just about money but about convenience, independence, and freedom; and I pointed out that we could simply stop hiring it if we got too poor—and that clinched the debate.

Jade ran over and opened the door to the courtyard, revealing the jeep outside on the track, and we laughed, and chinked glasses again. Then Sarah announced the steaks were done, and we dished out the food and ate like wolves.

"We've got *wheels*, I can't believe it," gloated Jade, as her chewing slowed. "This holiday is *made*."

"Oh, Jade, this *place* makes it," said Sarah. "The farmhouse."

"Well, yeah. I really want people here, I want to use it."

"We're using it now," said Sarah.

"Yeah, yeah I know we are, but—you know. Oh, *God*, this feels good."

"This is our *life* now," I said blissfully. "Just the beach, and the sea, and the heat, and the night, and whatever comes along."

"D'you remember, when you were like fourteen or so, just *dreaming* of a holiday like this?" asked Jade.

"I don't think I managed to even *dream* like this, when I was fourteen," I said. "I was deeply sad. I don't think I thought beyond two weeks abroad somewhere."

"God. You were sad."

"Yeah. I'd spend hours and hours getting ready just to go to this scabby youth center. *And* I'd be nervous about going there."

"Oh, right. Tribal terror. Will he talk to me, will she let me join her group, will I get ignored? We used to hang out in the kids' play park, didn't we, Sarah? Just for somewhere to meet. Talk about pathetic. In the winter it was bloody horrible weather and you'd stand about freezing, pretending you were having a great time—and in the *summer* it'd still be light till about ten o'clock so you'd get all these mums pushing toddlers on the swings while you hung about, trying to be cool."

"It wasn't that bad," said Sarah. "We had a laugh."

"It was the *pits*."

"So why did you come along then?"

Suddenly, I felt the atmosphere shift. Suddenly, Sarah was angry, glaring toward Jade.

"Oh, for heaven's sake." Jade laughed, oblivious. "I was fourteen. Staying in on a Saturday night was a *crime*. Even if it would've been a lot more fun to veg out in front of the box at home."

Sarah didn't say anything, just half-smiled,

131

then she started stacking the empty plates. "I'm going to bed," she said, in a sort of tight voice. "I've got this really bad headache—I think I had too much sun today."

"Oh, Sarah, we have too much sun *every* day," said Jade, impatiently. "I thought we might take the jeep out on a late-night trip."

"Not me," said Sarah. "Really. You go." Then she took the plates into the kitchen, and trudged up the steps to her room, calling out one last "Night."

"God, what is *wrong* with her?" I erupted, as quietly as I could. "Honestly, Jade, I know she's your friend and everything, but she can be such a drag. It's like she doesn't *want* to enjoy herself."

Jade shrugged. "She'll come around."

"But doesn't it bother you, the way she is?"

"Nah. I ignore her."

I frowned, perplexed. I wanted to ask all kinds of questions, like—what exactly is the point of asking someone on holiday if they're such a pain you have to ignore them—and as I was trying this out in my head, Jade suddenly slammed her wine glass down, and said, "Whoooops."

"Whoooops?"

"I've offended her. Saying how crap it was at fourteen. That's when I met her. Oh, shit. She took pity on me, and let me go out with her and—oh, shit."

"*She* took pity on *you*?" I repeated, incredulous.

"Yes. I was the new girl, just moved to her school, and she was just about the only person who'd speak to me. You couldn't blame people. I was dull. I was a dork. And I took netball *seriously*. Your street cred went down a whole notch if you were just caught *looking* at me, never mind talking to me."

"Jaaade." I laughed. "Don't exaggerate."

"I'm not. If it hadn't been for Sarah, and all the sports I was into, I'd've had no one to speak to at all. Oh, shit. And now I've just kind of thrown it back in her face."

"You could go up and see her," I ventured.

Jade shook her head. "Nah. No point. She'll've gone into one."

There was a long pause. I poked my knife into the charcoal on the barbecue, making it flare up again. "I can't imagine you as a dork," I said. "I mean—I really can't."

"Well, I was. I used to shuffle about, screaming '*victim*.'"

I gawped. "You did *what*?"

"I mean, my body language screamed it. You know. How I looked."

I stared at her. "So what happened?" I asked. "I mean—you're not exactly screaming 'victim' now."

"No. Well. When I was fifteen, I had this amazing conversion. Just out of the blue."

"Blimey," I said, imagining priests, archangels. "How?"

"Well, it was nothing really. It took about five seconds, but it was enough. It was a summer when lots of sporty stuff was being used in adverts—the whole hip-to-be-fit thing. You know, girls in big boots halfway up mountains selling lippy. Running along clifftops in lycra selling tampons. It was like—selling the idea of an active life. You saw the adverts, and you thought—I wish I was her. I wish I had her fitness. And that made you buy the stuff."

"Yeah, I know," I said. "Total crap. You could only be like those girls if you hacked up mountains and did fifty press ups a day."

"Right. But *anyway*—I was in this outdoorsy type shop one day, and there was this lovely poster of this girl, sitting on top of a big rock. And I got this kind of realization. I thought—I *do* that. That image they're trying to sell—I *do* it. I'd just done this abseiling course, and I'd been up a rock just like the one she was on." Jade laughed. "I didn't look like her of course, no way. But somehow, that thought—it had a real impact on me. I walked out of the shop and I was thinking, I can do it, I'm strong, I can abseil, and I could feel I was walking differently. Like, you know—my head was up."

"Ah," I said, and I suddenly saw it all—Jade walking tall, looking people in the eye . . . Jade *emerging*. Like a butterfly from its chrysalis. No, not a butterfly—too girly. A hawk-moth.

"I started to spend more money on my gear," she went on. "All sporty stuff still—I looked good in it—authentic. I started to like my body. It could do stuff. And OK I had no tits but at least I didn't spend half my life whining about being fat like most of the girls in my class. I got my hair cut. And then one day at the start of summer I was out on my bike in shorts, and these guys from the year above whistled, and then they realized who I was, and . . ."

"And what?"

"Well, nothing. Nothing actually *happened*. But—you know. *That* had happened." She sat back and smiled slowly, enjoyably, at the memory. "I didn't talk to them, I just rode off. But with *style*. And then there was this big party, just about everyone had been invited, and I bought a great dress, one that I'd hardly've *tried on* before, and . . .

whoa. That was it. I got off with someone already at college. Someone who didn't know my history. He was *deeply* cool. He gave me the confidence to take it all further, you know? I started really dressing up, to go out with him. Short dresses, high heels, the lot. Eye makeup that'd make Cleopatra look tame. He loved it. And I was getting all these looks from guys. It was magic—I'd never had *any* before."

"What happened to him?" I asked.

"Who?"

"The cool boyfriend?"

"Oh—I dunno. I dumped him. I met someone else. And then someone else. It was just—*brilliant*, Kelly. I wasn't a victim anymore."

No, I thought. *You were a predator instead.*

"That must have been weird for Sarah," I said, "when you suddenly took off like a rocket. You know—guy after guy."

Jade shrugged. "We still saw each other. On and off."

There was a silence. I stared into the dwindling coals of the barbecue. I was beginning to see why Jade had asked Sarah—and me—along on the holiday. Jade wasn't the sort who had good friends, who let anyone in close to her. I was beginning to see it wasn't how she operated. Maybe that was what was freaking Sarah out, making her so glum. Maybe she was finally seeing things, too.

"Shall we open another bottle?" said Jade. "Or d'you fancy going out in the jeep? I've only had one glass. I've kept myself deliberately sober, so I can chauffeur you."

"I dunno," I murmured. "It's—" I broke off. I'd heard a noise, in the silence. Something outside. Voices.

Jade looked up, listening, and then her face cleared. "That's Ross!" she said. And she ran over to the door and flung it open. "What the hell you doing out there?" she called. "We thought you were psychotic prowlers!"

"We are," said Ross.

"Ax murderers," put in Nick.

Then the two of them appeared in the doorway. I had a moment's panic. Two girls, two boys. *Why* d'you have to go to bed, Sarah?

"You weren't at the beach today," said Ross accusingly.

"No," said Jade, completely unabashed. "You see the jeep out there?"

"Yeah?"

"It's ours. That's why we weren't at the beach. We were hiring it, and then naturally we had to try it out."

"Naturally."

"In fact—we were just about to give it a night run—if you two want to come."

Ross's face, up till then a bit sulky, lit up in enthusiasm. "Yeah!" he said.

Jade turned to me and smiled, challenging me to back out. "What about Sarah?" I said, weakly.

"She'll be asleep. Let's go."

Ross got in the front seat next to Jade so fast I didn't have a choice but to perch next to Nick in the back, like we were on a double date or something. But as soon as the jeep got moving it was fine. Like me, Nick was absorbed in the drive: the narrow track, the night air rushing past. Then we hit the coast road; empty, dark stretches along the clifftops followed by areas lit up like Christmas trees, packed with people, crammed with clubs and high-rise hotels. We took a left, came inland a little, and arrived at a village with a central square that was absolutely buzzing. Jade circled it slowly, gears grinding, then Ross pointed out a parking place, and Jade swung into it, almost straight. We found an empty table in the square, and a waiter appeared, and we ordered coffee. The hot night settled around us, and the festive energy from the square sparked into us, and we grinned at each other, feeling great.

We sat there for ages as the nighttime street-life milled around us, chatting and laughing, ordering more coffee, fantasizing about finding a way to live and work in Greece and never have to leave. "Maybe a café," mused Jade. "One of those sexy little laid-back cafés on the beach. I fancy running one of them."

"Oh, come on," said Nick. "Slicing up about half a ton of tomatoes a day?"

"I'd have *staff* to do that. I'd just be there, at the front. Letting people buy me drinks."

"*Sure* you would. You'd be working your arse off. And you'd have to shut up shop in the winter and slog your guts out when it's hot."

"*God*, you're defeatist. OK—what could I do?"

"Clean?"

Ross burst out laughing at the very idea of Jade with a mop in her hand, and Jade gave Nick a withering look and said, "I don't *clean*."

"No, she doesn't," I put it. "I can vouch for that. You should see the state of the bathroom."

"Oh, sod off, Kelly. Bathrooms are self-cleaning. All that water sloshing around."

"Cleaning's a good idea," insisted Nick. "It means you have the whole day free. You get up *really really* early and . . ." He took in Jade's expression. "OK—it's a shit idea."

"Thank you."

"Bar work," suggested Ross. "Then you only work at night. I can see you in some hot club, Jade."

"Lap dancing," added Nick.

"Nick—you are asking for a smack in the *mouth*," Jade snapped. "No—a club's no good. I couldn't go back to the same place every night. I have to have *variety*." She laid enormous stress on *variety*, as though she got bored with everything very, very easily. Ross seemed to deflate on his chair, as though he knew she meant blokes, too.

"What I need," she went on, "is a job where I only work in the winter."

"Yeah, fine," said Nick. "There must be millions of 'em. All attached to the nontourist trade."

"Oh, ha ha. There must be *something* that'd let me spend all summer on the beach."

"You don't wanna do that. You'd look like a prune by the time you were thirty."

"No, I *wouldn't*. I use stuff." And she slowly raked her hair back with her fingertips and raised one eyebrow at Nick, as if defying him to think her skin was anything but superb.

God, Jade had such *style*. She had both the guys focused on her—Ross was so focused it was downright embarrassing. His eyes were out on stalks, slavering up her arms, her neck. I felt like a spare part.

Of course you do, I told myself virtuously, as I drained my coffee cup. You can't throw all that energy about, like Jade. You have a boyfriend. But somehow, this time, that thought failed to move me.

It was getting really late, but the square was still buzzing. Ross and Nick insisted on buying us both huge ice creams, Hollywood-style, to say thank you for the ride, and then they asked for extra spoons and swiped most of the cream and nuts and goo themselves. We paid the bill and piled back in the jeep and drove back the way we'd come, dropping the guys off at their apartment. Ross managed to jump a kiss on Jade; then he tried to pin her down about what she was doing tomorrow, which beach, which club.

"I don't know," she said. "Look—I know where you're staying now. Which number is it?"

"Thirty eight. That one right at the top, with the socks on the balcony rail."

"Nice design touch. We'll drop by—maybe tomorrow night. OK?"

And he had to be satisfied with that. I got in the front seat with her as we drove back, and I slid my eyes sideways and watched her. She was frowning and smiling at the same time. "You're really good," I said. "Driving, I mean. You haven't been driving for long, have you?"

"Nope," she said.

"D'you think Ross got the message?"

"What message?"

"Well—you know. That you don't want to get—involved." I could've bitten my tongue the minute that was out, it sounded so twee.

Jade's profile had taken on a sarcastic expression. "Why would he think I *did*?"

"Well—you know. He wants to see you and stuff. He keeps trying to snog you."

"That's not *involvement*, Kelly."

Oh, I thought. *Right*.

CHAPTER 15

THE NEXT DAY, SARAH WAS UP before any of us. It was weird—she was just standing in the kitchen, leaning against the counter, not doing anything. "You OK?" I asked.

She didn't answer. "Sarah? You OK?"

Her voice, when it finally came, sounded as though it came from the bottom of a pit. "Oh—just ignore me. I feel . . . er . . ."

"What's up—don't you feel well?"

"Look—I'm not ill or anything. I just feel like shit."

"Oh." The penny dropped. I'd seen Sarah sort of depressed before, at college, and as we'd been getting ready to go Jade had warned me she occasionally got glooms on. It was best then, Jade said, to give her a wide berth.

That seemed a bit mean though. I had to make some kind of an effort. "You feel down, you mean?"

"Yeah."

"Well—let me make you a cup of tea, eh? And some food. Get your blood sugar up a bit."

Sarah gave a crooked kind of smile, as though low blood sugar was the last of her worries and she blamed me for having no real idea what she was suffering. I ignored this, and began to bang about cheerfully, filling up the kettle, slicing up bread, slamming it under the grill. "Honey or marmalade?" I inquired.

There was a long pause. "Honey," she muttered.

Please, I said silently, as I got the jar down from the shelf and began smothering the toast. Maybe it would sweeten her up a bit.

I carried the tray of tea and toast out to the courtyard, and sat down at the table. Sarah was still inside the kitchen. I left it for a minute or so, poured milk into the mugs. Then I called "Sarah?" No answer. I took a large bite out of a slice of toast, poured out a splash of tea, decided to let it brew a bit longer. "*Sarah?!* Are you coming?"

There was a slow, shuffling noise from the kitchen, then Sarah made her way across the courtyard, head down. I poured her out some tea, and she sat and looked at it. I pushed a slice of toast toward her. No response. It was beginning to get to me. I was starting to feel like some kind of psychiatric nurse.

"Come on, Sarah," I said. "Eat something."

Silence.

"Have your tea, at least."

At long last, her hand stretched out slowly, picked up the mug of tea and conveyed it to her lips. She took a couple of sips, then she turned to look at me. Her eyes were hooded and lifeless.

"I'm sorry," she said. "I just feel so shitty I . . ."

She trailed off. We ate and drank breakfast in silence, then I cleared the table and stood up to carry the tray out to the kitchen. "Coming for a swim?" I said.

Sarah shook her head. I stood there for a minute, wondering if I should try and encourage her, then in the end I said nothing.

"Jade," I said with a hiss through her half-open bedroom door. "Jade? You awake?"

I could hear her turning over in bed, making I-don't-want-to-wake noises.

"*Jade!*"

"Whaaaat?"

"Can I come in?"

"Oh, *God*! Whaddyou want? I've only just gone to sleep."

"No, you haven't. Come on, it's late." I pushed her bedroom door open, and went inside. There was a sweet, dusky scent in the room, her scent. I crossed to the window and pulled open the shutter just a crack, so that the sun lasered in.

"Sadist," muttered Jade, rolling over in bed again.

I sat down on the edge. "Jade, Sarah's acting really weird. I think she's gone into one. You know—you said she got glooms on sometimes?"

"Oh, God. Tedious. What's she doing?"

"Nothing. Hardly speaking. Standing in the kitchen like a zombie. I made her tea and toast, it was like she didn't see it, I had to practically feed it to her."

"Oh, God, that's a gloom all right. Major by the sound of it. Just—*ignore* her. Seriously. She comes out of it in the end."

"But shouldn't we try and cheer her up, shouldn't we—"

"No point. Honestly. I *used* to—I used to sit there yakking to her, trying to get her to talk about what was wrong. But I pretty soon realized there was no point. There isn't anything wrong, usually. These moods just seem to come over her, and there's nothing anyone can do. You'd just beat yourself up trying to get through to her, end up feeling as bad as she does. She should go on Prozac or something. For everyone else's sake as much as her own."

"Mmmm. I dunno. It seems rotten, just to let her be. I mean—she needs help. If I hadn't fixed her breakfast, I swear she'd still be standing—"

"So feed her if you want to," said Jade, impatiently. "Just don't try and get through to her."

I stood up to go, and Jade said, "Hey, Kelly? If you bring me my breakfast, you won't have to feed me."

"Get lost," I said, and went to get my bikini on.

While I was pulling on my T-shirt, Sarah drifted by me and went through to her room. Then she shut her door, and I heard the sound of a chair being dragged slowly across the room, and pushed up under the doorhandle.

She'd barricaded herself in.

CHAPTER 16

"OH, FOR CHRIST'S SAKE, of course she's not going to top herself!" Jade snapped, as she rolled onto her front and started applying her third lot of bronzing cream that morning. We'd gone to the local beach—I'd insisted on it, because I felt awful about going too far from Sarah when she was in the state she was in. And I'd left her a note, pushed under her door, telling her where we were.

Jade was getting more and more fed up with me angsting about Sarah, especially when I reminded her it was probably her fault because she'd upset Sarah the night before. "Kelly, I don't *do* guilt," she snapped. "Anyway, I might have been the trigger, but I'm not the cause."

Which was true, of course.

Around lunchtime, Ross, Nick, and Megan appeared in front of us on the sand, wet from the sea. "I *told* you it was them," Ross was saying excitedly.

"OK, OK," said Megan. "You were right."

Ross threw himself down beside Jade on the sand. "I spotted you from out there. Didn't you see me waving?"

"Wasn't looking," said Jade.

"Oh. Anyway. How come you're *here*?" said Ross. "Not that I'm sorry you're here. It's just—you're not using that fabulous jeep."

"Yeah, well, Sarah's on a real downer, and Kelly says we can't go far."

"A downer?"

"Deeply depressed."

"In *this* place?"

"I know. Crazy, isn't it?"

Nick sat himself down, too, beside me. "It's insane. Maybe what she needs is a stimulating drive out to this fantastic place we know of. It's a bugger to get to by bus, but if you've got *wheels*. . . ."

Jade looked at him coolly. "Buy us lunch," she said, "then we'll go back to the farmhouse and get the jeep *and* Sarah—and drive there."

We had lunch, and got the jeep, but Sarah wouldn't come. Jade said she'd go and get her, but within minutes she'd run back downstairs, announcing, "She's asleep. We should leave her."

Somehow, I knew Jade hadn't knocked on her

door very loudly—if she'd knocked at all. But I decided against saying anything. The five of us took off, Ross in the front navigating and loudly criticizing Jade's driving, Nick squashed happily between me and Megan in the back. I was really glad Megan was there in her role as "honorary bloke." It took away from the foursome thing.

We had a great day, heading off to a different coastline, with scenery so stunning it left you speechless. The blue of the sky and the sea was vivid, unreal, with the white-hot sun hanging there. We parked the car and sat on the edge of the cliff and let it all burn into us, until it got so hot we had to move, had to find shade and a drink. We clattered through narrow, whitewashed streets, silent because it was siesta time, and wandered through ruins so old Nick said everyone in England had still been living in caves when they'd been built.

It worked, the five of us—it was fun. The only difficult bit was Ross was acting like Jade was his girlfriend and Jade was acting like she wasn't. It gave a mildly schizophrenic feel to things. And I was pretty surprised when Jade drew me aside and said, low-voiced, "Kelly—Ross wants to take me out tonight. To eat."

"Yeah? What'd you say?"

"I said yes. The taverna he's talking about sounds cool. Right up in the mountains. I drive—he pays."

"But it'll still be a date, Jade."

"*Yes*, it'll be a date—so what? We're not getting engaged. Anyway, I said we should ask you to come, too. With Nick."

I shook my head, furiously. *"No way."*

"Why not?"

"Jade—you *know* why not."

"*God*, you're boring. I bet Mikey's shagging anyone he can get his hands on."

"He's not like that."

"All guys are like that."

"Anyway, it's not just about Mike. What about Sarah? We can't leave her on her own all day and all night, too. In fact—we ought to get back soon. It's getting late."

Jade heaved a theatrical sigh. "OK. I guess you're right. I'll go out with Ross on my own then."

"Yeah," I said. "I really think that's best."

Then she walked off and I thought, *She goes out, I stay in with Sarah. At my suggestion. Great, Jade. Ten out of ten for manipulation skills.*

Sarah was still in her room when we got back. Jade shot off to colonize the bathroom, and I went and filled the kettle in a very sour temper. Once I'd made the tea, I poured out two cups and stomped off up to Sarah's room. I was getting ready to pound on the door and shout stuff like "Enough of all this nonsense, open up!" but there was no need. At my first knock, Sarah opened the door, and gave me a watery smile.

"Can I come in for a moment?" I asked. She nodded, and stood back from the door to let me by. I perched on the end of her bed, and handed her her tea.

"Feeling better?" I said.

She nodded. "A bit. Look—sorry about this morning."

"It's OK."

"You must've thought I'd lost it completely."

I gave a tactful shrug. "Well—I knew you were having a bad day. I just didn't know what to do to help . . ."

"Nothing. Honestly. When I get down like that I just have to kind of sit it out. If anyone tries to cheer me up it just . . . well, it doesn't work."

We both took a sip of our tea, and I said, "When you say 'down,' what do you . . . ?"

Sarah heaved a massive sigh, and I didn't think she was going to answer. Then she muttered, "Well . . . I woke up, and inside I was just . . . it was all stagnant, stinking, filthy. All inside me, every part of me, nothing I could do. And I felt like I'd be like it forever."

"God," I murmured. "You just woke up like that?"

"Yeah. I do, sometimes. And it's like the plug's been pulled on me, I can't move, hardly. It's like it's my *reality*, you know? I can't imagine another."

"God," I said, again.

"People say—'I feel low today'—stuff like that—and then they do something to cheer themselves up. I mean—how can they be so sure it's just *today* they'll feel like that? How can they be sure they won't feel like that from then on? That's how I get."

I stared at her glassily, and she stood up, walked toward the window, and looked out. "It's better in the evening. It's sort of—the day's over, and it's safe. The mornings are the worst."

There was another long pause. "Everyone gets depressed sometimes," I said, a bit helplessly.

"Yeah."

"I s'pose—what I think is weird is—how can you be depressed *here*?"

She shrugged. "I think it's *here* that's getting to me. I mean—it's just so beautiful—it's how life *should* be. But . . . I dunno. I'm just not up to it, somehow, I shouldn't *be* here."

"That's crazy. Why shouldn't you?"

"Because I'm not the sort of person who has wonderful holidays. I can't cope with them. My usual life is total shit. There's Jade—gobbling it all up, grabbing it—totally in *charge*—and I feel so inadequate I . . ."

Her eyes were swimming. Alarmed, I said, "Oh, *Sarah*. Jade makes everyone feel inadequate. We can't all be like her. And actually thank *God* we can't. Think of the noise level!" Sarah sniffed, smiled. "And anyway," I rushed on, "she's *not* always in charge. She goes on chocolate blinders sometimes, I bet you. And she must get days when she can hardly move from in front of the box. And booze—I've seen her pissed. God, remember that end of term party? She was *really* pissed."

"Yeah, but she *chooses* it. That's the point. When she got drunk that night—she'd decided to, she'd decided it was the way to go. And she wasn't that drunk, anyway. She's like—in charge of her life."

"Bollocks," I said. "No one is. It all depends on how you deal with what you're dished out, that's all. You just want to relax, Sarah. You're on *your* holiday, not Jade's. Now get your shoes on. It's a great evening, and you're coming for a walk."

I really had no idea what I was doing, but I had the strongest instinct that Sarah had to get out of that room and get moving, breathing in some different air. We walked along the coast road for a while, and I racked my brains for positive things to say. I ended up telling her she was a great cook, which I thought was pretty lame, but she smiled; and then I found a really lovely stone, kind of egg-shaped and mottled gray and red, and handed it to her. This started her looking around for more. We had five by the time we got back to the farmhouse, all beautiful, shaped by the sea. She arranged them on the courtyard steps, then she grabbed some crisps and a banana from the kitchen, and disappeared to her room again, saying she wanted an early night. I had the feeling she wanted to avoid Jade.

So I had that night on my own, sitting in the courtyard as the sky got dark. And actually, it was OK.

CHAPTER 17

SARAH WAS UP BEFORE ANYONE the next day and from the way she was behaving, it was clear she'd made some sort of change inside herself. She was more closed off, purposeful, and she seemed less twitched and anxious, too. She didn't say anything about the day before; when I asked her how she felt, she just said, "Fine."

Well, good for you, I thought. *And thank God.*

That day we drove along to three different beaches one after the other, so that we could give the jeep another real trial. We got lost five times and Sarah didn't moan once, not even when Jade tested the jeep down a steep cliff track and we had to brake and wait at a scary angle while a troop of donkeys trotted past. She didn't even complain when we picked up a breathtakingly fit hitchhiker who unfortunately only wanted a ride to the next town to meet his girlfriend.

Then as soon as we got back to the farmhouse, Sarah produced a flyer she'd picked up in a bar we'd been to at lunchtime, promoting a special "Hawaiian" night at a nearby hotel and suggested we go.

Jade and I stared at her, mouths hanging open. This was Sarah—seriously promoting fun. "Hawaiian?" said Jade dubiously. "Does that mean we have to wear grass skirts and stuff?"

"*No*, it's just *themed*. Fruity cocktails, half-price before 10 PM. And a special fish-based buffet, very cheap. We could get there early, and eat . . . there's live music, too. And a disco, with laser and smoke effects. Look—" she waved the flyer determinedly—"it's all down here."

"Right!" exclaimed Jade. "It sounds utterly naff but it could be a laugh. What d'you think, Kelly?"

"Yeah, let's go. It'll be a scream. And I reckon it's our bounden duty to take in all Special Events on offer. I mean—when you think about all the effort they've gone to—it's only *polite* to turn up."

"Do we call for Ross and everyone?" asked Jade.

"Up to you," said Sarah. "But I say we go on our own."

So we did. And it was eighty percent excruciating, of course, but that was part of the fun. As soon as we got there, an oily manager presented each of us with a rather ropy garland of flowers, saying, "Maybe later you'll do the hula-hula for us, yes?" ("Er, *no*," said Jade, well within earshot.) All night long guys kept pulling bits off the garlands, taking bites out of the flowers—it was quite a conversation opener. The place was packed with oiks spraying lager about and stripping half naked and tipping each other into the hotel swimming pool. They kept getting chucked out by Security, then they'd put their clothes back on and bluster their way back in. There was lots of seventies-style dancing. There was even, God help us, a *conga*—and you couldn't get out of it, you got grabbed wherever you tried to hide, you just had to go with it, like a kind of embarrassment-threshold bungee-jump. As for close encounters, I remained aloof, although I kind of liked all the attention I was getting; and Jade pulled five times and Sarah pulled twice and had to be rescued at the end. We were sore from laughing when we crawled out at 2 AM to go home.

But what was weird was when we all drifted down for breakfast pretty late the next day, Sarah said, "Um—I think—if it's OK with you—I'll give the beach a miss today."

"Hangover that bad, eh?" said Jade.

"Well—not good. But I sort of fancy just having a day off, you know."

"God, Sarah—you can't stay here all day!

You'll go demented! Look—we needn't go yet. Have another coffee and see if—"

"Jade—I'd really like to stay here. On my own. I want some—you know. I want some space."

"Oh," said Jade. "OK."

So Jade and I took off in the jeep and went back to the beach we'd liked best the day before. We were pretty tired; we both had a long siesta with our heads under the beach umbrella and our oiled-up legs stuck out to tan.

When we got back to the farmhouse, early and ravenous 'cos we'd slept through lunch, the most delicious savory smell wafted out of the farmhouse to meet us. Sarah came out to meet us, too, and she was glowing. "I've had the best day," she said, sounding almost apologetic. "I've been walking, and pottering about . . . I just wanted time out, you know? Look!" And she pointed to the stone steps. Lined up on one side, in the lovely old clay pots we'd discovered with the barbecue, were about fifteen green, spiky cacti, mounting the stairs like a chorus routine.

"Sarah, they look stunning!" I said.

"Like some kind of photoshoot," agreed Jade. "Where d'you get them?"

"Well—just out the back," Sarah explained. "By some rocks at the edge of the fields. There were loads—just growing wild. D'you think it's cruel—digging them up?"

"Look, I mash loads of cacti every time I park out there," said Jade. "You could say you're saving their little lives."

Sarah grinned. "I just—*enjoyed* it so much. I love plants. I know that's boring . . ."

"It's not boring. You're a gardener. The steps look ultra-classy now. And where did *they* come from?" Jade pointed to the old cracked urn at the foot of the steps, now filled with bright scarlet geraniums, and looking fabulous.

"The woman at the veg stall let me have them really cheap, 'cos they've gone a bit straggly."

"And that wonderful foody smell?"

"Dinner. Lamb casserole."

Jade advanced on Sarah, arms wide. "Sarah, you are a *star*. It looks fab, it smells *fab*. Any time you want time out—just take it, OK?"

Sarah looked at her, kind of grateful and glad and considering, all at the same time. "I will," she said. "I just can't keep your pace up, Jade."

Then they hugged each other, laughing, and I said, "No one can keep her pace up, Sarah. She's a freak."

Jade drew back, laughing. "Look—we're all different. OK—I'm a maniac—"

"Sure are," I said.

"—and *Kelly*'s like some kind of *nun*, vowed to remain faithful to that boring git Mikey."

"Oh, piss off!"

"And you, Sarah . . . well, like you say, you need your space. And what we all need to do . . ." (here Jade adopted a cringe-making American chat show voice) ". . . is value our differences! 'Cos it's our differences that make us truly human! We have to respect each other's *needs*, cherish each other's tender inner *child*—"

"Your tender inner child's going to get real kicking if you don't shut up," I said. "Sarah—when can we *eat*?"

As Sarah and I got the stuff on the table for dinner, Sarah said, "You were so sweet the other day."

"Me, *sweet*?"

"Yeah. When I was—you know."

"Sunk in gloom."

"Yeah. It was like you cared—but you let me get on with it. You didn't tell me what to do."

"Why should I?"

"Well, most people do. My dad does. He hates it when I'm down. He goes on and on at me, says I'm giving in and stuff . . . it all just makes me feel worse."

"Well . . . it would."

"He says, 'You start saying you're depressed, and you will be.' But he's not right. It takes so much energy, covering it up—it makes you feel ten times worse. I made myself go out yesterday, and it was fine. Today I just wanted to be on my own, so I was. I walked and walked and walked, and did the pots, and . . . I didn't feel I was giving in, I didn't feel a bit guilty. I felt like I was *curing* myself."

"Or maybe just *being* yourself."

She gave me a smile that upturned her whole face. "Yeah. I loved what you said about—you know—being on *my* holiday, not Jade's."

I'd actually forgotten saying that, but it didn't matter.

During dinner we talked about going to *Ariadne*'s that night, where they'd hopefully let us in free again. Then a fit of conscience overtook Jade and she said she thought we ought to go and call for Ross and Co. "And if they ask about last night, tell 'em we got free tickets, yeah? But only three. So we couldn't ask them."

"Jade—is lying a way of *life* for you?" I asked, pleasantly, while Sarah said, "What I don't under-stand, Jade, is if you're not keen on Ross—how come you keep seeing him?"

"Oh, *Sarah*," groaned Jade—which wasn't exactly an answer, but it was the only one she gave.

Ross and Co. did come out with us—minus Jodie and Chris, who looked very glad to have the flat to themselves—and we all had a good time. The only hitch for me was having to make it clear to Nick all over again that I wasn't up for anything physical. We had one slow dance and then when he tried to get a bit smoochy on the next one I took a deep breath and told him I was already involved with someone.

"Jesus, Kelly, I wasn't trying to *sleep* with you," he said. "I just wanted a snog."

Embarrassing. "Yeah, well. I don't," I mumbled.

"*OK*," he said, all offended, and wandered off on his own. Fifteen minutes later I spotted him dancing with this willowy black girl, and that was a relief. Sort of.

Sarah took off on her own, too. First, she really let rip on the dance floor, and then she disappeared, and we didn't see her for about half an hour. And then I clocked her necking with someone beside the bar. I cornered her in the bogs soon after, but she wouldn't give me any details—just told me it was the last night of the guy's holiday.

"So you're saying you felt sorry for him?" I asked.

"No. Just that I won't be seeing him again." And then she gave me a wonderful grin, went back out to the dance floor, and started dancing around with someone else.

BY THE END OF THAT FIRST WEEK I was totally in love
with the heat. I loved the way it dominated; the
way you planned the day around it. Sun, shade,
sun, shade; like slats in a Venetian blind. Sun-
bathing, swimming, rinsing off, creaming up, sunning again. It got to you and relaxed you, deep
down inside. It was like some great, growling god;
if you treated it right, it blessed you.

I nurtured my growing tan like a project, massaging in pre-sun and after-sun. Because I'm dark
I tanned well, whereas Jade had to take it easy and
had trouble with red shoulders. The bridge of her
nose was quite dodgy, too. I tried not to be glad
about this.

Sarah was tanning beautifully. Kind of tawny,
like a lion. She'd taken to clipping her hair back, and
it suited her. It slimmed her face, and showed off

her eyes. She didn't look the least bit nondescript anymore.

It didn't take me long to absorb some of Jade's beach style. I bought a sarong, and some elegant beach sandals, and a big raffia basket for my beach stuff. I dedicated one of my better, longer T-shirts to wearing over my swimsuit. I got some deep wax conditioner for my hair and one night when we stayed in I sat around for hours with a toweling turban on. It was all deeply trivial and Mike would have really despised me if he'd seen me doing it.

Mike. Somehow, he'd been shelved. Somehow, he didn't fit with what I was doing now. Whenever he drifted into my mind I'd push him away, tell myself I'd think about him later. Maybe week two, or three—when it was getting close to meeting up with him—then I'd let him in a bit. There wasn't time to brood about him now—things had settled into a wonderful, ever-shifting pattern, and the days were so full and everything was so new. We'd get up, and over a slow breakfast, decide what to do that day, which beach to go to. Sometimes we'd have to shop for food, which was dead easy now we had the jeep; sometimes we'd tour around a little. We'd let things happen. Then as the sun went down we'd usually make our way back to the farmhouse and get ourselves ready for the night.

Ross was around all the time, as keen on Jade as ever; and now she had Petros in love with her, too. Petros worked in a scruffy little bar ten minutes' walk from the local beach. We'd discovered it by accident and got hooked, mainly because Petros kept slipping us free drinks and crisps and stuff, on account of being besotted by Jade. He was about twenty, with gorgeous chocolate-brown eyes; he'd lived in the area all his life, knew everyone there. Jade said knowing Petros got us away from the superficial tourist stuff, got us into the real Greece. It didn't seem to bother her that now she had two guys she was stringing along, and they were both coming to our party.

Which was only days away now. Jade was fervent about it; to her, it wasn't just a chance to have a good time, it was part of a grand scheme. She was positioning herself at the center of things. She wanted all the people we were meeting to come and see where we lived, and see who else we knew, and realize what a hotshot she was.

"This party—it's like an investment," she said. "It'll get us into all the scenes out here. It'll get us invitations back. We can't keep going clubbing all the time. We'll run out of money."

"I thought we were going to get jobs, if we ran out of money." I said.

"Yeah, well, I've been thinking about that and I've decided I don't want a stupid job. I don't want to be stuck waiting tables."

"A few nights a week'd be OK," I reasoned. "It might even be fun."

"Kelly—you get a job if you want one. I don't want to be tied down like that."

"We could always stay in a bit more," Sarah piped up. "That'd save money."

Jade didn't even deign to answer.

The night before the party, the three of us agreed we'd stay in and make a huge batch of ratatouille. We were going to serve this up with French bread and Greek cheese—Jade felt this struck the right balance between sophistication and casualness. We'd organized everyone coming to bring the drink. Ross had promised to drop in that night with a crate-load of beer. So had Petros.

We got back early, with bags and bags of shiny Mediterranean vegetables from the roadside stall. Sarah bore it all off to the kitchen like treasure, told us not to help till we felt like it. I honestly felt she'd be happier doing it all on her own. She had cooking in her *soul*. So I left her to it and went and grabbed the shower before Jade could. Afterward, I didn't bother to dry myself, just wrapped a towel around me, enjoying the coolness of the water evaporating on my skin. I padded out to the courtyard, making brief, wet footprints on the sun-warmed stone. On the bottom step I sat down and wrung out my hair, wriggling my toes as the water splashed on them.

"Wouldn't it be great to have a bathroom in the open air?" I called out to Jade, who was on the sunbed, half asleep. "In the sun."

"Yeah," she mumbled back.

"Shower's free," I added, unnecessarily. I tipped my head back and started brushing out my hair. It was drying already in the warm breeze.

Jade stood up, and smiled at me, drowsily. "That wind is magic," she said. "The perfect hairdryer. It always seems to get up in the evenings."

"It smells of thyme," I murmured. "And jasmine. God—this is a sensualist's *heaven*. If I felt any better I'd be *obscene*."

Jade burst out laughing, just as Sarah poked her head out of the kitchen. "What's the joke?" she asked.

"Kelly's experiencing intense physical pleasure," said Jade.

I loped slowly up the stone steps, enjoying the ache in my legs, the spacey well-being that comes when you've swum a lot that day. I walked into my room and adjusted the shutters, so that the sun slanted like a spotlight onto the mirror. Then I dropped my towel, and twisted about in front of the mirror. In my opinion, I'd got a lot better-looking. Toned, tanned. Relaxed.

I flopped backward onto the bed, feeling so open, so good it almost hurt, and then suddenly Mike was there, the memory of him solid and strong, like he was there in the room with me, and I could sense him, but couldn't touch him.

And I was flooded with missing him. It was agony, that feeling, like amputation. I rolled over and got hold of the pillow and squeezed it half to death. All I wanted was him there, on the bed with me, wrapping himself around me. I wanted to make love slowly, while the sun sank down beyond the open window and the sky went dark.

After a while I slid to the floor, got down on my knees and dragged my case out from under the bed. Then I pulled out the photo of him and me and as I looked at it I could feel my eyes pricking, smarting with tears, and the ache inside me got worse. I sat for a while, amazed at the suddenness of all this, the strength of it. Not sure what to make of it. Then I left the photo lying on the chest of drawers, pulled on some shorts and a T-shirt and went downstairs again.

Jade was just coming out of the bathroom. She

took one look at me and said, "What's up?"

"Huh?"

"You look all upset. What's up?"

"Oh—I just—I just—" and then I couldn't help myself, I was crying, really sobbing. "I don't *believe* this," I sniveled, as she sat me down on the step, put her arm around me. "I was fine! And then I suddenly thought about Mike and . . ."

"You miss him," she said, gently.

"Yes. No. Shit!"

"You miss the sex. It's only natural, I miss sex."

"Oh, *Jade*, it's not *just* sex . . ."

"Course it's not. Sorry. Look—why don't I make you a cup of tea?"

She went off, and I sat on the step with my head in my hands and thought again about making love with Mike. He wasn't the only guy I'd ever slept with, but he was the only one that counted. I'd lost my virginity in the drunken aftermath to a bad party when I'd only just turned seventeen, and it was such a depressing experience it didn't get on the scale. Not compared to Mike. We'd made love exactly twelve times up till now. I could recall the place, and the details, of each and every time. It doesn't seem much, does it, twelve times? Sometimes it seemed like the world, though.

Jade came back and handed me a mug, and sat

down beside me on the steps.

"Jade," I said, "When you . . . when *you* start sleeping with someone, does it do your head in?"

Jade shrugged. "Only if they're crap."

"No—I mean, if they're *not* crap. If they're good. Do you go completely mental, start thinking you're in love with them and everything?"

Jade looked at me, smirking. "Oh, my God. Don't tell me old *Mikey*'s an expert in the sack."

Something told me Jade and I came at sex from totally different viewpoints. Something told me she wouldn't get what I was trying to say. But I so needed to say it.

"It's not *him*—it's not separate, like it's just *him*. It's me, what I feel—how it changes how I feel about . . . how we are together. I kind of—oh, God. Sometimes I think I slept with him too soon, you know? Like I let all . . . *this* . . . in too early, before I really knew him properly . . . I let myself get all besotted before I . . . oh, I don't know."

There was a long pause. Then Jade murmured, "Kelly, it's our party tomorrow night."

"I know," I sniffed. "So?"

"So that'll cheer you up. And—Kelly?"

"Yes?"

"I know you think sex and Mikey are the same thing, but let me *assure* you—they ain't."

CHAPTER 19

"OH, SARAH—WHAT ARE YOU *saving* it for? Honestly."
Jade turned and laughed toward me, showing all
her white teeth. It was seven o'clock and we were
getting dressed for the party. Everything was ready.
Petros had loaned us a load of glasses and plates
with the beer; he'd turned up, luckily, ten minutes
after Ross had left, so Jade had been able to give
both of them her full attention. The food was laid
out in the kitchen. The candles were lit, around
the steps, in amongst the cacti. And now Jade was
trying to make Sarah wear her sassiest outfit, one
that hadn't seen the light of day or dark of night yet,
and Sarah was worrying that it would get spoiled.

"She's still got best-clothes syndrome," Jade
went on. "She won't wear her new stuff because
she's saving it for a really special occasion. So then
it gets out of fashion before she's even had it in the
wash."

173

"I don't care about it getting out of fashion," said Sarah.

"Sure you do. Everyone does. We can't help it. We're brainwashed. Something just starts to look wrong, because you aren't seeing pictures of it everywhere anymore. Me—I wear my stuff to death the minute I get it. When I most like it. Then I get more."

"Yeah, you said it," snapped Sarah. "Then you get more. We're not all rolling in it, like you are. I just feel bad not to have something I can put on if I've got something great to go to."

"What's 'great'? Any time can be great! This party'll be great! Wear your good stuff and *make* it great!"

"Oh, shut up," said Sarah, smiling. "Idiot. OK, I'll wear it." And she scooted up to her room.

Five minutes later, she appeared on the balcony. "Come on," called Jade. "Let's see."

Sarah self-consciously started down the steps toward us. Her dress was absolutely simple: short, clinging, with very thin straps, and blue like the Greek sea. Her hair and skin shone against it.

"Sarah, you look wonderful," I breathed.

"You haven't got your shoes on," Jade said.

"I know," Sarah answered. "I don't have any that look right with this."

"That's 'cos it looks great barefoot. God, Sarah, you look *fabulous*. You ought to show your shape off more often, babe."

"Honest?"

"Honest!" Jade and I both said in unison.

The tension and excitement level was rising in the three of us. The courtyard looked like a stage-set now, waiting for the show. At seven forty-five precisely Jade went into the living room and put some very bluesy music on, loud. Then she uncorked a bottle of wine, poured out three glasses, and said, "Here's to a great night, OK?" But before she'd taken so much as a sip, she was off stalking through the courtyard, looking over everything once again, lighting a candle that had gone out, visualizing, anticipating, waiting.

"This is one huge deal to Jade," I muttered to Sarah.

"Yeah," said Sarah. "It'd better go well."

"She's just so *sorted*—the way she plans things. She has this kind of *overview*."

Sarah shrugged, and took a slurp of wine.

Underneath, I was oddly distanced from it all. I'd slept really badly the night before, full of frantic, desperate dreams about Mike. It was weird, like some kind of switch had been thrown inside me, turning me on to him again, sending my thoughts back to him.

Live in the present, I kept telling myself. You're here, now—and he isn't.

Ross and friends were the first to arrive, at five to eight—we'd asked them to come early. Ross had this set expression on—kind of determined but anxious at the same time. I think he'd decided that tonight was the night he really made it with Jade, but at the same time he was dead scared she'd get off with someone else. I felt quite sorry for him.

Nick, by contrast, was really hyper. He grabbed Jade, then Sarah for a hello kiss—then he grabbed me and kissed me three times, once on each cheek, once on the mouth. "You," I said, "have been drinking."

"Just warming up," he grinned, carrying a chinking carrier bag into the kitchen.

Then the first hitch happened. Petros turned up, and close behind him were about a million people that he introduced one by one at top speed—cousins, neighbors, best friends, friends of best friends . . . it was never ending. We'd asked him to bring a few mates but this was like a carnival coming through the door. There were lots of girls in bright clothes, some tight, some swirly, who'd all brought offerings of food on big pottery plates with teatowels wrapped around them. Then there were lots of guys, aged anything from thirteen to forty—three of them, I noticed, carrying guitars. And immediately, the whole cavalcade spread out into the courtyard and started opening beer and chatting (in Greek) and laughing so loud you could barely hear the CD player.

"Bloody *hell*," whispered Jade.

"Look on it as local color," I whispered back.

"But there won't be *room* for anyone else!"

There was, of course—there had to be. Five minutes later, while Petros was towing Jade past all his friends and relatives, introducing her to them this time, the people from the flat next to Ross turned up, with some people who'd moved in to the flat next to *them* only the day before—"We knew you wouldn't mind!" And then the guys from Birmingham we'd done watersports with rolled in. Half of them had girlfriends in tow, they were carrying a whole crate of beer, and they were noisily chuffed that they'd actually found the farmhouse. "Talk about off the beaten track, man!"

Jade escaped from Petros, and retreated to the third step up. I climbed up to join her and together we looked over the sea of people. And the courtyard door kept flying open. Jade's expression got more and more tense every time it did. The two girls from Guildford we'd met the other night at a club came, only there were four of them now. Ross's water-skiing friends turned up with what looked like the entire water-skiing club. "Is *everyone* going to bring someone else?" she muttered.

"Well, you kind of made it an open invitation, didn't you," I muttered back.

"Oh, that's right, Kelly, *blame me*," she snapped, and she stalked downstairs and off toward the kitchen, pushing her way through the crowd.

It was only when I saw everyone together, crammed into the courtyard, that I realized they were all still strangers. The longest we'd known any of them was ten days. It was kind of scary. I wondered who else was going to turn up; and what it would take for the whole thing to get out of hand.

Petros hailed me, a beer bottle in either hand. "Jade upset?" he asked.

"Um—bit tense I think."

"Tell her not to worry. Tell her—party get going soon."

I gawped at him. "I think it's more—she's worried about too many people. And—you know—gatecrashers and stuff."

"You want someone thrown out—you tell me," Petros shouted. Something about his ferocious expression cheered me up. I jostled through to the kitchen, and saw Jade and Ross standing together. He had his arm around her; I decided not to interrupt. Instead I squeezed out of the door again and got kind of shunted through the crowd, shouting hello to people, making myself hoarse trying to chat. At least half the people there I'd never set eyes on before, and I think I only knew half a dozen names. Still.

By this time, the party had surged up the steps and onto the balcony. We'd shut our bedrooms but there were only locks on the inside so there was no guarantee they wouldn't be invaded. A couple were sitting on the steps going up to the roof, arms around each other, faces a hair's breadth apart. As I watched, another couple climbed past them and went up onto the roof itself.

And then Sarah materialized at my side. "Look at that," she said. "A three-tier party. Cool, eh?"

"Are people still arriving?"

"Yes. But it's thinning out. It's weird, everyone came so early."

"Well, Jade told them there'd be food. Maybe they didn't want it to run out."

"I have *no idea* how it's going to get dished out. I mean—I thought people would just wander into the kitchen and serve themselves. But have you *seen* the kitchen? It's jammed."

"Kitchens always get that way," I said. "It's 'cos the booze is in there."

There was a pause, then Sarah said, "I think Jade's pissed off with everything."

"Yeah, well. She had such a clear idea of how she wanted it to go, and parties aren't like that. You always get too few people, or too many."

"I don't think anything could come up to the picture she had in her mind."

"What picture—a music video?"

Sarah laughed. "Yeah—with her as the star. Are you enjoying it, Kelly?"

"Not really. It's too much of a frug. And you can't just talk to people, you have to *shout*."

"Come on. Let's get the food out."

"What? *How*?"

But Sarah had already started elbowing her way through to the kitchen, so I followed in her wake. I got there to find her physically evicting people from the kitchen. She amazed me; she simply got hold of them, stuck a bottle of wine or beer in their hand, and shoved them out of the door. The door was one of these stable things, in two halves, and I was only just in time to get inside before she slammed the lower half of the door shut and shot the bolt in place.

"Right!" she said. "Start cutting the cheese up. And the bread."

We were like a pub gone crazy with lunchtime orders. She dolloped ratatouille on plate after plate, I added bread and cheese, then we passed them through the hatch to the sea of hands waving there. Ten plates on, we realized we'd forgotten all the yummy food the Greek girls had brought, so we started adding dollops of that, too.

The other side of the hatch, Petros was being a star. He collected empty plates, then slipped through the door and started washing them up at top speed, so we could serve the next batch. "Will the food last out?" I called out anxiously.

"Yup!" said Sarah. "I'm being *really* mean."

Comments started coming through the hatch back at us—"This is great!" and "Any more bread?" and "How come he's got a stuffed vine leaf when I haven't?" Then gradually, the hands waving outside the hatch thinned, and stopped altogether. And Sarah, Petros, and I scraped together some leftovers for ourselves and wandered back to the party.

Amazingly, the courtyard didn't look half as packed as it had done. "Have people just eaten and gone?" I asked, indignant.

"No," Petros assured me, mouth full. "They through there."

I followed his pointing finger and found that

everyone had discovered the living room; discovered that once you were in there, you could actually hear the CD player. And they'd started dancing, and left the courtyard free for people who wanted to talk and make contact and generally interact. I headed for the steps, uprighted two cacti and sat down to eat, while Petros relit the candles that had been blown out. It was suddenly looking quite civilized and elegant out there.

Nick emerged, and sat down next to me on the steps. "How's it going, hostess?" he asked.

"OK," I said.

"You going to give me another dance?"

"I'm eating," I said, forking in another mouthful.

"What about when you've finished *eating*?"

"Never jump about with a full stomach."

"You don't have to jump about. We could take it slow."

I took a deep breath, and said, "Nick—look—I told you I've got a boyfriend."

Nick pantomimed looking around. "Where? I don't see one."

"Not here, idiot. At home. In England. Well—not in England. Somewhere in Greece."

"I see. Separate holidays, eh?"

"Yeah."

"In the same country. Neat."

"He's touring."

"On his own?"

"In a van with four mates."

Nick laughed. "And you really think *he's* being faithful to you?"

My fork stopped halfway to my mouth. "Don't look so stricken," said Nick. "Course he is." Then he added, "Well—I would, if I was him."

I went a kind of garroted pink, and mumbled, "Nick—shut up."

"Sorry. Look—lighten up. Is it my fault if I think you're the best-looking bird here?"

There was a sudden yell from the balcony above, and we both looked up. And there was Petros, with—worryingly—the three blokes who'd brought their guitars. Petros shouted out a stream of Greek, arms waving furiously, and all his friends and relations in the courtyard below clapped and stamped. Then the three guitarists started playing, singing along loudly as they did.

It was really corny Greek-taverna stuff, but it was great. I put my plate down and stood up, and started clapping in time. People were wandering out from the living room, to see what was happening; some went back in again pretty smartly, sniggering; others stayed to watch and applaud, and move to the beat.

"Look," said Nick, pointing up at the roof, at a couple doing a joke flamenco, lit up by the white moon behind them. "Can you do that?"

"Yeah. Sure I can."

"Come on, then. This party is *ace*."

It wasn't until about three in the morning that the last straggling guests either went home, or collapsed in a heap on the ground somewhere to sleep away what was left of the night. I'd got drawn into the dancing, with Nick, with anyone, and then I'd done some singing with the guitar players and some pseudo-Greek dancing and all in all I'd had a complete ball. As I was waving off the blokes from Birmingham I realized I hadn't seen Jade for hours. Sarah said she must have gone to bed 'cos she wouldn't just go off somewhere without telling us. And she'd seen Ross leave, looking unhappy.

We stood wearily in the courtyard, looking around at all the cans and bottles and plates and glasses lying around. "We need another flood," Sarah said. "To wash it all out."

"I'll arrange one for you, in the morning."

"It *is* the morning."

"I mean—you know. Christ. After I've *slept*. I've got to get to bed. I've drunk too much."

"We should drink water," Sarah groaned. We wandered into the kitchen, and she said, "There's still some food left. Cheese and stuff. Maybe I'll clingfilm it."

"Well, I wouldn't bother with the ratatouille," I said, peering into the big pan.

"Why?"

I took a step back. "'Cos I think someone's been sick in it."

THE NEXT DAY I WOKE UP when the sun through the shutters got too hot and bright to ignore. I felt pretty ropy but I knew I wouldn't go back to sleep. I pulled on some shorts and a T-shirt and staggered down to the courtyard, where I found a few sad shapes drinking tea and shuffling off home. Sarah was up; a couple of guys were helping her to load a black binbag with empty bottles and cans. I got myself some tea; couldn't face breakfast. Then I collected plates and glasses, stacking the sink to overflowing.

We couldn't get Jade out of bed. We took her two cups of tea, but she was in a foul mood, and kept pulling the covers over her head, and telling us to go *away*.

"Great," muttered Sarah. "She throws the party, we clear up."

"Let's leave her the washing-up," I said.

"Oh, it's no big deal. And Petros said he'd be round at twelve, to pick the plates and glasses up. We'd better do it."

So we propped ourselves up against the kitchen sink, and Sarah washed and I dried, and we rehashed the best bits of the party, like when Petros had tried to teach the lads from Birmingham to dance, and when his cousin had done a mournful guitar solo up on the roof. We got into a rhythm together, plate after plate, and Sarah told me about this guy she'd really liked the look of, and how they'd kept kind of passing by each other, all night long, but neither of them had made a move.

"Oh, *Sarah*," I said. "You looked so gorgeous last night. Why didn't you just say *hi* to him?"

She looked at me, horrified. "I couldn't. Suppose he hadn't said *hi* back?"

"Well—then you forget him and move on."

"But I'd've been *crushed*. The whole party would've been spoiled. At least this way I had—you know, the *hope* of it."

"*Sarah!*"

We were laughing together when Jade appeared in the doorway, still in her flimsy dressing gown. "Any juice?" she yawned.

Sarah turned to the fridge and pulled a carton of orange juice out, but I refused to hand Jade a glass, and she had to squeeze past me to get one herself from the draining board. "About *time* you got up," I seethed. "We've just about finished."

She flipped a hand, dismissing my words. "You could've left something for me to do," she said.

"Like *what*? Petros'll be here soon to—"

"Oh, Kelly, give it a rest, *please*."

I turned back to the sink, stung. I'd heard her use that voice—the voice that said you were a total drag—to Sarah loads of times but it was the first time she'd used it to me.

"I don't know what your problem is," I snapped. "You've had more sleep than either of us. You must've gone up to bed at midnight."

"Eleven-thirty, actually. I couldn't stand it anymore."

"Jade—it was a great party!"

"No, it wasn't. It was a *scrummage*. Like some bloody student *hop*."

"OK, it was a bit packed. But that's better than being half empty. And everyone said how good it'd been, when they left."

"Oh, *goody*," she sneered. "That's all right then." And she drifted out to the courtyard.

I let out a kind of croak of annoyance, and slammed another plate down on the pile. "Don't let her get to you." Sarah laughed. "The party wasn't good for her, so it was total crap. She has this very subjective view of things."

"That's subjective, is it? Sounds like bloody

self-centered to me. Look—I know the party was a big deal for her. But it went *well*. God, anyone just walking *in* would've said so."

"Yes, but it would have gone well with her or without her. She wasn't *central*."

We were whispering now, hissing at each other across the pile of plates, in case Jade was just outside and could hear. "I can't *believe* you think she's that egocentric," I said.

Sarah looked away from me. "Well, she is. Everything is surface for her. You know what we were talking about the other night—when we were fourteen, when we first met?"

"Yeah. You got pretty upset by that, didn't you?"

"Yes, I did. I really tried to include her, you know, when she'd just moved here, and all she could say was how crap it had been. Anyway, I did some thinking after that. I've always told myself that she was a good mate, 'cos when she started getting popular, and all these boys started hitting on her, she didn't drop me."

"I should hope she didn't!"

"Yeah, right. It would've been really shitty, wouldn't it? After we'd been so close. Everyone would've thought it was shitty. And I reckon that's the main reason she didn't. 'Cos of the *look* of it."

"Oh, Sarah, that's not the only reason—"

"It's the main one. And it would've been more honest to drop me. More honest than this . . . this *compromise* friendship we've got."

"Sarah, that's not true. She thinks a lot of you, I know she does. God, only the other day, you remember, she said you're always there for her—"

"I'm beginning to think that's only 'cos I've got nowhere else to go," Sarah said, and plunged her hands back into the washing-up bowl.

Things got back to normal. Jade was sulky and deflated for a couple of days and when I asked her what had happened with Ross she told me, "He just didn't *do* it for me, OK?" So then I asked her whether he was still going to be around, and she acted so bored and irritated I dropped the whole subject. I got the feeling he'd walked out on her— he'd realized she was stringing him along, waiting for someone better to come along, and he'd walked out. Well, if that was the case I sort of congratulated him.

Jade wasn't the type to stay down for long, though. However disappointed she'd been with it on the night, the party had had the effect she'd hoped for. It was like we were established, we were hot. Three weeks after arriving in Greece, and at the time when most people would have been packing to come home, we were really getting into our stride. Now, when we went to a beach or a club, there'd always be someone to say hello to, and people would just turn up at the farmhouse and sit around with us, drinking beer, or take us off with them on an outing somewhere. I loved the variety, the buzz; Sarah kind of coasted through it. Sometimes, when people turned up, she'd just go off to her room.

Things were opening out between the three of us, too. When we'd first arrived in Greece, we'd been like this tight knot—going to the beach together, eating together, going out at night together. Sarah and I had hidden behind Jade, glad for her to deal with ordering drinks, finding the way to places. Then gradually the knot began to unravel, because Jade started to pull away.

At first, Sarah and I had felt like abandoned babies—threatened, unsure, but ashamed, too, ashamed of our dependency on Jade. Then we'd started to like it, and the best kind of pattern was set. We'd kind of fan out, do our own things for a while, and come back together again. Every day, fresh negotiations. Flexible, but in touch. Like the best kind of dance.

* * *

One morning, Jade came back from the mailbox outside the gate, and came into the kitchen sarcastically brandishing a bent-looking postcard. "Well, well, well," she said. "A missive from *Mikey*!"

I jumped to my feet, snatched it from her, scanned it hungrily, looking for words that said he missed me, wanted me, planned to meet up with me.

"What on earth are all those figures?" asked Jade, peering unashamed over my shoulder. "Looks like a maths problem."

I could feel my face sagging with disappointment. "It's distances and stuff. How many miles they've covered. Where they've been."

"Ro-*man*-tic," she murmured, heading for the fridge.

The card was signed: *Looking forward to seeing you, Luv, Mike.*

Luv Mike. *Luv* Mike. Jesus. What's wrong with the word, Mike? The real one. Afraid your backbone might collapse if you use it?

I flipped the card onto the kitchen table, let it slide into a pool of congealing milk. "What's the matter?" Jade murmured. "Aren't you going to prop it on your chest of drawers? Tuck it in your mirror frame? Stick it down your bra?"

"No," I said flatly, "I'm not."

IT DIDN'T TAKE JADE LONG to find a replacement for Ross. She met him at a new club we'd discovered; he was called Richard and he was well into his twenties, and very well-heeled. I didn't think much of the new club, it was attached to a smart hotel and it was kind of cheesily sophisticated. I had pretty much the same opinion of Richard. But Jade was keen. He asked her out for a posh dinner the next night and she was really excited about it.

When she told us, Sarah and I decided straight away that we'd stay in and relax. "Oh, for goodness' sake," Jade said. "You make me feel so guilty! I mean—you could get a cab. Or walk, to *Ariadne*. Or—"

"Jade," I interrupted, "we *want* to stay in, OK? We've been partying so much lately I'm going cross-eyed with it."

"Yeah," said Sarah. "And I love this place at

night. It's so quiet it's like—I dunno. A sanctuary."

"Yeah," I agreed. "We don't use it enough. And Sarah and I can have a really good chat. We can tear you to pieces while you're not here."

Jade tried to smile at this, but her mouth didn't quite make it. I regretted saying it—I hadn't exactly *meant* it, after all. She turned and ran up the stairs to her room, and came down soon after in one of her ultra-short, ultra-clingy dresses. "What d'you think?" she said.

"Too tarty," I pronounced. "Too clubby. It's *dinner*, remember."

She turned on her heel again and came down in something longer and looser but a lot lower in the front. "Better," I said.

She pouted. "I'm not sure about this dress. It needs a real cleavage."

I laughed. "Jade, if you had a cleavage too the poor guy would miss his mouth all the time he was trying to eat."

She shot off once more, came down in a third outfit—tight-fitting trousers with a cutaway top. She looked completely stunning as she descended the stairs, and I had a real pang that I wasn't the one looking like that, I wasn't the one going out. "Yes," I said, "that's it."

If the courtyard was Sarah's sanctuary, it was

Jade's stage. Her rehearsal stage, where she tried out everything she'd be for the evening. She sashayed up and down, practicing her walk. In her head she was already in the restaurant, impressing everyone.

"I don't understand Jade," said Sarah, once Richard had whisked Jade away in a predictably smooth little sports car. "You know—her *world view*. She's so into appearance. Not just her own, but what a club looks like, or a bar—whether it's cool or not. And yet she's the one least affected by this place, I swear she is. I mean—she likes the idea of it, the smell of the jasmine and all that—but she never seems to really *see* it. She thought we were mad, wanting to stay here tonight."

"Yeah, well we're not, are we," I said, and I realized what would have been a pretty grotty prospect three weeks ago—staying in alone with Sarah—was actually something I was quite looking forward to.

We got some food together and opened some white wine, and Sarah lit two candles to put on the table. I liked her doing that—sort of saying it was just us two, but it was still an occasion. She smiled at me across their light, and said, "And words, too. Have you noticed how Jade uses words?"

"Um—"

"Jade loves words. But she uses them like—I dunno. Objects. Separately. Haven't you noticed?"

I shrugged. "Well—she likes to throw off one-liners, yeah."

"For effect. Or attack. Like bullets. Ammunition. She never puts them together. She never lets them connect. And when she's talking with other people—she never exchanges them." Sarah's eyes had gone all wide as she spoke. "It's a bit like how she is with people, isn't it? Sort of . . . separate. She doesn't connect. She doesn't let herself get affected by anything."

"Blimey, Sarah—heavy. But you could be—I dunno. Right."

There was silence, while we each took a sip of the honey-colored wine. Then Sarah said, "That postcard you got—did Mike say when he was getting to Greece?"

I pulled a face. "A week or so's time. Nothing definite."

"So is it working," she went on, "this break from him?"

"It's not really a *break*," I said, defensively. "I mean—it's practical. I wasn't going to tag along with five blokes, walking up eight-mile mountains for fun and never getting a shower."

She laughed. "Jade can't stand him, can she?"

"No. He's not too keen on her, either."

"She thinks he pushes you around. She thinks he's a bully."

I picked up my glass, took a drink. "Takes one to know one."

"Yeah, she can be one."

"Always trying to override people—what they think, what they want to do."

"But you don't let her push *you* around, Kelly."

"I still feel the pressure, sometimes."

"And Mike? You feel the pressure from him?"

I sighed, closed my eyes. "Yes. Yes, I suppose I do. Look—he isn't a bully. He isn't at all. He's just—oh, God, I don't know. He *swamps* me. You know that mind game, where a psychiatrist says a word and you have to say the first word that comes into your head? Like—he says 'father' and if you say 'death—evil—KILL,' he has a kind of clue to your relationship with your dad?"

Sarah laughed, nodded.

"Well," I went on, "if you did it on me and said 'Mike Morris,' I'd come back with 'overwhelming.' Because that is what Mike is. And don't get me wrong, sometimes there's nothing I like better than being overwhelmed. It's just—not all the time. In every bit of my life. He has a *very strong* character. And the thing is, I agree with a lot of what he says and stuff, and I like the way he is . . . but sometimes when I've been with him all day I sort of forget who I am and what *I* think." I drew breath and glanced at Sarah. "Is this making sense?"

"Yes," she said. "It is." She looked as though it was, too. She surprised me, actually, how understanding she was being, what a good listener.

"It's never happened to me before, with a bloke. *I've* always been the stronger one. And the trip—it was the last straw," I went on. "I mean— it's not really my thing, roughing it and hiking and stuff, but if we'd planned it together, you know, if I'd had a say in it, I'd have felt differently, I know I would. It's just—it was like he thought all that mattered to me was to be with *him*. Which I could have dealt with if—"

"You weren't afraid it was true."

I smiled, ruefully. "Yeah. Maybe. Especially when he won't say what he feels about *me*."

There was a long pause, and this time I grabbed the wine bottle and emptied it into our two glasses, sharing it out fairly. Sarah laughed. "Well, you've proved you can have a good time without him, anyway."

"Yes. Yes, I have. It's been great, so far—and it's

going to get better, I'm sure it is. I just needed to do something alone, you know? Remind myself that I have a valid existence apart from him—and that it's *good*. I mean—we do seem to end up doing what he wants to do. Like he thinks my choices are . . . not interesting, or something. Not up to some standard he's got. I get the feeling sometimes he looks down on the other sides of my life. Like my friends. And art—you know I'm doing Art Textiles next year? He thinks that's a soft subject, I know he does."

"What's he doing?"

"Politics and Sociology."

Sarah groaned. "That figures." She indicated the empty wine bottle. "Shall we open another one?"

I pretended shock. "Sarah—what's got into you?"

"This place," she said, and she waved her hand at the white wall against the black night, and the vines stirring in the breeze. "Just look at those stars."

I smiled, looked up, inhaled the night scent. "OK," I agreed, "I'll get another bottle. Jade put one in the fridge."

"That's probably for when Richard drops her off. You know—a romantic nightcap."

"Well, we won't finish it, will we?" I said. "We'll leave them a glass each."

Jade arrived back at ten minutes to midnight, vibrating like a volcano about to erupt. "What a smooth *git*," she snarled. "What an arsehole!"

"Oh, dear." I laughed. "Not a success then?"

"We had dinner at his *hotel*. Not the restaurant he promised me. He bored me all through dinner. Monologues about his stupid business deals. Thought I was in awe of him, when actually I was trying to keep awake. And then at the end of the meal a waiter came and announced in this creepy conspiratorial voice that the coffee and brandy were ready in his *room*."

"Subtle."

"Yeah. Really subtle. So I told him: 'I've got nothing against sleeping with someone on the first date if it goes that way, but I don't like it planned out on some bloody timetable. Some *itinerary*. Because it's not exactly a turn on. Any more than you are, you jerk.' Then I stood up and walked out."

"Blimey, Jade—good for you! How'd you get home?"

"I had to get a cab. It was worth it, though, to make him look like a prat in front of all the hotel

staff. Oh, *shit*, I'm fed up. Why can't I meet someone *good*?"

Then she picked up my wine glass from the
table, downed it in one gulp, and stomped off
upstairs.

THE NEXT DAY WHEN I WOKE up I felt like I wanted some time alone. Jade was still in bed, no doubt sleeping off a hangover; Sarah was already stretched out on the sunbed in the courtyard with a book, and only grunted at me when I walked by her. So I grabbed my swimming things and went off to the local beach on my own.

I got straight into the sea and swam, swam for ages. The beach had only just started to fill up with sun worshippers. When I got out, I felt quite chilled; and more so after I'd rinsed off under the freshwater hose. So I wrapped my towel around me, padded up to the café, and shamelessly ordered a large bacon and egg sarnie and coffee. The kid who brought it to me sat and chatted to me, until his mother called to him to come and help out in the kitchen again.

Then I wandered back to the farmhouse,

wonderfully relaxed. Sarah had shifted into the shade. She told me Jade had headed off on foot soon after me, complaining how dull everything was.

I shrugged. "Right now, dull is nice. Peaceful. Want a coffee?"

The noise of a van rumbling its way along the track outside broke into her answer. It drew alongside our wall, then its brakes grated and it came to a standstill.

I looked up. "Who's that? Who do we know who drives something that size?"

Sarah shook her head, frowning. We heard the opening and slamming of doors and a man's laughter. And then Jade's voice. She sounded excited; there was a teasing, triumphant note to her words, but I couldn't catch what she was saying.

For no clear reason, my stomach had seized up into a knot of apprehension. I put down my coffee mug and made my way slowly across the courtyard to the great wooden door.

"Kelly!" Jade called, from the other side. "*Kelly!* Get out here!"

I reached the door just as it was pushed open in my face. I stepped back and stared through the opening.

Jade stood there, grinning, with four guys towering all around her. My eyes dilated in shock;

registered the newly-brown, familiar faces of Ben, Harry, Jim, and Andy. My heart thumped; my eyes spun outward, toward the van.

And there was Mike. Swinging down from the driver's seat. His hair was longer, bleached in streaks by the sun, and his neck was deep brown. He had on a creased blue shirt with the sleeves rolled right back, and on his forearm there was a long red scar, newly healed. His jeans had a jagged tear in them, just above the right knee. His boots were white with dust. His face was tanned.

I stared; I took him all in. I wanted him so much that for a whole thirty seconds I couldn't open my mouth, couldn't do anything but concentrate on keeping upright.

"WELL?" shrieked Jade. "Aren't you going to say *hello*, you daft cow? And then *thank me*?"

Mike finished cramming the van keys in his jeans pocket, then he put his head on one side, half-smiled and said, "Hi, Kelly."

"Hi," I croaked.

He shrugged, hesitated, loped over the space between us. Then he put his hands on my shoulders; I felt them right through me. I leaned toward him, and he bent down and kissed me on the cheek, quickly, too quickly, before I could sense him, before our faces could connect.

"Hi," he said again.

"Hi," I repeated, idiotically.

And then his hands fell back to his side, and he stepped away a little.

"Can we get a drink?" demanded Ben.

"Sure you can!" exclaimed Jade, and she led everyone into the courtyard, me and Mike following along, a whole arm's width apart.

I didn't know how to handle it. I didn't know what to *do*. My knees were weak from the shock of seeing him, being up close to him, wanting him. But we'd been as awkward as fifteen-year-olds on a second date. Worlds away from the wild, passionate reunion I'd fantasized about. I felt heavy with disappointment, and a kind of reluctance.

It's too soon, I thought. *I'm not ready for him yet.* I wanted more days alone in this climate, in this house, more days just being me . . . if we'd waited another week or so, it would've gone so much better.

I followed Jade, all laughter and extravagant hand gestures, across the courtyard. I stared at her back, and her profile as it turned from Ben to Harry and back again, and suddenly I was flooded with anger against her. *How* dare *you land this on me*, I thought. *How dare you just*—take over. *This isn't your show, these guys are nothing to do with you.*

How dare *you bring Mike here, with no warning, with everyone milling around and everything so exposed and public and me* not ready.

I could feel my face setting, expressionless, to keep all these jumbled feelings in. I couldn't look at anyone.

"We have everything here," Jade was caroling, waving her arms about. "Make yourselves at home. Experience *proper living*."

"Great." Ben laughed.

"A bit more space than that shitty van, yeah? Cold drinks, because we have a *fridge*. Mmmm. Shade. Chairs. Comfort. A *bathroom*, even. And if you play your cards right—probably the first decent meal you've had since you hit the road. What d'you say, Sarah?"

Sarah was still looking stunned by the invasion. With all five guys in it, the courtyard looked oddly crowded. They'd come to a standstill and formed a rough circle, looking around, grinning with appreciation. "But how did you—where did you . . . ?" she squeaked.

Jade was in her element. Center stage. "Yeah—I guess you want to know how this came *about*, don't you?" she said. "Well—happenstance. Coincidence. Totally serendipitous."

"Blimey," said Ben. "All three?"

"Yes. Sarah—let's get them some drinks, then I'll tell. Sit down, guys. You want beer, or juice?"

"Oh, fan—*tas*—tic," groaned Harry, greedily.

"Can we have both?" asked Andy.

Jade swept into the kitchen, followed by Sarah, and I found myself rushing in after them, overtaken by the instinct to escape. I pulled glasses out of the cupboard, beer out of the fridge, and smashed the ice tray out on the kitchen counter. Then I scooped all the ice cubes into a large tin jug that Sarah was holding out, while Jade added two cartons of juice, one of apple, one of peach.

Sarah kept peering at me anxiously, but Jade was smiling serenely, eyes averted, and before I could get it together to hiss any questions at her she swept back into the courtyard with a laden tray. Sarah and I followed, carrying an old kitchen stool each.

Mike had sat down at the table between Harry and Jim; Andy and Ben were on the other side. All five of them had sort of collapsed forward, arms sprawled. When Jade plunked the tray down in front of them, they gave a kind of collective groan of ecstasy, and for a while there was just the sound of ring-pulls and ice chinking and throats glugging.

Jade took the chair next to Ben. I plonked my stool down the other side of Harry, my stomach tight, my face rigid, and glared into my drink. Sarah perched on her stool and said, "OK, one of you—*please*—tell us the story."

"We rescued her," said Ben. "From this lust-crazed Greek."

"Ha!" Jade snorted. "More like I rescued *you*. From certain death by BSE in that grimy little shack you were going to eat in."

"*Jaaade!*" wailed Sarah. "What *happened*?"

"OK, OK," said Jade. "Well, I was so pissed off I wandered along to the Apollo bar. For a *coffee*, Sarah—don't look so disapproving. Only they do shit coffee, as you know. So I was grumbling away about this to Petros and telling him he should get a proper cappuccino machine and he said the bar in the next village but one did a great cappuccino and why didn't he take me on his bike. And I thought—nothing else to do—why not?"

Sarah looked huge-eyed with indignation. "Because the poor sod fancies you and he would have seen that as a *date*, that's why not!"

Ben growled with laughter, and Jade said, "Oh, balls. It was only a cup of coffee. Anyway, we got there. Just about. It took *three quarters* of an hour. *Far* further than he'd said. And we were swerving all over the place. It was *seriously* frightening. That bike should be turned to *scrap*, in my opinion.

Anyway. We came up behind this dodgy old van swerving even more than we were."

"No, it wasn't," said Mike.

"Yes, it was. And then the van stopped really suddenly—no signaling—"

"I *signaled*," said Mike.

"Not visibly you didn't. We had to *really* swerve then, to avoid going into the back of it, and Petros started yelling abuse, and Mike got out, looking like he was going to punch Petros's head in, and— *voilà!* I introduced everyone, and avoided a major violent incident."

"Just," said Harry, meaningfully. "Mike was in a shit mood. Jim's map reading is total bollocks and we'd just realized we were well lost."

"Yeah, it was a miracle, meeting Jade like that," said Ben.

Jade smirked. She liked being described as a miracle. And my head was ringing from the sound of her voice, and all the words from everyone flying back and forth.

"Anyway," she went on, "we all said hello and then they said the reason they'd done this *emergency stop*—"

"*Jesus*—" complained Mike.

"—was they were starving and they wanted to go in this *hole* across the road to eat. You could tell just by looking that it only served up diseased rats and stuff. So I warned them off."

"And this Petros geezer was getting all surly and possessive and wanting Jade to get back on the bike and go off with him," continued Ben.

"And get my cappuccino. So I invited this lot to come along, too. It was only another five minutes down the road. And we all had a drink and they got something to eat—"

"Nibbles," said Harry, scathingly. "Poxy olives and stuff."

"I'm starving," put in Jim.

"—and by this time Petros was getting really hostile. He kept grabbing my arm and trying to get me to get back on his bike."

"So I said: 'Why don't you let the lady make her own mind up?'" said Ben.

"Just like an old movie," went on Jade. "And as I didn't fancy an even longer trip in agony on the back of his bike, I said I had to show them here, and I got in the van."

"You are *so mean* to Petros," murmured Sarah.

"Oh, crap. He went off OK."

"OK?" guffawed Ben. "I thought he was going to ram us."

"Oh, *crap*."

At last there was a gap in the talk. I looked

across the table, straight at Mike, and cleared my throat, and said, "Were you trying to make your way here?"

"No," he said. "Well—yes. But not all of us."

"The plan was to drop Mike off nearby," said Andy.

"I thought you were going to send me an address to contact you at," I said, as evenly as I could.

"I was," Mike said, "but we never stayed in one spot long enough. I mean—we'd have moved on by the time my letter got to you. And then I thought I could send you the address of someplace to meet. But that seemed a bit unsure. So then I thought if I just turned up . . ."

There was a silence. I knew I should break it, I should be smooth and easy and welcoming and adult, but I couldn't. Somehow I didn't feel like his girlfriend anymore. So much had happened since we'd last seen each other; it was like there were no patterns or rhythms between us anymore, like we were starting over.

I wanted him. Even now, feeling so screwed up and shitty, I wanted him. But I needed to be on my own with him, and the time had to be right, the place had to be right. . . .

This wasn't right, it was a sodding circus.

The sound of three more cans of lager being opened broke the silence, and then Ben said, "Well, we can get going now. Mike can meet up with us later. Or we could drop back and collect him, or—"

"I thought you were starving," said Jade.

"We are," said Harry.

"So let's feed you. And *then* talk about what you're going to do."

Jade, butt out! I raged inside, glaring at her hard enough to knock her out of her seat.

But Jade was oblivious. "Sarah—why don't I go down to town? Get lamb, and stuff. We can barbecue."

"I've made ratatouille for tonight," said Sarah, a bit stiffly.

"Again?" said Jade. "Well—your rat's great with lamb."

There was a slight pause, and then Harry said, "I think that's the best idea anyone's had all day."

"Yeah, brilliant," said Andy. "If it's OK with the girls."

"'Course it is!" cried Jade.

"A barbecue, great stuff," said Ben. "I'm an ace barbecuer."

"So are we," I said, but Jade had gone all girly, and was saying, "Oh, *good*! You can come with me and choose the meat." Then she got to her feet, and Ben did, too, and together they walked out of the courtyard and we heard the sound of our Suzuki jeep revving up and heading off.

And we all sat there, a little dazed, in the quiet.

"Bastard," muttered Jim.

Harry smirked. "Just 'cos you got nowhere with her, and now she's taking *him* shopping. Come on mate, think of your other appetite. We're going to *eat*."

"Does anyone mind if I take these boots off?" asked Mike.

"I couldn't have a shower, could I?" asked Andy.

THE NEXT THIRTY MINUTES were taken up by more drinks and lighting the barbecue and the guys hefting several huge bulging rucksacks from the van and dumping them in the courtyard, then taking it in turns to lock themselves in the bathroom.

Between Mike and me there was so much tension it was like a forcefield. We couldn't get through it.

"Great," Sarah muttered to me in passing. "It feels like the blokes' changing room at a sports hall."

"Sorry, Sarah," I muttered back.

"And it *smells* like it. Jesus, when did they last wash?"

"Sorry, Sarah," I said again. "But it wasn't *me* that asked them."

"No," said Sarah, in a voice heavy with meaning.

Mike trudged past me on his way to the bathroom. He paused, and looked at me, half-smiling, and it went through my mind to say something cheesy like: "Hey, want me to come and scrub your back?" But I couldn't, I couldn't. I just smiled weakly back and he trudged on and I heard the door lock behind him.

You wait, Jade, I thought savagely. *First chance I get I'll mess up something for* you. I marched back into the courtyard, meaning to at least *glare* at her again, when I realized she and Ben still weren't back from the shops. And everyone else was busy and Mike was locked inside the bathroom and there was a very welcome kind of emptiness around me. I turned, thankfully, and ran up the stone steps to my room. I felt so scruffy and flung together. And if I couldn't do much about the mess inside my head and heart at least I could improve my outside a bit.

I slammed my bedroom door shut, crossed the floor and peered tensely in the mirror. And what I saw wasn't too bad, considering. Maybe crises vamp you up a bit. I ran a brush through my hair, and smoothed tanning cream on my face, the sort that makes you look browner. Then I outlined my eyes as finely as I could with pencil, and jabbed on some mascara and a bit of lippy. I blinked back at my reflection. Better. Much better. Gorgeous, in fact. Take charge, I told myself.

I couldn't change my clothes, because it would look all unrelaxed and obvious, but I did sling one of my favorite thin shirts over my beach top and shorts. Then I sprayed on some pricey duty-free cologne and ran down the stairs again just as Jade and Ben arrived back, hauling great bags of food.

It was immediately clear that while they'd been out they'd been getting on well. *Really* well. The space between their two bodies was perceptibly smaller now, and Jade kept laying her hand on Ben's arm and laughing, and he kept making little teasing comments, and she'd laugh even more.

Sarah appeared at my side. "Here we go," she muttered. "Jade's moving in on her target."

The target looked pretty happy about it. He winked at Jim, grinning.

"We've got enough for a *feast*!" Jade announced happily.

"Yeah, that woman is a serious pig!" put in Ben. "I dunno how she stays so skinny."

"Exercise," Jade said.

"Yeah? What sort?"

Jade didn't miss a beat. "All sorts."

Ben laughed and leered, while Sarah muttered

"Spare us" and retired to the kitchen with a bag full of salad.

"OK," said Jade, "is the barbie hot? We've got some fabulous lamb cutlet thingies here."

"Thanks to me," said Ben smugly. "All the butcher had in the window was these fly-blown little skanky bits, so I made him go out the back, and he brought out a whole carcass, and chopped off the bits we wanted."

"Yeah, yeah," said Jade. "Very macho. What about me and the tomatoes?"

"Oh, God. Big deal. She wanted only ripe tomatoes, but not ones that were split. She made this poor old dear go through the whole lot, hand-picking them."

"Ah, shut up. You wait till you taste them. With basil. We have basil growing here. And rosemary, for the lamb. It's like culinary heaven. Your taste buds are about to freak out in ecstasy."

"Not if you don't get on with it they're not. Let's get cooking."

And so on, and so on. Flirting as they unwrapped the meat, flirting as they rubbed it with oil. Their mouths didn't stop.

I decided I hated Jade. There she was, bantering away with Ben like she'd known him for months, while I'd managed only a few wooden sentences with Mike. He was still barricaded in the bathroom. Maybe soap and shampoo is really intriguing if you haven't seen it for a month.

In the courtyard, a happy, hungry atmosphere was infecting everyone but me. The noise level rose. Ben had brought a load of beer and wine— "On us guys," Ben insisted—and he went round loudly getting the money out of his friends for that and their share of the food. Jade was making a very big deal out of snipping basil and rosemary from the herb pot she never watered. Then Ben decided the coals were hot enough to cook on and he and Andy started slapping the meat on the grill. Mike came out of the bathroom, all wet haired and steamed up and gorgeous, but before I could even think about steeling myself to make a move toward him he got collared to move the van because Jim thought it was blocking the track too much.

So I picked up a bag bulging with loaves of Greek bread and went to find Sarah in the kitchen. She was at the sink, washing stubby cucumbers. A plate of sliced tomatoes was glistening on the table.

"That looks great, Sarah," I said, miserably. "Can I help?"

"Oh, I just need to chop these. Can you ransack that cupboard for five extra plates?"

"Sure. What about knives and forks?"

"I think there's enough. But they'll probably use their fingers anyway."

I was about to invite Sarah to join me cursing down Jade, when loud music suddenly pulsed into the kitchen from the courtyard. It had a fast, energetic beat. "Jade's decided it's party time," I said, sourly.

Sarah smiled at me anxiously over a huge bowl of lettuce. "Did you mind them all just turning up like that?"

"Sarah—they didn't just *turn up*. They were brought. Practically kidnapped."

"Oh. Er . . . yeah. But I mean—she didn't have a lot of choice, did she? They were making their way here anyway."

"She could've come on ahead, with Petros. She could've *warned* me."

Sarah sighed. "Jade doesn't think like that." The music had got louder, and the smell of grilling lamb was beginning to drift into the kitchen. "It's quite festive, though, isn't it? I mean—it'll be fun."

I didn't trust myself to answer. I got busy slicing the bread, and out of the corner of my eye, I saw Sarah drawing the cork on a bottle of wine. She poured out two large glasses and handed one to me. "Here you are," she said. "Cook's perks."

"Oh, Sarah, thanks." I took a large mouthful and swallowed. "I need this. Cheers."

"Cheers. It'll be OK, Kelly. You'll get some time on your own with him."

"Yeah, I know. It's just—it's happened sooner than I wanted. And it's been so *sprung* on me. If only I'd had a bit of time to—"

"Hey!" Jade's voice broke in from outside. "You two done the salad yet?"

CHAPTER 24

SARAH AND I CARRIED OUT the bread and salads, and put them down on the old table. The sun was going down fast, as it does in Greece, and dusk was making the corners of the courtyard shadowy. Jade had set out all the candles in their jars, some on the table, some on the steps, and now she was dancing around lighting them. Ben was standing over the smoky barbecue like a pagan priest, Andy was decorking wine, Harry was detaching cans of beer from their plastic loops. *Sarah's right*, I thought, *though I hate to admit it. It is quite festive. And once it gets dark, and the party gets going, Mike and I can—*

Where was Mike? I scanned the courtyard, and spotted a pair of long legs jutting out from the living-room door. Casually, I wandered over. Yes, it was him. Sitting on one of the old stools. Oiling his boots.

Oh, great. Oh, *seductive*. I turned on my heel, and headed over to Andy for a wine refill. My first glass had gone down at record-breaking speed. Andy smiled at me, and tipped the wine bottle up. "God, that lamb smells good," he said. "I'm like— *weak* with hunger. Ben—isn't it done yet, mate?"

"You wait, you greedy bastard," retorted Ben, flipping the cutlets over. "I'm just sizzling up the fatty bits."

Andy sighed. "The last four nights, we've had shit out of cans."

"Lovely," I said. "Why?"

"Well—it's cheap. And easy."

"And 'orrible."

"Yeah. Thing is, we're too knackered to get a fire going, most nights."

"But there's lots of cheap restaurants around."

"They have to be really cheap to let us lot in. Some do, yeah, but it's a hassle, sorting them out."

"And pretty crushing for your self-esteem when you get turned away, yeah?"

"Yeah. Ben always cries, don't you, mate? Throws a real wobbler."

"What? Shut up. OK. Get your plates, it's READY!"

Everyone crowded around the barbecue while Ben dished out the meat, then we all headed for the table. I wanted to turn and see where Mike was but for some reason I couldn't make my head move. I pulled out the chair next to Harry, willing Mike to be behind me; I was halfway seated when Jim yanked out the chair next to me. *Oh, sod it*, I thought, and started eating. Somehow all eight of us squeezed around the table. Mike was opposite me, over the other side. About as far away as he could be.

For several minutes the only noise was chewing and the occasional groan of enjoyment. I couldn't believe the speed at which the food on the guys' plates disappeared. I'd barely dished myself out some salad when Jim and Harry scrambled up from their seats, closely followed by the other three, and surged towards the grill again.

"We can divide these last bits up," said Harry. "You girls want any more?" He didn't sound exactly encouraging.

Sarah and I shook our heads, but Jade said, "Yeah, I do. A nice crispy bit." Ben brought it over to her and they exchanged a few more cracks and giggles. The eating pace was definitely slowing. Andy started slicing a third loaf of bread; Jim reached out for two slices then carefully started making himself a large lettuce and tomato sarnie.

I concentrated on tasting my wine, mopping

the oil on my plate. I looked up once to see Mike staring at me, but he immediately looked down. *Something has to happen now,* I thought. *It's got to. Now everyone's been fed.*

Andy pushed his plate blissfully away from him and leaned back in his chair, arms stretched behind his head. "That was brilliant," he announced. "Now I just need another beer."

"Yeah, well hang on," put in Jim, mouth full. "Don't get too pissed."

"Why not?"

"'Cos who's gonna drive, that's why not. Mike isn't."

There was a silence. Saying Mike wasn't going to drive was saying Mike was going to stay the night, and it must have dawned on even the thickest, least observant of the party that Mike and I weren't exactly intertwined like lovers.

Jade broke the silence. "No one has to drive," she said. "Come on! I thought we were going to have a party?"

Ben looked at her and grinned. "Yeah?"

"Yeah! The night's just started! There's stacks of booze left! And you can crash out in the room downstairs or if you're *really* wedded to your stinking van, you can go and kip in that. You just don't have to *drive* it anywhere." She turned to Sarah and me, but I was so rigid with indignation that she'd taken over *yet* again that I just stared past her in a kind of blind fury. "That's OK, isn't it?" she went on. "You want to have a party?"

"Well . . . yeah, OK," said Sarah. "If Kelly—"

"Then they can take us out to breakfast in the morning. To say thank you for this *fabulous feast*." And she waved her arm with a flourish at all the empty plates.

I got to my feet, amid cries of, "Yeah, *great*! OK! Party *on*! Where's the rest of the beer?"

I strolled, as casually as I could, over to where the carrier bag of drinks had been dumped. I pulled out a bottle of red wine, and a six pack of beer. I strolled back to the table, deposited the six pack in front of Andy, and picked up the corkscrew. Then I uncorked the wine, poured myself a glass, put the bottle down on the table. I could feel myself giving off waves of anger, swelling, threatening. I looked at no one.

Jade stood up, saying, "I'm gonna switch this music. Change the *atmosphere* a bit." And she was off before I could tell whether she'd made a dig at me or not. All around the table, chairs were pushed back, and the guys stood up and began moving.

And I walked over to the stone stairs and

began climbing them. Slow, steady, deliberate. I'd had it, I'd had enough, I was sick of putting on an act. I bypassed the balcony, went straight up to the roof.

Then I sat down, back against the stone balustrade that bordered the edge, and looked up. Nothing above me, just the great, empty, star-crowded sky. I tried to keep the anger at Jade going. I muttered things like "interfering cow" and "thinks she's running the show," but they tasted hollow. It was me I was angry at, not Jade. I'd acted like an unsophisticated sap. I'd been knocked sideways, I'd failed to *take control*. And as for *Mike*—

If he doesn't follow me up here, I thought, fuming, *if he just stays down there opening cans of beer and making idiotic conversation, that's it, it's over, I don't want anything more to do with him ever again.*

There was a step behind me, echoing over the flat roof. I sat rigidly, not looking around.

And then Mike's voice said, "Kelly? That you?"

CHAPTER 25

"'COURSE IT'S ME," I MUTTERED.

He moved into my line of vision and stood looking down on me. "So what's up?" he said.

"What d'you mean? Nothing's up."

"Why d'you come up here? Away from everyone?"

I let about five seconds beat past, thinking how to answer a question as phenomenally stupid as that, when Mike broke in with, "Kelly, what's bugging you?"

I gritted my teeth, tried for restraint, failed, and let rip. "OK, Mike, I'll tell you what's been *bugging* me. *Since* you ask. It's been *bugging* me that you just turn up out of the blue, no warning. It's been *bugging* me that we were s'posed to meet up alone, and instead it's like Piccadilly Circus down there. And it's been bugging me how . . . how . . ."

"What?"

"How uptight we've both been together. How . . . *fake*. Like we're just friends. Like we're . . . like we're not . . ."

"Sleeping together?" he said. And he dropped down on his hunkers right in front of me.

"Yeah," I breathed. Desire hit me like a wave, mixing with the anger. "That."

"Well, we're not, right now, are we? We haven't been for the last four weeks."

"No, but—"

"That's a long time. If you set the time we have been sleeping together, against the time we haven't—it's longer that we haven't. Proportionately, it's—"

"Jesus—H—Christ," I exploded, *"if you start working out proportions I'll—"*

He leaned toward me, grinning. "You'll *what*?"

"I dunno. I'll think of something. Maybe I'll poison you. *No*—I'll batter you to death with those stupid walking boots you're so obsessive about."

He laughed, and there was all kinds of relief in his laugh. "Oh, come on, Kelly," he said. "Calm down."

"Yeah, well. Sitting there polishing them when I was—"

"When you were *what*? You were ignoring me.

You wouldn't talk to me, you wouldn't hardly *look* at me."

"*So?* It threw me, all of you arriving like that. What d'you expect?"

"A snog?"

"Oh, piss off," I said, but I smiled, I couldn't help it. All the tightness in my chest had gone. I could feel my heart beating, strong, fast, steady.

Mike shuffled a bit closer on his haunches, then he sat down beside me. "Look Kelly, I meant to get in touch, give you an address, but I couldn't pin the guys down. They never wanted to plan the route—or if they did, they didn't stick to it. And then when we started heading in this direction I thought, right, problem solved, I'll find the farm-house, just me, and well—we can go from there. Only then . . ."

"Jade happened."

"Yeah. Look—I didn't think. I just wanted to see you. I didn't think about what you'd feel about the whole pack of us just turning up until you opened the door and I saw your face. Shit, I thought you were going to faint or something. And then when I tried to kiss you—Jesus. Talk about freezing me off."

"I wasn't freezing you off. I was in *shock*. I mean—it was so totally *unexpected*."

"Yeah. Well. It threw me, too. I mean—we've been apart a long time now. I didn't know if you'd—you know—changed toward me. I thought you had, the way you kept turning away. I reckoned I'd really loused things up, coming here. I kept waiting for you to talk to me, but you wouldn't."

"Yeah, well. I was waiting for *you* to talk to *me*."

"I did talk to you! When I explained what had happened, you wouldn't even answer me—"

"I meant, talk to me in *private*, Mike. You know—on our own?"

"How? You were never *there*. You kept rushing off to the kitchen and chopping things up."

"*You* were never there. You kept doing things to the van—and showering—and—"

"I thought you were really mad at me. I thought you didn't want me here. I was thinking all kinds of things. I thought . . . she's met someone new, she's having this hot romance, he's up in the bedroom right now, hiding out. . . ."

"Oh, *bollocks*." I laughed. "You didn't."

"Yeah, well, you weren't exactly welcoming, Kelly. I started to think something was really wrong."

There was a silence, then I said, "We both acted like jerks, didn't we? Freezing each other off. Everyone'll think we're jerks."

"I don't give a shit what everyone thinks."

"Me, neither."

"It just matters what you think."

"Yeah. Look—I'm sorry. I'm sorry I was so weird. It just—*threw me*."

"I know, I know. It was stupid. Just turning up with everyone like that."

There was a sudden shout of laughter from the courtyard below, loud over the thumping music. Mike and I didn't move. Surreptitiously, I swiveled my eyes around to look at him. He was staring fixedly ahead, eyes locked on the ground. I loved his profile. All strong lines, dead macho. And these wonderful raggy eyelashes, softening the effect.

"So, d'you wish I hadn't come?" he said, finally.

I made him wait for about five seconds, then I said, "No. Not now you're here."

"So can I stay?"

"Yes."

He gave a sort of half-groan, half-sigh, and then he turned toward me. "I've missed you *so much*, Kelly," he said. "Every day, I'd wish you'd come along with us, in the van."

"Oh, *Mike*," I muttered, and he put his hand up to my face, and I grabbed it, holding it to my skin.

"Aren't you going to say you missed me?" he said.

"I missed you. I did."

He'd slid his hand to the back of my neck now, and he was gradually pulling me toward him. "Kelly?" he said.

"What?"

"Gimme a kiss, for Christ's sake."

I shut my eyes and let my senses get flooded. By his taste, his touch, the scent of him—everything I'd been starved of for the last month. He wrapped himself tight around me, as if he wanted to fuse with me, traveling over my face and neck, kissing me, and I kissed him back, his skin, his shirt, everywhere my lips made contact. Then he stopped, and looked right at me, as if he was asking something. He pushed my shirt back off my shoulders, and slid the straps of my top down, pulling it down around my waist. Then he fell on me with his mouth.

"Oh, Kelly, you're beautiful," he muttered. "And you're so *brown*. Everywhere. You've been going topless."

"Only up here. On the roof."

"So it's OK to get naked on the roof?" His mouth was muffled, words lost against my skin. I twisted around, kissed his neck, moved down to his chest, making it all mine again.

His hands were around my waist, tugging at

my shorts. "Mike, wait," I groaned. "We should go to my room."

"There isn't *time*." He was struggling out of his jeans. And suddenly I wanted him so badly I reached out and helped him strip, and we collapsed down together on to the hard roof, kissing, and somehow, with incredible speed, still kissing, he'd grabbed a Durex from his jeans' pocket and maneuvered it on and pushed inside me and from a long, long way away I heard myself crying out.

As though my life had just been saved.

I held on to him like I might drown, tighter, tighter. He was all I wanted, right now he was the whole world. And then I realized he was mumbling into my neck, "Sorry, Kelly, sorry."

"Shut up," I whispered. "It's OK." I wouldn't let him move. I made myself heavy, lead heavy, and wrapped myself around him, weighting him down, tying him down on top of me.

We lay there, suspended, between the roof and the sky. I couldn't move. I looked up, watched the stars moving. I knew we'd make love again, soon, and I felt glad.

Suddenly, there was another explosion of laughter from the courtyard, followed by clapping. I heard Ben's voice shouting, "Go, Jade!" And it was like the spell was broken. Slowly, I let Mike pull away from me, and we both sat up and peered over the balustrade.

It was unreal, down below, like a film. Old seventies music was playing, and everyone was dancing except for Sarah and Andy, who were sitting together on the steps. Jade was strutting up and down, swaying and arm-waving, sexy and funny. Ben was opposite her, eyes never leaving her, setting her off like a backdrop. And over by the wall, Harry and Jim were lurching about, swigging lager in rhythm with the beat.

I felt Mike's arm go around my shoulders, and I snuggled in against his chest, lost in how much I felt for him.

"Sorry, Kelly," he whispered again. "But it's been *four weeks*."

"Mike, it's *fine*. It's just so good to be . . . you know."

He squeezed me in closer. "What were you saying about your room?"

Just then, I saw Harry lurch backward and as he did, he looked up—and pointed. "Oh, *shit*, they've seen us." I gasped. Then I dropped to the ground, giggling, pulling Mike with me.

We started grabbing our clothes, pulling them on. I had visions of a drunken stampede up the stairs to the roof. "Seriously, Kell," Mike breathed, buttoning his shirt, "can't we just slide down to your room and lock ourselves in?"

"Well, we could. But my room has a drawback. Sarah has to come through it to get to her room."

Mike looked stricken.

"See, I thought it'd be fine," I went on. "I was planning to be totally celibate—*here*."

Mike's face softened. "OK, OK."

"Unlike *you*. With your pockets crammed full of condoms."

"Aw, Kelly, come on. That was just—"

"Opportunistic?"

"Responsible. In case my prayers were answered and you still liked me."

"Yeah, yeah. Look—we'll sort something out. Maybe we should go down and join them for a bit."

"Yeah," he said, reluctantly. "I could do with a drink." We were both dressed now, standing hand in hand at the top of the roof steps.

"Everyone's going to laugh at us," I said.

"Yeah."

"*We-know-what-you've-been-doing*."

"Sod 'em. Come on," he said, and together we wound our way down to the courtyard once more.

"*At—fucking—last*," crowed Jim. "They're actually touching each other."

"Shut it, Jim," said Mike.

Jade sashayed over. "*Hi*, you two! Want a beer?"

If she sneers, I thought, *if she crows, if she shows by the slightest twitch of her mouth that she thinks I'm a naive, fumbling, awkward* . . . She'd drawn up right next to me. "You can have my room tonight," she whispered.

My eyes widened. Jade could be amazing. "Thanks," I whispered back. And then she was spinning off, heading for the last few remaining cans of beer propped on the table, picking up two and handing them to me and Mike.

I felt kind of dream-like and mesmerized as I sat down on the steps next to Mike, and pulled the ring on the can of beer. I was more aware of him next to me than of anything else in the courtyard.

The embers in the barbecue were nothing but a soft glow now, and everyone looked like they were slowing down. "Come on," said Jade, suddenly. "Let's go down to the beach. Let's go swimming."

There was a general groan, and Harry slumped down in the corner, muttering about sleep.

"Oh, come *on*," said Jade. "OK—we needn't swim. Just take a look. It's great by moonlight. The sea gets all kind of glowy and phosphorescent."

"I'll go with you," said Ben.

"OK," said Jade immediately. "These losers can stay here. Sort out their boring old sleeping bags."

"Yeah," mumbled Harry.

And the two of them left. Not quite holding hands—close enough not to need to.

Mike twisted around, put his mouth practically inside my ear. "Did she say what I think she said?"

"Yes. She's not such a cow as you think she is."

"She's a star. Let's go."

"Already?"

"Yeah. Already."

If we'd been rushed and frantic on the roof, in Jade's room we were slow-motion. Lazy, luxurious. Mike remembered everything I liked; he covered every centimeter of me as though it was the greatest pleasure in the world. Utterly indulgent, utterly pleasurable. I felt completely linked to him, completely besotted. Then, wound around each other, as though it wasn't the end, just part of the whole experience, we drifted into sleep, and the night closed around us.

I didn't feel I'd been asleep for five minutes when I jerked awake. By what? I couldn't hear anything. Mike was still breathing like a baby, his face crushed into my neck. Heart pounding, I listened, alert, waiting. Everything was silent.

Then a low, urgent tapping sounded at the door. And Sarah's voice, quavery, far higher pitched than usual, saying, "Kelly? *Kelly*?"

I untangled myself from Mike's arms, and grabbed Jade's kimono that was hanging on the back of the door. "Just coming!" I hissed, as I wrapped it around me. Then I opened the door a crack.

Sarah's eyes were wild, frightened. "It's Jade," she said. "She's not there. Oh, God, Kelly. I think she's been *drowned*."

CHAPTER 26

I STEPPED OUT OF THE ROOM, got hold of Sarah's arm with one hand and shut the door on Mike with the other.

"I'm sorry," she was burbling. "I didn't want to disturb you."

"Look, it's OK," I said.

"It's just—she's not in your room. And your bed hasn't been slept in. I woke up about five minutes ago with a really bad thirst. Too much to drink. So I crept out, to go down to the kitchen, and . . . and she wasn't there. Your beach stuff was still all over the bed. She hadn't *been* there."

Sarah's voice was getting shriller, and it was making me feel panicky. "Look, Sarah, it's OK," I insisted. "You know what Jade's like. You saw the way she was after Ben. She's probably—with him in his van. Or making love on the beach."

"Yeah but—she said she wanted to *swim*. You

know she did. And she'd had a load to drink. People drown when they're drunk. My aunt lives by the Thames, she says loads of people die every year in the summer, jumping in when they've had a skinful and not getting out again."

"She's with Ben," I insisted. "He'd save her."

"Maybe he tried to," Sarah said, her voice thin with fear. "Maybe he tried to and she struggled and *he* drowned too—otherwise—otherwise—why aren't they *here*?"

I'd heard enough. I knew now we had to find them or neither of us would sleep. I was just wondering whether I should wake Mike when the door opened behind me and Mike looked out. "Kelly? What's going on?"

I told him, briefly, while Sarah stood wringing her hands, averting her eyes from his chest and the one naked leg you could see around the door. He was great. He went back into the bedroom without a word and pulled his jeans on and then the three of us went down the steps together.

"The guys were going to sleep in your living room," Mike said. "You don't think Jade decided to—"

"Look, Mike, I know you think she's a bit of a slapper but she's not exactly into gang-bangs."

"Let's check the van first."

The van was locked; when we peered through the windows we could see it was empty. Mike went through into the living room and came out reporting that neither Jade nor Ben was there. Sarah by this time was wringing her hands so hard they looked in danger of breaking off from her wrists.

"I bet they're on the beach," Mike said. "They sat and snogged under the stars and then they had it off and then they fell asleep."

"But we can't just *assume* that!" cried Sarah. "They could be washed up on the beach, dead! We have to go there!"

I could positively see Mike wrestling with himself, wanting to make some flip comment like "What's the point if they're dead?" But he didn't. He sighed, and said he'd get a couple of torches from the van.

I put my arms around his neck and kissed him, marveling at the way a kiss is charged with everything that's gone before. He smiled at me, happy, knowing. Then I turned back to Sarah. She was gone.

"Sarah?" I squeaked, casting my eyes about. She was heading up the stone steps. There was something weird and determined about the way she was climbing them. Hurriedly, I set off after her. She crossed the balcony, and went on up to the roof. And then she stopped dead.

I reached her just as I heard the sounds. No mistaking those sounds. And then I looked over Sarah's shoulder and saw Jade straddling Ben.

My eyes goggled. My face froze. "Sarah, come away!" I whispered.

She looked like she'd been rooted to the spot. "Sarah!" I took her arm, dragged her to the steps again, and she started sleepwalking down them.

I looked down into the courtyard. Mike was there, head rotating as he looked for us. "Mike!" I whispered. "We're here. Panic over. Jade and Ben—they're very much alive. On the roof."

"Yeah?" he said. "Asleep?"

"Shagging," I blurted out.

"Yeah?" He started up the steps toward us.

"Don't even think about it, Mike," I gabbled. "You bloody voyeur. They've already been disturbed once. Although we didn't actually *disturb* them. We could've put on a three-ring *circus* and not disturbed them. Right, Sarah?"

Sarah didn't reply. She was still looking shell-shocked as she slowly descended the steps.

I sighed, and said, "I'm going to make some tea."

Once we were perched in the kitchen with the lights on and the kettle heating up, Sarah seemed to come to. "Sorry," she muttered. "It's just—God. I've never walked in on someone—um—*doing* that before. Never."

Mike shrugged. "Not much different to you doing it. Just it's—you know. Them and not you."

"Brilliant, Mike," I muttered.

Sarah stared at him, uncomprehending, then she looked away. Her eyes looked oddly wet. I made the tea and we sat and watched it brew, then I poured it out and we each sipped, in silence. A streak of sun, stale, tired, too early, was making it into the kitchen underneath the drawn blind.

"I think I'm going back to bed," said Mike. "You coming, Kelly?"

"In a minute," I said. I didn't think I could just walk out on Sarah right then, not with her looking so disturbed and everything.

"All right," Mike said, then he wandered, yawning, from the kitchen.

I reached over the table and put a comforting hand on Sarah's elbow. "You OK?" I asked.

She turned and stared at me. "It's the energy," she said. "It's the same energy."

"What energy?" I asked.

She didn't answer me right away, just stared at me. I felt spooked. It was like it wasn't me she was seeing. "The . . . you know I said this place had lots of energy? Vibrations? From the past?"

"Yeah," I said, reluctantly.

"Well—when you were on the roof with Mike—and then when Jade was there—it was like—all the energy just—I don't know—*doubled*."

"Whoa. Well, it was pretty good up there, Sarah. Maybe you were just picking up on—"

"No. No, you don't understand. It was the *same* energy. The old, original energy. It was like it intensified. It—you know—moved up a pitch. The steps—I could barely move on the steps. It was like a force field or something." She turned and looked at me again, and at last her eyes focused. "I reckon someone had a real big love affair here, years ago, maybe centuries ago. And it was broken off abruptly. That's when you get a real atmosphere in a place—you know, like when someone dies suddenly?"

I shrugged, looked toward the thin light at the window. I was beginning to wish she'd shut up.

"I reckon the memory's still in the stones here," she went on. "And it gets wakened up when you . . . when you . . ."

"When you have it off with someone? Oh, please, Sarah. Get real."

"I am real. I felt it." She glanced down, offended.

"OK, OK. It's just a bit creepy, that's all, when you talk like that."

"Oh, it's not creepy, honestly. It doesn't feel bad. It's just so powerful. God, I'd love to know what happened here. Who those lovers were."

"Yeah, well, I'm not sure I would," I yawned. "They probably got stabbed by a jealous ex or something. Look Sarah—I have to go to bed now."

"Oh—in a minute," she pleaded. "I'm still feeling really freaked. Finish your tea."

I subsided over my mug. "Freaked by the energy?" I said.

"Yes. Well, no. Not so much that, as what I *saw*."

"Oh, come on Sarah. I mean—Mike's right. It's only natural."

"Yeah but—*God*. She looked like she was *riding* him."

"She was," I said, dryly.

"*God*. She's so . . . *God*."

"She's had a lot of practice."

"Yeah. Sorry. It's just . . . when Mike said it was the same as *me* doing it . . ." She trailed off.

"Oh," I said.

So Sarah was a virgin. Well, of course she was.

"*God* knows how Jade and I got to be friends!" she exploded. "We're different down to the bones. Her attitude to sex is just—is just—"

"Totally easygoing?" I suggested.

"That's one way of describing it. She *set out* to lose her virginity, you know. Like it was something to just—get shot of. No idea of waiting for the right boy. She was fifteen. Not even nearly sixteen. It was that first guy she met, the college one. Oh, I know lots of girls are young but they're often . . . you know, doing it for the wrong reasons. Pushed into it. Wish they hadn't afterward. Not Jade. She seemed to know exactly what she was doing, she was proud of it."

"Yeah, well—that's her, isn't it? You don't have to be like that."

"No. And I don't want to be. It's just—weird sometimes. Jade and I used to joke that between us, we'd make the national average for losing your virginity. You know, seventeen. Only . . . only it's becoming true. *More* than true. And I don't find it funny anymore."

"Oh, Sarah." I sighed. "You shouldn't worry. It's not a competition."

"I know. I know that. But I just feel so—ignorant. Out of it. As if everything's passing me by. As if I'll never catch up."

"Don't be daft. You're waiting for the right guy, aren't you? It'll happen. It'll . . ." And then I couldn't help it, a massive yawn just about split my face in two.

She looked at me, all wry and rueful. "Oh, Kelly, sorry. Get back to bed. Go on. I'm fine."

I climbed up to the balcony in a coma of exhaustion, never sure if I'd make it up the next step. I felt like great weights were pressing on me. Finally I reached the top—and stopped. I could hear noises from my room. I paused for a moment, listening. It was Ben and Jade, laughing together. They'd moved from the roof.

Oh, Jesus, I thought, *what a night*. If Sarah walks in on them again she'll—oh, sod it. Why is it my responsibility? She'll hear them before she goes in the room, won't she? And then she can just creep away and she can always sleep—she can always sleep . . . oh, *sod it*. She's had a lot more sleep than me.

I staggered into Jade's room and collapsed down on the bed next to Mike. "Mmmmm," he said, half awake. "How long you been gone?" Then he reached out and started sleepily unwinding the long silky belt to Jade's kimono.

"Don't even *think* about it," I groaned, and I tugged the belt away from him and wound it back around me. Then, with the sunlight bursting through the shuttered window, I went to sleep.

CHAPTER
27

I WOKE THE NEXT DAY completely smitten by Mike, with a tiny hangover and a body that felt fabulous and the pleasurable knowledge that no one, *no one* could expect me to get up until I was good and ready. Mike was over by the door, pulling his jeans on. "You stay there," he said.

"I'm gonna," I mumbled.

"You wait there, 'cos I'm getting breakfast, OK?"

Total bliss. I dozed off, curled up pleasurably, and when I came to it was to the sound of the door being gently barged open and the lovely sight of Mike with a laden tray.

"Coffee," he said proudly, "and muffins. Jade and Ben must've bought them last night."

"Oh, *brilliant*," I said, and I snuggled up against him as he sat on the bed beside me. I wanted to tell him I loved him, but I didn't. "Is anyone else up?" I asked.

"Saw Harry staggering into the bathroom. No sign of the others, though."

"Oh, God. I wonder where Sarah ended up. I s'pose I should—"

"Not yet. Stay here. Let's hide up here until your friend demands her room back." And he handed me a muffin on a plate.

I bit into it happily. "Jade won't dare demand her room back. Not after the scare she gave us last night. Well—gave Sarah."

"Yeah. I'm not sure which freaked her more—thinking Jade was dead or seeing her with Ben."

"The last. Definitely, the last. Open the shutters, Mike."

He walked over to the window and swung the shutters open, and the sun streamed in. He looked beautiful, in all that brightness. I breathed in the new morning air and I thought—we'll have breakfast, and talk, and then maybe make love again.

Mike came back to the bed and sat crosslegged, facing me. "That good?" he said.

"Delicious. Oh, this is *great*, Mike. I can't believe we're—you know. Like this, now. We were so *weird*, when you first arrived. Why did we do that? Why did we act like such idiots?"

"Oh—I dunno. Because we've just had three weeks apart, I s'pose, no contact at all, and anything could've happened. *Did* anything happen, Kelly?"

"No." I laughed.

"Just checking. And we've been doing something completely new, completely different. We're bound to have changed."

I felt these stabs of threat, of jealousy, when he said that. Like I was allowed to move on, but he wasn't. "How have you changed?" I asked.

"I dunno. I dunno yet. It's just been like—a totally different life. All these things crack open in you, it's like you're tested every day . . . it's brilliant. You're not just sleepwalking through the day. You've got to make it happen."

"Sounds exhausting."

"Yeah . . . well. What about you?"

"I love it. I love it here."

"It's a great place. This house—it's wonderful."

"I know," I said proudly. "And you should see the beaches . . ."

"Well, I can, can't I? You're going to let me hang about for a bit, aren't you?"

"Yes, course I am. At least until Jade wants her room back."

He laughed, and nudged the tray to one side, and then he stretched out beside me, pulling me down, too.

* * *

We finally left the room at two o'clock in the afternoon and went to take a shower together. Even just walking through the courtyard I knew something was up, but I blocked it out and locked us into the bathroom. We had a nice, splashy twenty minutes, then emerged out into the blistering heat of the courtyard to dry off.

"Anyone about?" said Mike. "Can I drop this towel?"

"I dunno," I said. "I can't see anyone but—"

Just then, Sarah came out of the living room and walked over to the kitchen. She had a fixed, strained smile on her face, a bit like a medieval saint being tortured to death.

"Hi, Sarah," I said, breezily. "Where is everyone?"

"At the beach."

"Didn't you go, too?"

"Yes—for a bit. But I came back early. I've got a dreadful headache."

"Oh, dear."

"I didn't sleep too well last night."

"Ah. Did you . . . did you . . ."

"I got my bedding out of my room, and went up on the roof. But there were mosquitoes. And bats."

"Hunting the mosquitoes," put in Mike, as though that zoological explanation made it all all right.

She looked at him coldly. "I hate sleeping in the open."

"Oh, shit, I love it," Mike said. "When you look up and it's just like this *black infinity* and—"

"Leave it, Mike," I whispered.

"I couldn't sleep," Sarah insisted.

There was a long, awkward pause. I wondered how she'd got her bedding. Whether she'd knocked, and waited for Jade to open the door, and then swept into her room, exuding reproach. Or whether she'd just burst in, in a rage. But I didn't dare ask. "So—Jade, and Ben—and everyone—you all went to the beach together?"

"Not exactly together," said Sarah, cryptically. "But they said they'd be back soon because—"

The door to the courtyard swung open and crashed against the wall, and Ben stomped through.

"Hey, mate," said Mike, cheerfully. "Had a good time?"

Ben turned a face on him that could quell a football crowd, and marched into the living room. Three seconds later, he was out, towing about three sleeping bags in one hand and five rucksacks in the other. He went out of the door, and we heard the sound of the van being opened and the sleeping bags and rucksacks being hurled with great force into the back of it.

"Oh, shit," muttered Mike. "They've had a row."

The next sound we heard was Jade's voice. It was not the voice of someone who'd had a row. She drew nearer and nearer to the farmhouse, laughing loudly, chatting happily. Then she glided into the courtyard with Harry, Jim, and Andy close behind.

She looked carefree. They looked awkward and downright confused.

"Hi, you two!" she caroled, spotting me and Mike. "Just got up? Typical. We've had a great time at the beach. And I've been offering these guys lunch but they say they have to go."

Then from outside, a roar of impatience from Ben. "Are you lot coming or what?"

Mike detached his hand from mine and went out to the van. Jade drifted up the steps to her room. No, my room. Sarah tottered into the kitchen. Harry, Andy, and Jim shuffled into the living room, and came out with the last of their gear.

"Thanks, Kelly," said Harry. "Last night was—"

"What's going on?" I whispered.

Harry shrugged, eyes wide with not understanding anything. Then the other two said goodbye and all three went out to the van. Minutes later, I heard the engine start and the van drive off, and I stood there, wondering in a daft, helpless kind of way if Mike had driven off with them.

But he walked back in.

And I pounced.

"**LOOK, KELLY, I DON'T UNDERSTAND** what's going on anymore than you do!"

"Yeah—but you've *seen* Ben! What did he say to you?"

"Not much. God—I've never *seen* him that cut up before. Ben's like—easygoing. Easy come, easy go. Jade is just—*God*, what a bitch."

"But what *happened?*" I squawked.

"All I know is, he suggested staying on here for a few days, like I was doing. And Jade laughed in his face."

"Oh, come on. Jade wouldn't—"

"Ben thought the time they'd had last night was pretty special. And he said it was just as good in the morning, too. And then they went to the beach, and she had a swim, and it was like—switch off. Sorry mate, time's up. When he asked her what was wrong she looked at him like he was

255

stupid. He said it made him feel like shit. He tried to talk about staying on, and she just blanked him. So he came back here, and left, fast."

"Oh," I said. "Well—I dunno. Maybe she thought he understood it was only for a night. Maybe she thought they were on the same wavelength."

"She's a bitch, Kelly."

"Oh, come on, Mike. Guys do that to girls all the time. Have one-night stands, I mean. And now just 'cos it's a *girl* doing it to a *guy*—"

"Ah, don't give me that neo-feminist crap."

"*Whaaat?* What the hell is neo-feminist?"

"All the crap about it's the girls' turn to dump on men. It sucks."

"Only as much as it sucks when guys do it to girls."

"I'm not *arguing* with that," Mike said heatedly. "If Ben had done that to Jade I'd feel pissed off with *him*."

"Only not quite as much."

"*Look*—" He broke off as I nudged him, sharply. Jade was coming down the steps. Her expression wasn't nearly as pleasant as it had been going up. I wondered how much she'd heard. Mike's voice isn't exactly muted.

"Oh, dear," she said, looking coldly at Mike,

"one of the boys got left behind."

I decided to treat that as a joke, and laughed.

"Does that mean you won't be clearing out of my room yet?" she went on.

"Well . . ."

"Only Sarah isn't exactly happy having me as a close neighbor. She probably told you."

"Yes," I admitted. "But it'll be all right now—you know—Ben's gone." *Good one, Kelly,* I thought. *Ten out of ten for crassness.*

There was an awkward pause, then Jade said, "Well—another night or so, OK? Then I want my space back." And she drifted elegantly into the kitchen.

"Selfish cow," groused Mike.

"Come on," I said. "Let's get out of here. Get your swimming stuff, yeah?"

Mike went into the living room, and I ran upstairs. It wasn't going to work, camping in Jade's room, that was clear. Not with her treating us as some kind of charity case. The way things were, it was going to be awkward enough just having Mike around.

Then, in my room, the obvious solution hit me. Immediately, I went along to Jade's room, stripped the bed, and bundled the sheets under my arm. Then I picked up the clothes we'd left strewn around and bundled them under the other arm. I dumped the clothes in my bedroom, went downstairs, tipped the sheets in the bath and turned the taps on. Then I got the soap powder from the kitchen, and added some of that.

"What are you doing?" asked Mike, coming up behind me.

"Washing Jade's sheets," I said. "Can you take all your stuff up and leave it in my room?"

"*Your* room? We can't stay there. Sarah'll go into seizure. She'll end up on the roof again, fighting off the bats."

"No, she won't," I said, "'cos that's where *we're* going."

Mike's face lit up. "Brilliant!" he said.

"You said how you loved sleeping in the open."

"Yeah—I do!"

"Well—shift your gear up to my room, and then put my mattress on the roof. Then you can help me wring these sheets out. And *don't salute*, you prat!"

Mike headed out the door, and I started energetically pummeling the sheets. I wasn't going to give Jade one reason to complain.

I'd rinsed them by the time Mike returned, and together we heaved them into the courtyard, took an end each, and wrung them out. The water splashed on the stones, running toward the thirsty vines. Steam started rising from the ground. "There's a washing line on the roof," I said. "They'll dry in about ten minutes in this heat."

Mike had put the mattress up against the balustrade, the same place where we'd made love the night before. I couldn't meet his eye as we pegged the sheets on the line. "What now?" he said, grinning.

"Well—I think we should scarper to the beach."

"I'm starving."

"Yeah, me, too. We can get lunch there. And then we can stay on, and swim and stuff, til the evening. Sound good?"

"Sounds wonderful. Let's go."

I searched out Sarah and Jade to tell them we were going, but when I found them they both seemed to be asleep. Sarah had reclaimed her bedroom and shut the door, and wouldn't answer my quiet tap; Jade was stretched on a lounger in the courtyard with her eyes jammed shut. So I scribbled a note saying: *Gone to beach—don't wait*, propped it against a geranium pot, and pushed Mike out of the door.

Freedom.

"Don't wait for what?" Mike said, as we walked hand in hand along the track.

"Eh?"

"Your note. You said don't wait."

"Oh, I dunno. We've been doing things together. I just meant they should eat, go out, whatever."

"So we can be on our own tonight?"

"Yup."

"Great."

We went straight to the shack café and ordered bacon and egg sarnies, done to order on a hot griddle, and the coldest possible beers. Then we found a table under the thatch of palm leaves and sat there holding hands, relaxed right down to our bones. We didn't say much, just kept looking from the seashore to the blue horizon to each other, hearing the waves, and the chatter and laughter from the other tables.

"I love this café," I murmured, at last. "I love the way all the chairs are different, and the tables are made out of old packing cases. If that happened in England it would be part of some gruesome theme-bar. Here, it's just 'cos it's cheap. It just *is*, you know? And I love the way they grow those plants, in oil drums. All the green against the sand. Like an oasis."

"Um," said Mike. "Yeah."

"And the *view*! Just look at it."

But Mike kept on looking at me, with a grin that made me go hot.

We had the best time. We swam, and stretched out on the sand and kissed, and oiled each other up; all the things I'd dreamed of doing. By some silent agreement we didn't talk about how long this could last; we didn't start to make plans for tomorrow. We just lay there, sometimes silent, sometimes talking, always touching, as the sun dropped lower and lower toward the horizon.

"Shall we go back?" Mike said.

"Back? Why? It's still hot."

"Yeah, but so am *I*." He nuzzled his nose into my neck. "And there are all these *people* about."

I pushed him off, laughing. "Go and have another swim."

"Oh, God, it's the *beach*. It makes me so *horny*."

Pretty soon we packed up and made our way back to the farmhouse. "Will the gruesome twosome be there?" Mike asked.

"Are you talking about my *friends*?"

"Sorry. Will they?"

"Don't expect so."

"Good," Mike said.

But I was wrong. Jade and Sarah were sitting at the table in the courtyard with the teapot between them, like a couple of visiting aunts. "Hi," said Jade, disapprovingly. "We were just talking about which club to go to tonight. I want to go somewhere *different*. It's all got incredibly *samey*." And she glared at Mike, as though he was solely responsible for that.

"D'you go to a club every night?" asked Mike.

"No," I said. "'Course we don't."

"I hate clubs," he said.

"Been turned away from too many, have you?" asked Jade, sweetly.

"It wouldn't bother me how many I was turned away from—it's all a pile of shit. Those apes of doormen who check you out, turn you away if you're not dressed right—it's pitiful."

"No, it's *not*."

"Yes, it is. Like the people who reckon they're something if they get in."

"Oh, don't take it so *seriously*, Mike!" said Jade, in her most irritatingly superior voice. "It's only dress codes."

"Jesus. Dress codes. What a standard to rate yourself by."

"Anyway, I don't mind the doormen," Jade went on smoothly. "They never turn *me* away."

Mike looked at her as though he wanted to bite her, and not a nice bite either. "Yeah, well, some girls'll always get in."

"I'm taking that as a compliment."

"It wasn't meant as one."

"Will you two *stop* it!" I exploded. "Jesus, we've only been back here five minutes and you're getting at each other. Look—I want to take Mike out to eat tonight—so we won't be clubbing, OK?"

"Too right we won't," Mike muttered.

"'Course it's OK," said Sarah, hurriedly.

"I thought we'd go to that little fish place, down by the harbor. . . ."

"Groovy," drawled Jade. "Feed him lots of oysters."

"WHAT *IS* THAT COW'S *PROBLEM?*"

"Oh, just ignore her, Jade's just like that. She—"

"If I was to go on at her the way she does at me—"

"You *do* go on at her."

"She starts it."

"Mike—you sound like a ten-year-old."

"Bollocks. And the way she keeps sizing me up and making little smutty comments . . . if I did that to her, I'd get clapped in jail for harassment."

"Oh, God. Well, maybe that's it, Mike. Maybe she fancies you."

There was a pause, while Mike seemed to be considering this.

"I was *joking*," I said, acidly.

We were in my room, getting ready to go out. Even Mike had felt too inhibited to head straight up to the roof and make love, with Jade sitting in the courtyard "like some evil bloody Praying Mantis" as he put it. So we'd just showered and got dressed.

"Oh, come on," I said. "Cheer up. This restaurant is gorgeous. Don't spoil tonight."

As it turned out, it would have taken a tidal wave swamping over us to spoil that night. We walked along the shore to the harbor, hand in hand, barefoot through the waves. "This is soooo corny," I said. "I love it."

"If we were in some crap film," Mike said, "we'd stop right now and snog."

So we kissed and giggled. "Stop laughing into my *mouth*!" Mike said, and then we wandered on to the end of the beach and climbed up ancient, shell-strewn steps to get to the fish restaurant. It was perched right on the edge of the quay; the nightly catch went straight from the boats to the kitchens. The place was packed and festive, but the table we were given was somehow totally private. We ordered the fish of the day, and local wine, and felt there was no hurry about anything.

Over our meal, Mike talked about his trip and his mates—the great times they'd had, and all the risky and challenging things they'd done—and I took the piss out of him for being straight out of the adventure section of a *Boy's Own* annual. I told him about Jade and Sarah, and how different they were to each other, and then we lapsed into a highly enjoyable slagging off session, and he had me in hysterics describing all the macho bust-ups they'd had. I told him how fabulous it was, living in the farmhouse, how part of me would like to live there forever.

And then we talked a bit about how we'd missed each other, and we leaned closer and closer together over the table, hands intertwined, and underneath the table, he'd pushed one of his legs between mine, and I trapped it there. The night got darker, and our talk grew more and more sketchy, because there was nothing left to say. We both knew that soon we'd go back to the farmhouse and escape up onto the roof. We ended up just looking at each other, over the half-empty wine glasses and the fish bones.

The farmhouse was dark and silent when we got back to it. And the door to the courtyard was locked.

"They must both be still out," I said, dismayed. "Clubbing."

"Great." Mike grinned.

"Great? We're stuck out here!"

"No, we're not," he said, then he shinned up the wall and sat on the top. "Come on, Kelly. Gimme your hand." I put one foot on the wall, and held out my hand, and he braced himself with one hand and hauled me up with the other.

"Ouch." I gasped, landing on the top. "*Thanks.* I've think I've just scraped all my tan off."

"Don't be so bloody ungrateful. God—I'm strong. All those workouts've paid off."

"You saying I'm heavy?"

"No, Kelly, you're perfect. Now jump." We landed in the courtyard, and Mike said, "It's easy to break in here, isn't it?"

"Yeah. Don't tell Sarah. D'you think they've left a note, saying where they are?"

I stooped down in front of the steps, looking to see if they'd propped a note among the cactus pots. Mike came up behind me and wrapped his arms around me, pressing his chest to my back. "Come *on*," he said, lifting me up a step. "Let's go to bed." And he lifted me up another.

His cheek was against mine now, and I rubbed against him. "Smooth," I said.

"I shaved before we came out. Just for you."

"Mmmm. You smell gorgeous. You smell— *Jesus*!"

Something white and huge had swooped at

our heads. I leaped backward, knocking into Mike.

"It's OK!" He laughed. "It's not Jesus. It's Jade's sheets."

"Oh, *shit*, I'd forgotten—they're drying on the roof. Oh, *shit*, that scared me."

"You thought it was a ghost, didn't you? Chicken."

"Yeah, well, you were scared, too."

"Wasn't."

"Was. Damn. We have to make her bed up. I'd forgotten."

"Why do we?"

"D'you want her trooping up to the roof in half an hour's time?"

"No. OK. But let's just dump the sheets in her room."

"No," I said firmly. "Come on." We shot up to the roof, unpegged the sheets, went down and made up Jade's bed at top speed. Then I hurried along the balcony into my room, to collect my pillows.

Mike followed me in, and kind of rugby tackled me onto the bed. "If they're all out," he said, face an inch away from mine, "why can't we stay in here?"

"Because they'll come *back*. You want Sarah walking in on us?"

"God, that would finish her off, wouldn't it, after seeing Jade the other night. We could do a sixty-niner. We could—"

I clapped my hand over his mouth. I'd noticed the tiny thread of candle light coming from under the door into Sarah's room. "Sarah?" I called nervously.

"'Night!" she called back, in the kind of voice that said—Go away. *Now*.

Mike and I creaked off the bed, and headed for the steps, giggling. "Sarah's locked Jade out," I hissed. "She's gonna have to climb over the wall!"

Mike grinned. "That'd be worth watching. If we didn't have something a lot better to do." Then he got hold of both my hands and towed me up to the roof.

It was still so warm up there, and when you took off your clothes the night breeze flowed against your skin.

Dawn was breaking by the time we got to sleep.

We got half-dressed when the sun was too hot to bear, and trooped down to the kitchen, hoping it would be empty. But Sarah was in there, a bit apologetic, a lot self-righteous.

"I'm *sorry* you had to climb over the wall," she

said, busying herself with the teapot and bread and stuff. "If you'd shouted I'd've come down and let you in. But I *had* to lock it—I had this awful cab driver, really creepy—it was horrible having to take a cab on my own anyway—I really thought he was driving me into the middle of nowhere at one point, I thought this is it, my time's up, I'm going to be murdered, and my body'll never be discovered. . . ."

Mike yawned, massively. We were standing side by side in the kitchen doorway, leaning on each other. "So Sarah, what happened to Jade?" I asked, trying not to yawn myself.

"She got drunk. She said we'd have to leave the jeep, collect it tomorrow. Then she picked up this fabulous-looking bloke. Then she came over and told me she was going back with him and could I get a cab."

"Nice friend," said Mike.

Sarah looked at him gratefully. "I was really pissed off with her. And I have no idea *who* he is, *where* she is, whether she's still *alive*. And I don't care."

Mike laughed. "Sarah, come down to the beach with us today," I said. "Jade'll turn up."

"No—you two go. I'm fine. I'm going to get a bus into town, mooch around. Then have a siesta."

She sounded so sure we didn't argue. It wasn't as though we exactly wanted a threesome.

.

It was after a long swim, when we were lying entwined just at the waves' edge, that the subject of the future came up. "I have this number," Mike said. "It's a bar. In Turkey. I have to phone it later today and the guys'll be there."

"Right," I said. "So you can discuss what's happening?"

"Yeah. You know. And arrange when we'll meet up again and everything."

"Ah," I said, and I was just about to broach the subject of how long away he thought that could be, when he suddenly reared up on one elbow, and craned forward over my head, muttering "Bloody *hell*."

I turned around, stared where he was staring.

"Is that—that's *her*, isn't it?" he breathed. "That's Jade."

She was swaggering along the shoreline, head tilted back toward the sun. She had her lizard-skin dress on, the shortest, tightest one she owned. In one hand she swung her glittery bag, and in the other her spiky high heels. Her earrings flashed in the sun. Her mouth was midnight red. Everything about her screamed *I didn't sleep in my own bed last night*.

She drew closer, and I called out, "Jade?"

"Oh, hi! Hey—you got any money? I need a drink!"

"I'll get you a Coke," I said.

"No—come on. It's so *hot* out here. Let's go to the café."

Only Jade would feel no embarrassment sitting in a beach café at midday with her party gear on. "All right," I said. "You coming, Mike?"

"Yes," he said, nastily, standing up.

She looked at him scathingly. "Nice bathers, Mike. *Roomy*."

"They need to be."

"Oh, *God*, he's trying to be funny."

Mike bared his teeth at her. "*Your* dress is about three sizes too small."

"I'm inside it, aren't I?"

"Most of you isn't."

"Shut *up*," I wailed. "Both of you. *Please*."

We found a table at the café. Jade was indifferent to all the gawping and sniggering—she even seemed to be enjoying it. Once we'd been served, she downed her lemonade in practically one gulp, and wiped her mouth. Then she opened her bag and reapplied her lipstick. "I should get back," she said. "I need a shower. *God*, that was a night."

"So who was he?" I asked.

"He's Brazilian. He's *beautiful*. And he dances—God, you should see the way he dances. Men who dance well are always very, very good lovers." And she sneered at Mike.

"So, are you seeing him again?"

"Oh, *Kelly*. You and your thing about *commitment*. It's so boring. I've got his number but—I dunno. I like men when they're *new*." And she sneered at Mike again.

"Sarah was pretty pissed off with you," I snapped. "You just leaving her, and everything."

Jade groaned theatrically. "Oh, *God*. She was OK. She had the cash for a cab. And what's all this about 'just leaving her'? You 'just left her,' too. At least I started the night with her."

"Yeah, but—"

"Oh, *look*. I've got to go. I've had *no* sleep." Then she stood up, said, "Thanks for the drink," and was off, dress scintillating in the sun.

"Don't say it," I muttered, as Mike let out a great, disgusted breath and snarled, "*Jes*us. What a *slapper*."

TWENTY MINUTES LATER, and we were back on the beach, and Mike was still growling about Jade. "She's not happy. All this slagging about—it doesn't make her happy."

"Well, she looked pretty pleased with herself to me."

"That's not the same. She's made a conquest— she's chuffed. How long will that last?"

"I dunno. Till the next time, probably."

"Yeah. She makes out she gets tired of guys easily, bored easily—it's *her* she's bored of. It's *her* she keeps trying to move on from."

"Oh, Mike—blah, blah. You and your sodding amateur psychiatrist theories."

"They're not amateur. I'm right, I bet you. She's *empty*. She's empty and she's waiting for someone to fill her up."

"Great image, Mike. Look—can we just drop

it? She hasn't done this all holiday. She's had two guys, that's all."

"Both of them in the last couple of days."

"Yeah. *So?* Why does it bother you, what she does?"

"'Cos you're spending the summer with her."

"And you think she'll influence me? You think I can't think for myself? Well, *thanks*."

There was a long silence. Mike rolled onto his front and put his head on his arms and said, "I'm going to sleep for a bit, OK?"

"OK," I snapped. "I'm going for a swim."

It wasn't the same, in the sea on my own. Jade's appearance had somehow ruined the taste of the day.

After I'd sluiced off under the freshwater hose and got back to Mike, he was sitting up. "I'd better make it to a phone," he said. "I have to make that call. What am I going to tell them?"

"Well—how long can you stay on?"

He gave me a long, cool look from under his eyebrows. "I don't think it's a good idea, me staying on, do you? What with Jade hating my guts."

"And you hating hers. No—maybe not."

"It doesn't work, mixing friends and boy-friends."

"You see?" I said triumphantly. "That's what I

275

said. That's why I didn't want to come along with you in the van."

"Blokes are different."

"Oh, *don't* give me that."

"Look, Kelly—I really wish you didn't see it that way."

"What? Why?"

"'Cos I was just about to ask you to come along with me again."

My mouth dropped open. "You are *joking*! We've been through all that!"

"Yeah, but you've had a month here now. I thought that might've been enough. Don't you want to see some different places?"

"Mike—I can't just clear off. I can't just leave Jade and Sarah."

"I thought you said you weren't paying rent. You won't be landing them with anything."

"But that's not the point. They're my *friends*."

"So if they're your friends they'll understand, won't they? They'll want you to do what you want to do."

I took a deep breath. "OK. Yeah, maybe they will understand. Not for the rest of the holiday but just—just for a week or so. Will *your* friends understand? If you tell them you and I are taking off, just for a bit . . ." I trailed off. His face had grown all dark and closed off.

"We haven't got anything to *take off* in," he said.

"That doesn't matter. We can take buses. We can walk."

"My money's all tied up with the van."

"I've got money." I shifted closer to him on the sand. "And we can sleep on the beach. We can—"

"Oh, *Jesus Christ*," he exploded. "I don't understand why you're being so fucking *stubborn*."

I flinched away. I felt like he'd hit me.

"I can't just opt out," he went on. "I don't *want* to."

There was a long pause. My throat had gone all tight. "Not even for a week?" I croaked. "We agreed we'd meet—back in England, we said we—"

"We've *met*. Here. If I take off for longer it'll screw everything *up*. And I want to *be* there with them, I want to see all those places—"

"Yeah, well, I don't want to leave here," I said, my voice rising, "but I'm prepared to, to spend time with you—"

"It's different!" He was practically shouting now. "You're just in one place!"

"So *what*? I want to spend time here, really get to know it—"

277

"You sound like an old-age-*pensioner*, Kelly!"

"Yeah, well you sound like a stupid *tourist*! Ten minutes in each place, see all the sights."

"Don't give me that. We're not tourists."

"Just 'cos you don't have cameras and stupid *shorts* doesn't mean you're not tourists. You're *touring*, aren't you?"

"Yes. That's the point of it. We move on. We came away to *travel*."

"Fine. We came away to stay put. In that beautiful house."

"Jesus, Kelly, it's just a *building*—"

"Yeah? Well, your van is just a van and the roads are just roads and all the places you go to are *just places*. . . ." I felt like I was choking. I was desperate for him to see my point of view, to rate what I was doing.

He was looking out at the waves, sullenly scraping at the sand with his thumbnail, silent.

"Look—if I can give up a week, I don't see why you can't," I went on, as evenly as I could. "What I'm doing is just as important to me as what you're doing is to you."

"Yeah, but you could just pick it up again—"

"So could you!"

"I'd've missed out on stuff."

"So would I! *Jesus*. What it comes down to is—

you don't think what I'm doing is important. But it is. We've really got into the life here. We've dug down into it—we're *part of it*. I mean—why d'you think *your* sort of holiday is the only valid one?"

There was a long pause, then he said, coldly, "I don't. It's just—different to yours, that's all. Like you're different to me. I mean—it looks as though we want completely different things, doesn't it, Kelly? Face it."

FACE IT. FACE IT. Words that start a split. Words that mean you're about to break up.

I felt that panic again, that little desperate voice saying *back down, back down, or you'll lose him. Reverse, retract, go back. Paper over the split. Keep him.*

I pushed the voice down. I fought down the huge need to say something that would make everything all right, make him put his arm around me, keep the feeling of the last couple of days.

"You're doing it again," I said.

"Doing what?"

"Trying to . . . *frighten* me. Trying to make me go along with you, because otherwise we'll split up."

"No I'm not."

"You are. It's the exact same argument as the one we had back home."

"I'm just trying to get at the *truth*. If we're

hat different, if we think that differently about
hings . . ."

"We think differently about some things. Jesus,
what d'you want—a clone for a girlfriend?"

"No. Of course not. But these are important
hings. If you really want to stay stuck in some
armhouse rather than come with me . . ."

"Like you want to stay stuck in that van with
our mates rather than come with *me*."

Mike's face was clenched up in anger, like a
ist. "It's not the *same*. Jade and Sarah wouldn't
are if you took off. Jesus—Jade wouldn't even
otice for days, she's too busy having it off with
alf the locals."

"That's not *true*!"

"Oh, *shit*, I'm sick of this!" he suddenly ex-
loded. "I should've finished with you back in
ngland. When you wouldn't come away with me."

I could feel my jaw drop, dumbfounded. "*What
id you say?*"

"You heard. It was clear enough then that you
idn't care about being with me."

"Oh, Mike, you *arsehole*! I don't believe I'm
earing this. Not again. It wasn't you. It was the
rip."

"Whatever. I should've just dumped you."

I looked at his mean, set profile as those words

sunk into me, and suddenly, I felt almost hysterically angry. I was sick of my words not counting, sick of being pounded like this. It was like being knocked about physically. I could lose him and survive, but if I lost *me* . . .

That was it. That was the edge that I was balanced on. Lie this time, compromise . . . and it's just the start. You're not you any longer, you're what he wants you to be. A shadow person, a non-person, no center, no wholeness. Just a limp hotchpotch of what someone else once wanted you to be.

I didn't say another word. I stood up, and walked away, back to the farmhouse, on my own.

When I got back, the courtyard door was locked, and no one answered when I pounded on it. So I scrambled over the wall, grazing my shin badly, trying not to remember how Mike had pulled me over it the night before. I went straight up to my room and collapsed on the hard wooden slats of the bed. I couldn't face fetching my mattress from the roof.

I cried solidly, angry and frustrated at first, then bitter, miserable, all through the hottest part of the day. I heard Sarah come in, call out—I heard Jade answer her, explain how she'd been crashed out for the past two hours. I didn't move. I didn't want to speak to them. If I told them what had happened it would make it real, and I couldn't bear that. Part of me was waiting to hear Mike arrive, so he could say he was wrong, he was sorry, so he could make it all all right and undo what I was feeling. He'd left some stuff here, after all. He had to come back.

I fell into a horrible, anxious sleep, and when I woke up Mike's clothes and his wash-bag were still there, in the corner of the room. I looked over at the window and saw it was already getting dark, and I knew he wasn't coming back.

Jade and Sarah were brilliant, once I'd stumbled downstairs and choked out an explanation. They hugged me and listened and handed me tissues; they plied me with tea and toast and then wine and peanuts. They said all the right things—Sarah said he was an idiot, and Jade said I was far too good for him. "It's great you just walked off," she said. "I'm proud of you!"

I managed a wavery smile. "He couldn't even *listen* to me. He started shouting, and I just—I'd had it."

Sarah looked at me, eyes wide. "He shouts because he's scared of losing you," she said.

"Oh, *bollocks*," snapped Jade. "He shouts 'cos he's a bully. An inarticulate prat who thinks if he ups the volume no one'll notice he's talking rubbish."

Sarah shook her head. "No . . . it's more than that. It is, I just know it is."

"Oh, shit," groaned Jade. "She's getting all mystical again."

"He's scared of how much Kelly means to him—so he tries to cut her down to size, fit her in to *his* life."

"Yeah, yeah. The guy's an idiot, that's all. *God*, it's great being able to say this at last. I mean— I saw him on the beach. He was all—"what *is* the point of just *lying* here?" His idea of fun is swimming out to the rocks at high tide and taking bets on how much of his body is left at the end of it."

Despite myself, I laughed. "He just likes to stretch himself. You know, test himself."

"Yeah? And when does he *relax*? His idea of a *party* is downing half a dozen bottles of beer in complete silence then giving you a monologue on how there's no meaning to life. And how *dare* he try and get you to just dump us? Jesus, Kelly. Dumping *him* is the best thing you've done in *years*."

There was a pause, then I said, "I didn't feel like it was me dumping him."

"Well, it was. No doubt about it. Now why don't we all go out and get blasted to celebrate? Sorry. That was insensitive. But shall we?"

"No," I said. "Not tonight. Tomorrow, maybe."

Jade didn't push it. She went and got more wine and bread and cheese and made me eat some; and we talked generally about how hard it was working it out with blokes and how maybe you were better off without them. I felt so warmed by Jade and Sarah, by their support—I wanted to stay near them. It was one o'clock in the morning before we turned in, and I went up the two flights of steps to get my mattress from the roof.

As soon as I saw it lying there in the moonlight, I started crying again. I pushed my fist into my mouth to muffle the noise, and sat down on the edge of it, and gave way to the tears.

I didn't want to face what I was thinking. What I was beginning to know. That I shouldn't've started sleeping with Mike. I should've waited until we'd worked all sorts of other things out, until we'd been down different paths together. Not that main path, right away. Not that path that overrode all the other ones.

My mind went back to that night we decided

to . . . *come on, Kelly, be straight. There was no "decided" about it. There was just his house, empty, and his room, with the door shut and the curtains drawn and the music on, and us together, lying on his bed, his weight on top of me, and our hands and our mouths.*

And this sudden revolt I felt at this endless, endless petting. This getting worked up, coming down slow, only halfway good, never satisfied . . .

I felt cheated, aching, starved . . . I said, "It's OK, Mike, it's OK, I'm sure . . . let's . . . let's . . ." And Mike muttered, "You sure? You sure?"

He had condoms there, of course he did. We made love. And oh, God, the relief, the exhilaration, the *power*. *I'd* said yes, *I'd* decided, *I'd* been ready. Now there was nothing holding back, no mind watching, keeping a check on things, just the body, just feelings, sensations, better than any drug.

Mike was a good lover, right from the start. He pleased me, he pleased himself, and I remember laughing from the sheer pleasure of it, the perfection of it. It wiped out that first awful time completely. He was very gentle, very slow, and he could read me, he knew when to get stronger. He knew when to push inside me, and then stay there for a while, not moving.

And afterward, lying there, perfect. "You sorry?" he said.

"You know I'm not," I'd answered, the words sounding weird, unreal, from my mouth.

"God, Kelly. Oh, *God* that was good."

Sex kind of took over after that. *Sex is us.* It was why we were together, what we thought about, planned for. And along with it came the kind of assumption that because we were fused physically we were fused in every other way, too. Mike would make plans, accept invitations, and then tell me about them, no discussion. Part of me liked it. Part of me liked being his girlfriend first and foremost. But part of me started to feel kind of obliterated, like I wasn't me anymore, like I was thinking his thoughts half the time.

Got to stop brooding, I thought, as I stood up, picked up one end of the mattress, and started bumping it down the steps from the roof. It reminded me of the day we'd first got here, when I'd helped Jade to drag the mattresses out to air and get rid of the smell of insecticide. And I had a sudden strong memory of how I'd felt that day, how I'd been so glad to get here, glad to escape.

That was why I hadn't gone with him in the van, I knew that now. I'd needed to escape. All the closeness and the passion had just got too much for me. *He*'d got too much for me. Always there, always wanting me, always crowding me, pushing me into what he wanted. Somehow, I never relaxed. With Mike—when you pleased him, it was great; when you didn't, it was awful. That was a pressure on you, a weight, the whole time.

I dragged the mattress down to my room and heaved it back on the bed. Then I looked in the mirror, wondering how grim and wasted I'd appear after all that crying. There was something there, in my eyes, something I hadn't seen for a long time. I looked closer, and I realized it was me. Back again.

WHEN I WOKE UP THE NEXT DAY, I felt like I'd finished my crying over Mike. The anger had come in instead—anger over his anger, his refusal to listen. Everyone has a song they sing to themselves— "Poor me, life's so hard," or "Look at me, I'm so great." Well mine was short and to the point, those few days after I walked out on Mike. It was "Sod you," and I sang it all the time—in the shower, in the sea, walking, dancing. It helped a lot.

Sarah and Jade were so kind to me over the next few days. It was the best sort of kindness— just there in the background, ready if you needed to talk, which I did, a lot, but carrying on as normal, so that I felt I could carry on, too. Jade kept shoving us in the jeep, taking us off to different beaches, touring the clubs. Sarah insisted we have a huge barbecue, and we invited people to just turn up and bring something to grill, and the night turned into a party.

Ross, Megan, and Nick arrived, halfway through, Ross with his arm ostentatiously and tightly around the shoulders of a curvy, brown-haired girl. "D'you mind us gatecrashing?" asked Megan. "We heard about it, on the grapevine."

"'Course not," I said. "It's good to see you again."

"Heard about something else on the grapevine, too," said Nick, raising his eyebrows at me.

"Yeah? What?"

"From Petros. He said your boyfriend turned up, and you had a big fight."

"How the hell did Petros get to know about that?" I snapped.

Megan moved away tactfully, murmuring, "I'm going to put this chicken on the barbie," while Nick grinned and said, "Petros knows about everything. He has spies."

"Yeah, well he can just mind his own business, OK?" I didn't need to add—*And you can, too*. Nick got the message, and gave me a wide berth all evening. Then, at the end of it, he said, "We're leaving in six days."

"Are you?"

"Yeah. It'd be nice to see you again, before we go."

"OK," I said, and when he brought his face down to mine, to kiss me good-bye, I didn't back off.

Soon the three of us were back to normal, back to the pattern we'd plotted out for ourselves before Mike and everyone turned up. We fanned out, did our own things, came back together again. The money was lasting out—just—though one night we had a big discussion about car costs and Jade ended up agreeing to pay for half the rent of the car, because she was using it more.

"OK," she said. "That's fair. And now—what about the key? If Sarah locks me out one more time, I swear I'm going to murder her."

"So, don't stay out so late," said Sarah. "I'm not going to bed with that door unlocked."

"Well, I'm not coming back before *you* go to bed. We need somewhere to hide the key. A stone. By the courtyard door."

The three of us stepped outside, and looked around at the ground. "We need a stone we'll remember," said Jade. "Look—how about this one? It looks like a frog."

"Oh, it does!" squealed Sarah, reaching out her hand for it. "Oh, it's *cute*. We could paint it green—we could paint *eyes* on it—on that little ridge there."

"That," said Jade dryly, "would rather defeat the object, don't you think?"

"Oh . . . yeah."

"*Oooh* look—a stone painted like a frog. *Oooh* look—there's a key under it."

"OK, *OK*! Don't rub it in. I just think it's cute, that's all."

In some ways, it was Sarah who was really branching out. Doing something different. Jade said it was weird, because she'd been so uptight and nervous at the start of the holiday, but I think I understood. Something had broken free, inside her. She got into exploring, taking off on the local buses, or just walking, inland, a bag with a water bottle slung over her shoulder. She said she met all kinds of people, had the best conversations.

"You want to be careful," Jade warned. "All on your own like that."

"That's rich," she'd answered, "you telling me to be careful. Anyway—I'm not always on my own."

She wouldn't enlighten us any more, but that night we heard her come back very late on the back of a scooter, and it was a good thirty minutes before the scooter drove off again. When we asked her about it the next day she told us in the friendliest possible way to mind our own business. "I'm superstitious, you know that," she said. "I don't want to talk about it, in case it gets jinxed." And we had to be satisfied with that.

I joined her on one of her hikes once, and had a great day. Bussing out to the mountains, walking over them. It was like, after the first mile or so, my mind cleared, and I felt soothed, relaxed, just letting my eyes gorge on the scenery around us.

"Jade thinks we're mad, doing this," I said. "She said walking was *dull*."

A lizard skedaddled across the path right in front of us, and Sarah laughed. "It's Jade who's mad. It's stunning."

"I know. It's a trip. An all-round sensory experience."

"You going out with her tonight?"

"I dunno. She's so desperate to fix me up with someone new it's awful. I can't just have a dance anymore, I'm on some kind of talent quest. I tell her I want a break from all that, but she can't seem to accept it."

"You know," said Sarah, "Jade goes on about being free and stuff, but have you noticed her idea of freedom always has to have endless blokes in it? I mean—it's like she only feels alive if she's got some guy paying her attention."

"Yeah," I said. "She's addicted."

"And you've just kicked the habit."

I laughed, and Sarah started singing, "Might as well face it, you're addicted to *lurv*," and we set off along the track again, with the mountain dropping away in front of us, and the sky blazing, and the goats watching us from the rocks.

I did go out with Jade that night, and Sarah came, too. We met a whole crowd of people we knew, and there were a couple of new lads in it, both pretty sweet looking. Jade got off with the best one so fast he barely had time to blink.

"He's gorgeous," she gushed, when we collided in the bogs halfway through the evening. "They're *both* gorgeous. They're sharing a hotel room, though."

"*God*, Jade—you asked, did you?"

"Yeah. Look—I want to take him back with me. He's hot."

"You mean, you're hot."

"Same thing. What about yours?"

"*Mine?* I've only danced with him."

"Kelly—let yourself go, for Christ's sake! Do what your body tells you!"

"Jade—I'm doing it, OK? Exactly what it tells me. I'm saying good night."

"*God!* Well, I'm glad I've got my body, not yours."

"Yeah?"

"Yeah. It's a lot more fun."

I smiled. "It's different fun. Believe me."

Inside me, there was still this grief for Mike. I couldn't've even have kissed anyone else.

CHAPTER 33

JADE DID TAKE HER PICK-UP back with her. We heard him escape about seven in the morning. "He was shy," said Jade, as she made a pot of tea. "Of seeing you two gorgons. *God*, he's sweet. I might even see that one again."

Just then there was a scratching at the courtyard door. "There he is, back for more," I said, and went over to open it. Waiting there was a poor, thin, little white dog with black patches. It looked up at me, ears drooping, one paw lifted like it was prepared to scarper if we shooed it away.

"Shut the door!" Jade called out. "It's a stray— don't encourage it!"

The dog looked up at me. Its tongue was hanging out, parched. Sarah appeared at my elbow. "Shut the *door*!" repeated Jade.

"I'm going to get it a drink," said Sarah, hurrying into the kitchen.

"*No!*" shouted Jade. "You do that—you'll never get rid of it."

Sarah reappeared out of the kitchen with a bowl brimming with water. "*Sarah!*" screeched Jade, heading for the door. "I'm *warning* you!"

There was a brief scuffle. Jade tried to push the door shut but Sarah got her shoulder in front of it and managed to slip out just as it closed.

"Oh, for *Christ's* sake!" Jade looked at me, face vivid with indignation. From the other side of the door came the sounds of frantic lapping, and I couldn't help it, I smiled.

"God!" said Jade. "You're as soft as her." She pulled the door open. Sarah was crouched beside the thirsty dog. "It's not coming inside, Sarah!" she snapped. "I mean it."

Sarah shrugged, pushed her way past Jade, disappeared into the kitchen again. When she came out she was carrying the remains of the chicken we'd cooked the evening before.

"Sarah—what are you *doing*?" Jade absolutely exploded. "You'll never get rid of it now!"

Sarah turned on Jade, eyes blazing. I'd never seen her so determined. "I don't want to get rid of it, OK? I'm going to take care of it. It's starving, and lost, and it's *come to us*. It's knocked on the door and—"

"Dogs don't knock, idiot."

"Whatever. Scratched. It's *chosen* us!"

"Oh, Christ. Are you getting all mystical over a *mutt*?"

"I'm not going to turn it away, Jade. I'm going to find out if it's got a home, and if it hasn't, I'm going to get it one."

Jade's mouth opened, as though she was going to let loose an absolute torrent of abuse, then she shrugged silently, and stalked off upstairs. Sarah opened the courtyard door, and I saw the little dog lunge at the chicken as though its life depended on it. Which maybe it did. I stood and watched it eat, ravenously. Sarah sat beside it, steadfastly refusing to look up at me. So after a minute or so I followed Jade upstairs, to get ready for the beach.

By the time we'd come down again, both the dog and Sarah had disappeared.

When Jade and I got back from the beach late that afternoon, the dog was stretched out in the shade of the shrubs just outside the farmhouse. Next to it was a brimming bowl of water. It wagged its tail hopefully as we walked by, and I stopped to pet it.

"It's probably riddled with fleas," snapped Jade.

"It's not," called Sarah over the wall. "I've bathed it."

"Where?" shrieked Jade, slamming through the courtyard door. "Exactly *where* did you bathe it?"

"If you can find *one dog hair* in the bathroom—"

"Oh, *shit*—she used the *bathroom*!"

"—then I'll clean it all again. I got special stuff from a vet in town."

"Tell me you didn't use my towel," groaned Jade.

"Oh, for Christ's sake," snapped Sarah, "did I go on about that little jerk you brought back last night?"

"Sarah—he was *human*."

"Yeah, and I hope he didn't use *my* towel. Humans carry diseases, too, you know. *And* they murder you in your bed and . . . and steal stuff. Dogs don't."

The dog was peering hopefully around the door. "It's not even attractive!" snapped Jade. "It looks like a *cow*. A scruffy, skinny *cow*!"

"Yeah," said Sarah. "You're right. *Sweet!*"

That was how the dog came to be called Moo. That night, I heard it whining and whimpering, outside the wall. Then I heard Sarah creep downstairs, and come up again, treading more heavily. I knew she was smuggling Moo up to sleep on the end of her bed. I smiled, and pretended to be asleep as she walked past me.

* * *

"I think I've found Moo a home," Sarah announced the next evening. "*And* I've got myself a job."

Jade and I gawped at her, completely stunned. Then I croaked out, "A *job*? Where?"

"That bar on the main road into town. It's perfect, 'cos I can walk it. They want me two nights and three afternoons a week. To start off with."

"Whaaat?" squawked Jade. "That's all your *time*!"

"No, it's not. Just Wednesday and Thursday, four till eleven—and Saturday afternoon. I have to work, Jade. My cash is right down. And anyway, it's fun. I did a trial shift yesterday and I really liked it."

I was speechless. The Sarah who had come out on the plane would never have done that. She'd've barely gone into a bar on her own, let alone got herself a job.

"Anyway, I told them about Moo, too. They said they needed a dog to keep the rats away from the kitchens at the back—"

"Nice," murmured Jade.

"—so I'm taking her down there, just while I work at first—see how it goes. What I'm hoping is—she'll be able to stay on. When we go back."

There was a pause. Jade turned and looked at me, eyebrows so high they practically disappeared off the back of her head. "Aren't you going to congratulate me?" asked Sarah.

"Yeah . . . *yeah*," I answered. "It's—great! It's just—I had no idea you were planning to get a job."

"It was kind of an impulse thing."

"Well—well done! Do we get free drinks?"

Her face lit up. "Oh, yeah. You'll come and visit, won't you?"

Just then there was a noise on the balcony, and Moo trotted down the steps and bounded over to Sarah.

"She's been asleep on my bed," Sarah said fondly.

"What the *hell* is it doing in here?" spluttered Jade. "*I* said there was no way it—"

"Yes, but you're not in total charge of this holiday, are you, Jade?" said Sarah, fiercely. "Why is it up to just *you* if we have a dog or not? I think we should take a vote."

And then first Sarah, and then Jade, and finally Moo turned and stared expectantly at me. "Oh, let it stay," I croaked.

"Sorry, Jade," I said a bit later. "Outvoting you, I mean."

"Yeah. *Traitor.*"

"But it means so much to Sarah and it's not doing any harm."

"Trust her. To get gaga over a *dog.*"

"She's really bonded with it."

"She *loves* it. She loves the stupid way it rolls onto its back. She loves its *smell.* When she cuddles it I swear to God she *inhales.*"

I laughed, and said, "Sarah's changed, this holiday. It's like she's—I dunno. Enjoying being who she is, at last."

Jade gave me a cryptic look, and said nothing.

The next morning, really early, a scooter turned up outside the farmhouse—the same scooter we'd heard at night a few times, dropping Sarah off. It parped quietly, and Sarah hurried stealthily through my room, Moo at her heels. I waited for thirty seconds or so, then I shot out onto the balcony, nearly colliding with Jade.

"Can you see who it *is*?" she hissed, craning over the stone balustrade. Sarah was just shutting the courtyard door behind her.

"No. That helmet's too big. Clothes are too loose. It could be any age, any sex."

We watched as she hugged the unisex figure on the bike. "And any relationship," said Jade, gloomily. "God, I got out of bed before dawn to learn *nothing*."

The unisex figure handed Sarah a helmet, which she put on; then she climbed on the back of the bike. Then Moo jumped up between them, and the bike puttered slowly off.

"Groovy," said Jade, grumpily. "A threesome."

We felt too awake to go back to bed, so we had breakfast in silence, with the unspoken fact that Sarah seemed to be having more action than we were hanging over us. "Sometimes," said Jade, "I really miss having a *phone*." Then we wandered down to the local beach, because that was the place where we'd be most likely to bump into people we knew.

Nothing happened for two hours. Then Ross, Nick, and Megan called to us from across the sand, and came across to join us.

Ross was conspicuously solo. "Where's your girlfriend?" Jade asked, offhandedly.

"She went home. She was only here for two weeks."

Jade raised a very smirking eyebrow, and said, "Only two weeks? Shame."

"Yeah, well. Everything has to end. We go back the day after tomorrow."

For a moment, Jade looked quite upset. "That's

so soon! We ought to *do* something. On your last night."

"Our last night is only going to be about four hours long," said Megan, bitterly. "The flight's at five in the morning. We're eating out tonight."

"Want to come?" said Ross.

"Where?" asked Jade.

"Well—if you came, you could drive us. We could go out to the mountains and—"

"Oh, that's right—exploit me!" cried Jade.

There was a long, uncomfortable pause, during which me and probably everyone else was waiting for Ross to say something damning about how *he* wasn't the one who exploited people. But he just looked at Jade steadily, then he shrugged.

"Only joking," she said hastily. "'Course I'll drive. What you got in mind—that taverna we went to?"

"No," he said. "A better one. And Jodie and Chris want to come out with us, too."

"Well, there won't be room in the jeep for . . . what . . . eight? If Sarah wants to come, too?"

"It's OK," Nick said. "I don't give my bike back till tomorrow."

"You've got a *bike*?"

"Yeah. Had it for the last week. It's brilliant. You really get the place in your face." Jade mimed throwing up. Nick laughed, turned to me and said, "Want to ride pillion?"

"Um . . . no thanks. Ross can."

"Oh, go on, Kelly," said Jade. "Let rip a little."

"That's what I'm afraid of," I said. "Getting ripped."

Ross was right, the taverna was excellent, and we had a great evening, ordering just about everything on the menu to make up for it being the end of their holiday. I only had one moment of upset, when the waiter brought us a huge platter of shellfish, and it reminded me of that last, perfect night I'd had with Mike, down at the little restaurant by the quay. I got up from the table and headed off to the bogs, where I blew my nose a couple of times, put on two lots of lipstick, and mouthed *"Sod you"* in the mirror until I felt better. When I got back to the table, nobody said anything, and Sarah had saved me a big heap of prawns.

Ross had backed right off from Jade and was treating her as a friend now. Maybe he thought she just liked to keep things on a non-physical level— it's not as though he knew about the three guys she'd had one-nighters with. When we left the taverna, Jade linked her arm in his and said, "Want to sit up front with me?"

"I'm on the bike," he answered.

"But Kelly wants a go on that." She turned, looked straight at me. "Don't you, Kelly?"

Then Sarah, of all people, said, "You ought to, Kelly. See the mountains on the back of a bike. It's an amazing experience."

"Yeah," said Nick. "Come on." And he jammed a helmet on my head.

I didn't feel I had a lot of choice. Five minutes later, there I was, behind Nick, doing a ton down a steep mountain track. Face scrunched into his back, eyes shut tight, legs pressed against his legs, arms wound tight around his body, half-scared out of my wits, hanging on for dear life.

"You OK?" he shouted back over his shoulder.

I gave a kind of squeak of sheer terror, and he yelled, *"What?"*

"I'm OK . . ." I wailed.

Ten more minutes of the road rushing past, though, and my backbone unlocked a little, and I dared to look up. I started to enjoy the movement, the speed; I loosened my vice-like grip on Nick just a little. "That's better," he shouted. *"Relax!"*

It was far too exciting to relax. Trees tore past like trains; the wind nearly took my face off. We traveled on down the mountain, straight at the horizon. The night view was stunning. And then suddenly it was like the bike bucked, and my heart seized up, and we were lurching and swerving across the road and Nick was swearing, horribly. Then, before I actually passed out from fear, he careened off the road into the wasteland at the edge, and jammed his legs down onto the uneven ground. The bike slowed, swayed, toppled.

And we toppled with it.

CHAPTER 34

"OK."

"You all right?"

"Ooww!"

"God, that was lucky."

"Lucky!"

"Yeah. The tire—the back tire. It's gone. Burst."

"Oh—*God.*"

"Must've been something on the road. Just as well I'm such an ace biker—"

"What?"

"—or we'd probably be dead by now. Well, OK, not dead. But a lot more damaged."

I let out a low moan. "I think I'm going to pass out."

"No, you're not. Put your head down. You'll be OK."

After a few minutes the feeling of nausea went away, but I was still very shaky. *We could've died,* I kept repeating to myself, *we could've died*. Slowly, I sat up, rubbing at my leg, and peered around about. It was pitch black; no lights anywhere. I could just about make out the shape of a few stunted-looking trees in the anemic moonlight.

Nick was bent over the back wheel of the bike. "How can you *see* anything?" I said. "Haven't you got a match?"

"*DUH!* Suppose there's been a petrol leak?"

"Oh. Right. D'you know where we are?"

"Yeah. Somewhere between the taverna and your place. About—halfway between."

"Great. Where's the nearest town?"

"God knows. Let's get on the road, and start walking. Maybe we can hitch a lift."

So we set off, in the direction of the farmhouse. I was wearing my least comfortable shoes—pretty soon I took them off and walked barefoot, praying there was no glass underfoot. There were very few cars on the roads, and the ones that there were didn't stop for us. "In the last ten minutes," I said, "only two cars have gone by."

"Yeah, well, it's getting late," said Nick. "It's well after one."

"They'll be really worried by now," I muttered. "Sarah and everyone. They'll think we've had an accident."

"Kelly—we have had an accident."

"No—I mean, they'll think we're *hurt*. Really hurt. They'll think we've come off a cliff and we're spattered across some rocks somewhere."

Nick stopped walking and looked at me; then he reached out and took my hand. "Come on, Kelly, cheer up. We'll get somewhere soon. We have to."

We walked for what felt like hours, and I kept hold of Nick's hand. My mind had gone kind of blank, but I just kept putting one foot in front of the other. We didn't say much—we were focused on getting somewhere, somewhere we could get help. The night got blacker and blacker. I was worried we'd taken the wrong route—that we weren't going in the right direction for the farmhouse, but I didn't say anything to Nick. What mattered was to find someone still awake, who could help us.

At last the bleak road we were on straightened out, and led us into a tiny village. There were shops, all shuttered, and houses, all asleep, but— *miracle!*—a tiny bar was still open, with a group of men sitting around on wooden chairs outside, smoking and chatting.

As we walked toward them they all turned to us and stared. "I feel like I've just got off a spaceship," I muttered. "Why are they *gawping* like that?"

"They're looking at your legs," Nick said. Then he took a deep breath and marched over to the men, and in a mixture of English and pidgin Greek he explained what had happened to us.

The men all started shaking their heads, and kept shaking them. No, no garage was open at this hour. No, there were no taxis. No, there was nowhere to stay. But there was a telephone.

"That's no use!" I hissed. "There's no phone at the farmhouse—is there one at your apartment?"

Nick frowned, shook his head—then his face cleared and he asked to be shown where the phone was. One of the men pushed through the bead curtain to the bar, beckoning him to follow. The remaining men stared at me and talked very fast Greek to each other, so I stumbled past them and followed Nick into the bar.

He was at the far end, at a wall-mounted phone, and he'd obviously got through to someone. "No . . . yeah, I know it's late, yeah . . . look, I'm *sorry*. It's an *emergency* . . . OK? An *emergency*. Petros! That *you*, mate? Oh, *great* . . . terrific! Look, mate—you sober? Sober enough for your bike? You are? You do me a big favor, yeah? We're stranded mate—me and Kelly—yeah, yeah. No, I didn't. My bike's bust. The back wheel—*no*, I didn't. Look, mate—we need to get a message to Jade, tell them we're OK. *Yeah*.

Can you? You'll save my life. Tell them what happened. Then you can take another crack at Jade. Yeah, yeah. We're staying here—it's a bar, it's OK. No, I'm not. I'm not that lucky. Great. Cheers. You're a star, Petros. Thanks."

Nick put down the phone, and turned to me, grinning. "You're brilliant," I breathed. "What a brainwave."

"I remembered the name of his bar. I got the number from the directory."

"And he doesn't mind?"

"He thought it was a big joke. He's going straight over. He'll milk it for every bit of drama going."

"I don't care what he does, as long as he tells them we're OK." I paused, then I asked, "Why did you say 'I'm not that lucky'?"

Nick smirked. "Oh, never mind. Want a drink?"

"Yes. But a bed more. What're we going to *do*?"

"Sit outside? Wait for the sun to come up and the taxi rank to open?"

Just then the bar owner blundered through the bead curtain once again. "You married?" he barked. "I have one room free. You stay here."

CHAPTER 35

HE ROOM HE SHOWED US to was tiny, with a narrow
on bedstead and a sink in the corner, which I
nmediately went to, put in the plug, and turned
n the tap. Then I balanced on my right foot, stuck
iy left foot into the water, and scrubbed it.

"Oh, *great*," grumbled Nick. "I was just going to
vash my face."

"Shut up," I said. "Oh, God, they're *filthy*.
huck me that towel from the bed."

"He knows, that guy," he said, throwing it at
ie. "He knows we're not married. I saw him
ocking your ring finger."

"Why should he care? He gets paid."

"Yeah. It's ironic, really. Pretending to be mar-
ed. When we're—you know. Viceless."

And suddenly it was really awkward, crowded
iere together in the tiny room, by the narrow
:d. I stopped drying my feet, and glanced up.

"Look, Nick . . ." I began.

He came over, put his hands on my shoulders, rested his forehead against mine. "Don't say anything," he muttered. "I'm just glad it's over. I'm glad I didn't kill you."

Then he kissed me on the eyebrow, and I knew I had only to make the slightest movement toward him, and we'd be kissing properly.

But I couldn't. About three seconds passed, and then I said, "Nick. Sorry. You're great, and I really like you, but—"

"It's OK." He turned away, pulled the thick, shiny eiderdown off the bed, spread it out on the floor, and threw himself down on top of it. "Lob me one of those pillows," he mumbled.

"Oh, Nick, you can't sleep there. Look—the bed's not that small—we can—"

"No, we can't. *I* can't. OK? G'night." And he rolled himself up in the eiderdown like some kind of chrysalis. I picked up one of the pillows, and went and slid it under his head. "G'night," I said. "Thanks, Nick."

We slept like the dead and the next day the sun came up like a festival, and filled the little room. Ever since I'd split up with Mike, waking up had meant opening the gate to this flood of misery, but today—well, it was hardly a trickle. I was alive, and I felt great. I got off the bed and padded out to the loo in the corridor outside, then I came back in and brushed my teeth with my finger and some soap and ran my fingers through my hair. Jade had taken my bag off with her in the jeep last night but somehow, that morning, in the great scheme of things, makeup and stuff didn't seem that important.

Nick woke up and started emerging from his eiderdown, so I tactfully went downstairs and waited for him. The bar owner—who looked like he'd been up all night—pointed across the road to the local cab driver, and said he'd be open in an hour or so, then he directed us to a café, five doors down.

We wandered down to the café and got served fresh coffee and bread and wonderful honey, with nothing to do but wait. "Well," said Nick, through a mouthful. "What an adventure, eh?"

"Yeah. I can enjoy it now it's over."

"I was impressed, Kelly. By the way you coped and all. You're tough."

"Is that meant to be a compliment?"

"Yeah. Yeah, it is, actually."

I laughed, and looked down at the table, and his hand, holding his coffee cup. I remembered the way he'd reached out and held my hand, last night—how good it had felt. The sun had started to burn down on the back of my head. All around us, shop front shutters were going up, and the day was beginning.

"Look," said Nick, "the cab guy's opening up. Let's be first in his queue."

It was a only short ride back. "You know, this would only have taken us about an hour to walk," said Nick, as the cab turned on to the track leading up to the farmhouse.

"Yeah," I answered. "If we managed not to get lost in the dark."

"I s'pose. Look—mind if I come in with you? I want to see everyone's faces, when we walk in."

"Sure. D'you reckon there'll be a welcoming committee? Champagne on ice?"

"Or at least a Bud. Here—" He thrust a folded bit of paper at me. "I wrote this down for you. In case I don't get a chance later."

I opened it. "Your phone number?"

He nodded. "You don't live that far from me. I checked with Sarah. And—it would just be nice to see you again sometime, that's all. I know you're still brokenhearted over the wonderful boyfriend. I'm not trying to push anything. I just—" he broke off, and shrugged.

"Thanks, Nick," I said. "I mean it. Thanks." Then I folded it again, and put it carefully in my pocket.

The cab driver ground to a halt. "No further!" he exclaimed. "Too bumpy! Why you want to stay along here?"

"'Cos along here," I said, clambering out, "is one of the best houses in the whole world, that's why."

The cabbie grunted, unconvinced, and Nick and I pooled our money and paid him off. "I wonder if Ross is here," Nick said, as we started to walk toward the farmhouse. "I wonder if he came over, to find out if his best mate was alive or not."

"Yeah. I bet he hasn't slept."

"I'm going to have to sort out collecting the stupid bike today, aren't I? Hey—I wonder if we'll get compensation. For the trauma. I'm still traumatized, aren't you, Kelly?"

I stopped dead in the road. "I am now," I croaked.

In front of the farmhouse was parked a very familiar old van.

CHAPTER 36

"HEY!" CROWED JADE, her eyes alight with malice. "You're back! *Together!*"

Mike was sitting at the table in the courtyard, next to Jim. He rose to his feet as Nick and I walked through the door, but he didn't say a word.

"Is that your boyfriend?" whispered Nick.

"Ex-boyfriend. Yes," I hissed back.

Ben, Harry, and Andy were sprawled over the steps. They all turned to stare at us. Then Jim stood up, too, and both he and Mike took a step toward us. And I found myself thinking, *If I was Nick, I'd be seriously intimidated right now.*

And inside me, there was all this hope, and wanting, and confusion batting around—so much, so sudden, I didn't know what to think, what to feel. I lowered my head at Mike and blurted out, "Why are you here?"

"He arrived *last night*," interrupted Jade, with massive satisfaction. "So I told him you were on the back of Nick's bike. And then when it got later and later and you didn't get back—well, we were so *worried*! Then Petros turned up. Said you were—*both*—staying the night somewhere."

"Did he tell you the tire on the bike burst?" I squawked.

"Well—yeah. Petros told us what Nick said." Then she pushed her top lip up with the tip of her tongue, and laughed. "Was it good, Kelly? The place, I mean."

"Kelly, can we go somewhere?" said Mike. "And talk?"

"Oh, for God's *sake*!" cried Jade. "At least let me say hello. She nearly *died* last night!" She sprang at me and gave me a huge hug, then she turned to Nick and hugged him, and said, "You *both* could've been killed—it's awful!"

"So what happened?" said Mike, looking straight at Nick.

"Like Kelly said—the back wheel burst," Nick replied.

"How?"

"Something on the road, I guess."

"So how fast were you going?"

"Oh, for God's sake, what is this—a tribunal?"

burst in Jade. "She's alive, isn't she? Nick took good care of her."

Nick sighed, turned to me, smiled, and muttered, "I think I should go now."

"Um—OK."

"I've got the bike to sort out, and I've got to pack."

"Oh—right. Your flight's first thing, isn't it?"

"Oh, don't *go*!" shrilled Jade, grabbing his arm. "Stay for lunch—stay for—"

"Look, *Jade*, will you *butt out* of this?" growled Mike.

Jade whirled around. "*Me* butt out? *You're* the one who should butt out. I don't know what the *hell* you think you're doing here now—she's finished with you!"

Mike turned on me. "Come *on*, Kelly. Let's *go*."

"Don't you order her about!" shrieked Jade. "Who the hell do you think you are?"

"Look—I've come back here to see my girlfriend—"

"She's *not* your girlfriend!"

"Let *her* tell me that, OK? We've still got things to sort out—"

"The only thing Kelly needs to sort out is how to get shot of *you*!"

The courtyard felt like it was shaking. I had this

huge desire to jam my fingers in my ears. "Will you two SHUT UP!" I yelled. "GOD! I feel like a bit of old rope pulled between the pair of you!"

There was a stunned pause. And then Nick stepped forward and got hold of my arm and looked straight into my face. "I'm off, Kelly. Goodbye. Good luck."

"So I won't see you again?"

"That's up to you." He ducked and kissed me on the cheek, then he walked out of the courtyard door.

"Kelly—why are you letting him *go*?" wailed Jade.

"Mike—shall we go for a walk?" I said.

Then I turned and went out onto the track, without looking back.

Mike followed me, of course. We walked in silence along the cliff path, and my pulse raced. I was waiting for him to say something, to speak.

"I was ready to strangle that bitch," he muttered. "And who was that scrawny geek you turned up with? Don't tell me you like him."

I stopped dead, and turned to face him. "Mike, if you're going to go on like that, you can piss off again."

He glowered, starting walking. "I mean it,

Mike," I called after him. "I'm sick of you slagging off my friends."

He turned around and faced me. "Do *you* think we're too different?" he demanded.

"What?"

"You and me. Are we too different to work?"

He'd skipped any idea of apologizing, excusing himself, explaining why he was here. He'd just gone right back to the row we'd had that day on the beach. I liked that. I stared at him, and didn't answer. I was waiting.

"I know all that kak about opposites attracting," he went on, "but if we like completely different things, if you hate all that stuff I do, what was it Jade called it? All that prove-yourself macho-crap . . . if you think it's a load of shit, how can we—"

I took a deep breath. I had this feeling that every word counted now, every word I spoke had to be true. "I don't think it's a load of shit," I said, carefully. "I don't, honestly. I quite like you doing it. It's just—*I* don't want to do it. Like . . . like *you* don't want to dance."

"But I *can't* dance."

"And that's fine. You don't have to dance. But I don't have to *not* dance."

He screwed up his eyes, as though the light

hurt, and said, "Look—can we sit down for a bit?"

"Yeah," I said, and we both flopped down at the cliff's edge, with an arm's width space between us. I gazed down at the sea, and out at the heart-stopping blue sky, and decided to let him have it. Once and for all.

"Differences aren't the problem, with you and me," I said. "I've been doing a lot of thinking since we split up and I've come to the conclusion you're *afraid*. You're scared of getting involved with someone who's different to you. You've put a lot of work in trying to convince me that *I'm* the one who's afraid, too afraid to break out of my rut, do stuff you want to do, but actually it's *you*. Everything's got to go your way or it freaks you out, you can't cope with it."

There was pause. I waited for Mike to start in on me, tell me I was full of crap, but he didn't. He just sat there, head down, staring at his hands that were slumped on his knees. He looked as though he might be waiting for what I'd say next.

So I said it.

"I used to think you were a typical selfish bloke, wanting your own way all the time, but it's more than that. You're a control freak. Scared to let us have differences. You won't just let go, relax, follow me for a bit. You remember, the third time we went out together, to the cinema?"

There was a pause, then Mike grunted yes.

"You wanted to see that heavy war film, and I said I wanted something lighter, 'cos it was so near my exams, and I needed cheering up?"

He grunted again.

"Well, you made me feel like 'lighter' was some kind of *decay*. You made me feel *terrible*, like I was some soppy, giggling girly with—"

"Yeah, well that's the point," he broke in. "I was disappointed. I wanted to—*admire* you. I didn't *want* you to want to see that braindead shit."

"OK, OK. I could understand if I'd wanted to go to karaoke bars every night, or . . . or *bingo* or something. But Christ—a funny film? What's so dreadful about that? And it wasn't just films. You *policed* me—my friends, clothes, books I read—"

"Oh, Kelly, don't be so fucking melodramatic. I didn't tell you what to do."

"No, you didn't *tell* me. You made it so *damn clear* what you approved of and what you didn't, you didn't need to *tell* me. I mean—I felt *judged*, all the time. Like you wanted to cut out the bits of me you didn't like. And for a bit, I went along with it. 'Cos I was crazy about you."

He grimaced. "Well, at least you've come to your senses over that."

"No, I haven't. Not completely. But I *have* started thinking that I'm not some sodding pic 'n' mix bar, where you can choose what you like and lob back the bits you hate. OK?"

He laughed, and for the first time he looked across at me. "OK," he said.

"I mean, I see you as a person, as a *whole*," I went on. "And the bits that piss me off—like when you're pompous or blokeish and want to spend hours going on about some stupid rugby game with Jim or someone—well, I accept that because it's part of *you*. And I make *compromises* with you. I adapt—I listen to you."

"I listen to you."

"No, Mike, you don't. You act as though you do but nothing I say ever goes in, ever affects you. It has to be *your* way. It's like it's a serious, serious problem if you don't get your way. It's like you can't compromise on *anything*."

"That's not true."

"Yes, it is. And if I won't back down it's always—'You think too differently to me, what's the point, I'm off.' That's *fear*, Mike. Control-freak fear. It's like you're afraid if you go along with what *I* want you'll—I dunno—stop being you or something. You'll be weak, handing over the control. And that is just *shit*, Mike. I have no interest

325

in controlling you. Tying you down. That doesn't attract me in the *slightest*."

Mike was staring at me intently, listening, with the beginnings of a grin. I was on a roll. I went on: "You know—the stupidest thing is you wouldn't want me if I kowtowed to you all the time. If I'd come on your touring trip, I would've been a drag, 'cos I would've resented it. It wasn't what I wanted."

"Look, I don't want you to do stuff just to please me," he broke in. "It's just—maybe I'm looking for someone who—you know—*wants* what I want. And—you know—thinks like me more."

"I see. Like you, only female. You, with tits. Groovy, Mike."

"All right, all right," he said, laughing. "It's just—I've got this stupid idea of . . . of *perfection* that—"

"Yeah, well, I think *we've* got perfection," I said in a rush. "A lot of the time, we've got perfection, and you know it. When we're together, those two days we had here, when we're . . . *well*. It's the nearest I've ever got to perfection. Not that I want something *perfect*, actually, because that would be bloody boring. I want something alive, and exciting, and . . . and we've got that, and *you're afraid*, you are. You throw up this idea of perfection because it's something that will never, ever happen, so you can hide behind it, and never get involved with anyone. And you can drop me when it gets difficult and just say—she's not right, she's not perfect, 'cos you're afraid to take risks, you . . ."

I trailed off. Suddenly, I felt drained. All talked out.

There was a long, long silence.

Then Mike said, "D'you really think it's that good, what's between us?"

"Yes," I answered.

"Really?"

"Oh, for Christ's sake. *Yes—I—do.* I'm in love with you. I always have been. And all you do is hurt me and I'm tired of it. So there."

Whoa. I'd said it. And the sky hadn't fallen in, the sun hadn't darkened. The waves were the same, lapping on the shore, the cicadas were chirping in the shrubs behind us.

I lay back on the sandy ground, put my hands behind my head, closed my eyes. And this wonderful, incredible feeling of relief and pride and self-sufficiency flooded into me. Mike's reaction to what I'd said was almost unimportant beside it.

At long last, I thought, *I've said what I feel.* And for all him going on about his freedom and not getting tied down, I'm more free than he is. Because

I'm honest, I'm straight. And I'm not scared any-more. I've stated who I am, and who I am is OK.

I lay there and let the sun and the silence soak into me, and I felt invincible. Then I was aware that the sun wasn't burning down on my eyelids anymore, and I opened them just a slit to see Mike's face, about ten centimeters away from mine.

"Kelly?" he said.

"What?"

"Look I—I—OK, yeah, I am afraid. You're right. I'm afraid of . . . what I feel for you some-times. It scares me shitless. Last week, I was a mess. I don't want it, Kelly. I mean—it's great, yeah, but . . ."

As I listened to him stumbling over his words I tried to prevent the smile that was spreading over my face, spreading like butter. But I failed. The smile was there, and suddenly I wasn't feel-ing drained anymore. I stayed stretched out on the ground, hands behind my head, and smiled up at him.

He was propping himself up on a fist on one side of my head, glaring at a spot on the other side. "I'm scared of you getting too important," he mut-tered. "I'm scared of—losing what I'm about. I've seen it happen, Kelly. I've watched guys get totally axed by girls. You know—pushed off-course. Like my cousin. He dropped out of college and everything, just 'cos of this girl he was in love with who wasn't in love with him."

There was a pause, and then I said, "Why has the word *overkill* drifted into my mind?"

"You're not taking this seriously, are you, you cow?"

I beamed up at him. "Yes, I am. And don't call me a cow."

"Sorry."

"It's overkill 'cos you really don't have to try that *hard*, Mike. I mean—all those barriers you slam up, just to protect yourself from me. I s'pose it's flattering in a way. Mike—you are the *last* person to . . . lose what you're about, or whatever you said. Get pushed off-course. You're strong. That's one of the reasons I like you. It's just—I'm strong, too. In my own humble way."

"I know. I know you are, Kelly. Well—not humble. Strong. That's why I like you."

"And I'm not such a coward as you."

"What?"

"'Cos I'm prepared to take a risk. I'm prepared to get involved with someone strong like me and not be shit scared all the time that I'll get *swamped* and lose my *identity*."

Mike had started laughing. And he'd maneuvered himself on top of me, elbows either side of my head. "I'm a bit more *substantial* than that," I went on, ignoring him. "I mean—I can tell people how I feel without being scared I'm going to blow up or something. I can—"

I broke off. His mouth had landed on mine, rather hard. I was laughing, too, now, gurgling far back in my throat, gurgling with triumph.

He pulled away and grinned at me. "You're a bossy cow," he said. "And I—and I—"

"Go on, Mike, say it."

"I can't."

"OK. Weakling. Coward. Worm."

He landed on me again, full force, and I laughed with what little breath I had left in my body. "I win!" I wheezed.

"I love you," he said.

CHAPTER 37

"HI, KELLY," BEN SAID, materializing beside me. It was an hour later; Mike had disappeared into the shower, and I was kind of floating about in the courtyard. "You're looking disgustingly happy and pleased with yourself."

"Am I? Yeah, well, I am. Happy and pleased with myself. I've really thrashed things out with Mike."

"Yeah? Lucky Mike, getting thrashed. Deep down, that's all a macho guy like Mike really wants."

"Oh, ha ha. Don't be so *puerile*."

"Whoa. Jade been giving you a vocab list?"

"Look—you want to hear this, or not?"

"Yeah, yeah."

"I mean—he's your friend. I would've thought you cared about him and what was happening with me. I would've thought—"

"Kelly—shut up. Tell me."

"It's just—I finally had the courage to tell him some home truths, you know? About our relationship. I told him he was afraid to just trust, let go. I told him he was a control freak."

"Yeah? I've been telling him that for years."

"What?"

"Well, it's pretty obvious, Kelly. He's always the one with the map in his hand, the plan worked out, the ideas—thing is, he's pretty good at it—most people are happy just to follow along. The problem starts when you come up with an idea of your own. Or disagree with one of his. Then he can be a real wanker."

"Oh," I said. "I see."

"I sorted him years ago. I just threatened to smash his face in if he didn't take my views into account." There was a pause. "That what you did, Kelly?" Ben asked.

"Not exactly," I said, and I smiled, remembering how we'd made love, right there on the edge of the cliff, with the great fireball of the sun hanging in space just in front of us, not knowing or caring if anyone walked by.

"We've all been taking bets on how long you two would last. You see, you Kelly—you're the first all right girl who's stuck him. And we knew you were having fights. I told him to back down, I told him he'd be crazy if he screwed up things with you. But it's like in his bones, you know? He has to try and get things his way."

"Well—I think we've made a start. On working it out, I mean. I really think we have, Ben."

"Yeah? I'll believe that when I see it."

Just then the bathroom door opened, and Mike walked out, wearing only a red towel, looking all brown and utterly desirable. "Hey, mate," Ben called out. "Just been telling your girlfriend what a tosser you are."

"She knows," Mike answered, grinning, then he came over and put his arm around me, and I put my arms around his neck, and Ben said, "Oh, knock it off, you two, for Christ's sake. Look, Mike. I want to get going soon. What're you doing?"

Mike looked down at me. "What am I doing, Kelly?"

"You're going," I said, firmly. "Because that's the way it was planned. You're going to finish your holiday, I'm going to finish mine. And then when we get home, we'll see, OK?"

"OK," he said. "You're the boss."

Ben gave a disbelieving snort and trudged out to the van, and Mike buried his face in my hair and muttered, "Unless you want me to stay."

"I don't think that's a good idea."

"No. Maybe not. Oh, Kelly—that was amazing, what you said on the cliff. About me being a jerk and everything. Why didn't you say all that before?"

"'Cos I hadn't worked it out before."

"And it was *amazing* what happened afterward. . . ." He slid his hands onto my shoulders, resting against my neck. "What about going off somewhere, just the two of us?"

"Oh, *Mike*—"

"Come on, Kelly—I came back, didn't I?"

"Yeah, about a week late."

"I was a mess last week. I was miserable. You ask the guys."

"Well, it wasn't exactly carnival time for me either."

"I had to come back. I had to see you."

"Yeah. I'm glad."

"Let's go off somewhere. Just us. Like you wanted."

I shook my head. "Not now. It's been good, this time apart. For both of us. And maybe . . . maybe we need longer. We were in so deep, so soon, and I'm . . . well, I'm not going back to how it was before."

"But I've changed, Kelly. I really have."

"I've changed, too."

"I know. I like it. That's why I want to be with you now."

I took a deep breath, and said, "Mike—you're doing it again."

"What?"

"Pressuring me. Not listening to me. Oh, *look*, Mike, it was fantastic, up on the cliffs, the talking and the . . . it was *magic*, but it doesn't mean everything's solved, you know? It doesn't mean everything's changed at a stroke. Things don't work that way. And I need these two weeks. I want them."

"*Why?*"

"Consolidation. Of us. Of *me*. And when we get back to England we'll . . . we'll see."

There was a pause, then he said, grinning, "OK, you win. I'll see you back home. But you'll want me. I guarantee it."

Then the van outside parped impatiently, and I reached up and pulled Mike's head down to mine, and kissed him. Then he went back into the farmhouse and got dressed, and we walked together to the courtyard door, and I didn't cry as I waved him off.

I had the farmhouse to myself. I climbed up on the roof, walked right over to the far side, and sat side-saddle on the balustrade, looking out over the parched landscape, all hazy in the sun. I felt like my mind was flying in the heat and the silence. It was perfect, too perfect to even move.

Some time later, the jeep rattled to a halt outside the wall, and Jade, Sarah, and Moo clattered through the door. "Sarah has *huge* news!" cried Jade. "Tell her, Sarah!"

Sarah looked searchingly into my face as I came down the steps to meet them. "You've got huge news, too, haven't you, Kelly? You're back with Mike."

"Oh, *shit*!" exploded Jade. "Kelly, you *idiot*!"

Sarah turned on her. "Jade, it's *you* who's the idiot. She loves him—he loves her. That was perfectly obvious, right from the start. They just had to get—balanced."

"Oh, God," said Jade. "You and your *balance*, and *harmony*, and all that kak—"

"Er—excuse me," I interrupted. "Before this develops into a major discussion—I'm *not* back with Mike."

"You're not?" said Sarah.

"Not exactly. We're going to get back to England . . . and see."

"Oh, *Kelly*," snapped Jade. "The minute he gets his hands on you again you'll go all smitten and it'll be *just* like before and you'll be a *total pushover* and—"

"No, I *won't*. Sex isn't everything."

"Isn't it?"

"No. I was out of my depth then. Now I'm not."

Jade shrugged. "So what's made the difference?"

"Being here. This holiday. Me." There was a pause, then I grinned and said, "Look—just trust me, OK? Now come on, Sarah, what's happened to *you*?"

Sarah took a deep breath. "I'm staying on. Here. I'm doing a gap year. I'm going to carry on working at the bar, only I'll be doing the cooking."

"Sarah, that's *wonderful*!" I squawked.

"She made her famous ratatouille the other night," Jade crowed. "And they offered her a job on the spot."

"I get more money, and a room . . . they want to start expanding the whole food side of the place, kind of easy bar food, and they want all my ideas. And that's practical experience, for the catering course I want to do."

"Isn't that *brilliant*?" enthused Jade. "She's going to be a real cook! She was all set up for this grim secretarial course in September. Her dad really pushed her into it. But now she's just going to cut loose. Have a year out—get on a Cordon Bleu course—and end up running her own restaurant!"

Sarah laughed, pleased. "You will, you will!" Jade crowed.

"That's amazing, Sarah," I said. "Just deciding like that . . . it's so *brave*."

"Not really. The thought of going back and living a gray life was the really scary thing. It's just been so brilliant here. It's so beautiful, and open . . . I've never had a summer like this. The three of us here, everything we've been through . . . it's been incredible."

"Yeah," I said. "I know."

"I feel so different, and I like what's happening to me—you know, inside."

"She's escaped!" said Jade triumphantly. And then her face crumpled a bit and she said, "I feel left out. You two have had amazing things happening this holiday. What about me?"

I smiled dreamily at her. "Don't worry, Jade. We've still got two weeks left. With your fast work, that's plenty long enough."

CHAPTER 38

SARAH HAD AGREED TO START working full time almost immediately, and the next night Jade and I went down to her bar to see her in action and maybe blag some free food. We turned up early, before the place got too full. And when we got through the doorway both of us stopped short.

Sarah was sitting at the bar, talking, all animated, looking kind of fluid and wonderful. On one side of her was Moo, balanced on a stool. On the other was a boy with a beautiful profile, and jet black hair. He was leaning in toward Sarah, listening intently, and when she stopped talking, he smiled, and moved in even closer to her, and said something very caressing. And Moo was nosing up over Sarah's shoulder, looking as though she was listening, too, and Sarah laughed at whatever he'd said, and reached backward to cup Moo's snout in her hand.

The whole scene was perfect. It had the kind of cool you could never, ever set up. "Doesn't she look gorgeous?" I breathed.

"Yes!" hissed Jade. "Blimey. That must be the mystery bike rider. No wonder she didn't want it jinxed."

Sarah spun around in her seat. She must have sensed us, because we were far too quiet to hear. "Hi, you two! Come here!"

We went over, making our way through the little wooden tables and chairs. "This is Jack," Sarah said.

He turned around and smiled. White, slightly pointed, very sexy teeth; dark, sloe-shaped eyes; and so sensual-looking you could feel yourself melt. "Hi," he said. "I've heard all about you two." As he spoke I noticed his hand slide along the polished bar, and unseeingly take hold of Sarah's.

"So, are you the guy with the scooter?" demanded Jade.

"Yes. Well, I guess I am. I've been showing Sarah the island."

"We've been to some beautiful places," said Sarah. "Hard to get to, and so they're empty . . ."

"You live here?" asked Jade.

"A lot of the time," said Jack, ambiguously.

"Jack's dad's American," said Sarah. "And he's

there some of the time, too."

"I'm supposed to be going back there, to start at UCLA this fall," Jack said. "But I might—"

"Not be," finished Sarah, and they both laughed.

"Oh, wow," said Jade, "are you staying on to work, too?"

Jack turned to look at her. "I'm not sure what I'm doing." He shrugged, happily. "It'll work out."

There was something blank, secret, about Jack's face as he spoke to us. Like a beautiful mask. And then when he turned back to Sarah, it fired up, like a light was going on inside. It was like he had a private face, just for her. It was incredibly sexy.

Sarah got us both a drink, then she took us out to the back and proudly introduced us to the proprietor and showed us the kitchen where she'd be working. Then she led us up some winding back stairs and showed us her bedroom. It was large, low-ceilinged, with whitewashed walls and a bare pine floor. There was a chest of drawers, a deep porcelain wash basin in the corner and a generous bed with a graceful iron bedstead. I knew Jade was looking at the bed, like me, and wondering about Jack, but there was no way we could ask. Not with Sarah.

The double window opened over the street, with a tiny balcony that Sarah would be filling with pots of flowers in the spring. "Isn't it perfect?" she breathed.

"Perfect," I agreed. Already, it seemed to belong to her, even more than her room at the farmhouse. "When are you moving in?"

"Well—I thought I'd move in gradually," she said. "Maybe starting . . . tonight."

"Ah," said Jade.

We went downstairs, and Sarah dished us up some delicious quiche and salad, and when we'd eaten Jade looked at me and said, "Ready to make a move?" and I nodded. We kissed Sarah good-bye, and waved to Jack, and left.

"I liked the bar and everything, it was just—I dunno. Too quiet," said Jade.

"Too Sarah." I laughed.

"Yeah. God, she's changed, though, hasn't she? I mean—she's come out of her shell all right."

"Yes. It's wonderful."

"She came into my room last night. To have a chat, she said. And she was all on about how we were so different but that was OK, and how she was glad she knew me. And then she *thanked* me. For bringing her here. So I said, well, I was glad you could come, and then she said I'd changed everything for her. She said it might have been inadvertent, but I'd still done it."

"So what did you say?"

"Nothing much. I wasn't too sure what inadvertent meant, to be honest."

I laughed. "Whoa. Fancy Sarah using a word you didn't know. Inadvertent is kind of—not meaning to."

"Ah. That makes sense. Anyway, she gave me this huge hug, and then just . . . wandered off. With her dog. It's weird, it was like she was saying good-bye."

"God—I thought the same at the bar just then. When she kissed us."

"It makes me depressed. I want to keep seeing her."

"Well—you will, then."

"I dunno. She seems all wrapped up in what's happening to her now."

"So maybe you'll have to make more effort to see her now," I said. "But you will if you want to. Sarah isn't the sort to drop friends."

"I s'pose not." There was a pause, then Jade said, "D'you reckon Jack's all mystical, like she is?"

I shrugged. "Dunno. But I bet he likes that side of her."

"Yeah. He's all kind of dreamy, too, isn't he? God. The way he was *looking* at her . . ."

"And *touching* her . . ."

"Yeah," Jade agreed, gloomily.

"Come on. Let's get back and get tarted up. You need to go out tonight."

We had our usual race for the bathroom, and I let Jade win. Which meant she was half made up and shouting at me to hurry by the time I'd got through with the shower.

"All right!" I yelled, running up the stone stairs. "I'm going as fast as I can!" I combed out my hair and jumped into my underwear, then started making up. It was one of the good days. Everything seemed to glide on, everything I did looked great. Then I raced over to my wardrobe and my foot went crunch on something on the floor.

I stooped and picked it up. It was the framed photo of me and Mike—I'd hurled it at the wall a few days ago and just left it there, symbolically. The glass was even more shattered now I'd stood on it. I sat down on the edge of the bed and examined my foot, relieved not to see any blood. Then I set the frame back on the chest of drawers. The photo was still unspoiled—me and Mike, intertwined, staring out. It still made me smile.

There was a folded bit of paper lying next to it. Nick's phone number—I'd dropped it there when I'd undressed last night. I picked it up and pushed it into the picture frame. There was room for it now the glass had gone.

"Kelly?" Jade yelled. "You ready? Only if we don't get there soon all the great guys will be taken."

I laughed, pulled on a dress, shoved on my shoes. "I'm ready!" I called back.